"I want you out, Carlisle,"

Brenna muttered at him. "Do you hear me? I want you out of my house, my office and my life."

Mitch leaned forward. "Did you know that when you're angry, your eyes get these gold sparks in them?" he observed lazily. "Interesting, really interesting. The blue shade darkens, and then these little, sparkling flecks show up and kind of dance around."

Brenna stared at him, stunned by the outrageous comment. "That's the stupidest thing I've ever heard," she ground out when she found her voice. "My eyes, gold flecks or not, are none of your business!"

"Stupid!" Mitch theatrically placed a hand over his heart. "And here I thought I was being charming."

His declaration summoned up the mental image of his half-naked body holding hers. "I don't want you charming," Brenna managed to say in a furious whisper. "I just want you gone!"

Dear Reader:

We at Silhouette are very excited to bring you this reading Sensation. Look out for the four books which appear in our Silhouette Sensation series every month. These stories will have the high quality you have come to expect from Silhouette, and their varied and provocative plots will encourage you to explore the wonder of falling in love – again and again!

Emotions run high in these drama-filled novels. Greater sensual detail and an extra edge of realism intensify the hero and heroine's relationship so that you cannot help but be caught up in their every change of mood.

We hope you enjoy this Sensation – and will go on to enjoy many more.

We would love to hear your comments and encourage you to write to us:

Jane Nicholls
Silhouette Books
PO Box 236
Thornton Road
Croydon
Surrey
CR9 3RU

LYNN BARTLETT
Heart and Soul

Silhouette Sensation

First published in Great Britain in 1992
by Silhouette Books, Eton House, 18-24 Paradise Road,
Richmond, Surrey TW9 1SR

© Lynn Bartlett 1991

Silhouette, Silhouette Sensation and Colophon are
Trade Marks of Harlequin Enterprises B.V.

ISBN 0 373 58642 6

18-9209

Made and printed in Great Britain

Other novels by Lynn Bartlett

Silhouette Sensation

The Price of Glory

Worldwide Books

Defy the Eagle

For Mary Genco,
who for twelve years
greeted each new creation with
sweet words and lavish praise.
This book is dedicated to you,
dear aunt.

Chapter 1

The graceful old château crowned a rise in a heavily wooded area an hour's drive from Paris. When twilight descended, as it had several hours ago, the electric sensors positioned around the château and immediate grounds perceived the lessening sunlight and activated the exterior lighting, bathing the snow-spattered front lawn with harsh, artificial illumination. Within the château, its owner and sole resident sat in a leather wing back chair, his booted feet resting upon a matching ottoman. His left hand held a crystal tumbler half-filled with Scotch, his right a lit, unfiltered cigarette. The room was filled with the resonant tones of the final movement of Beethoven's Ninth Symphony. From time to time he indolently lifted either the cigarette or the tumbler to his mouth, but his eyes remained closed.

To an outsider, the scene was deceptively tranquil, belying the extraordinary security precautions that protected the château both within and without. The final notes of the symphony reached their crescendo and echoed into silence, then came the soft whirring of the compact disc player as the Beethoven disc was returned to the magazine and the next fed into the player. This time the selection was a Scarlatti invention for harpsichord that began simply enough but grew increasingly complex as it continued. The harsh line of the man's mouth relaxed, not enough to be labeled a smile, but into a less severe expression.

The harsher line returned only moments later, when the phone on the bar across the room jangled for attention. Cold green eyes opened to regard the instrument with an expression just short of utter hatred. After the fifth ring, he gave a resigned sigh and set aside his drink to rise and cross the room. This phone number was unlisted and known to only a select few. Mitch Carlisle was a very cautious man.

"Yes?"

"Hello, teach." The male voice carried clearly over the line. There was none of the distortion that usually marked a transatlantic phone call. This line did not bear the usual, public, usage. "Got a minute?"

The casual tone of the caller's voice sounded forced. Mitch crushed out his cigarette and turned off the music. "For you, always."

"Remember that Icon you were interested in acquiring a few years ago?"

Mitch's grip on the receiver tightened at the hated code name. "I remember."

"Word is, it's about to come up for auction in the next week or so."

"Where?" The question was a harsh demand.

"Here. The fact is, teach, that I'm supposed to hold a seminar about the Icon for members of a rather well-known national investment house, and I could use some help. Would you be willing to act as consultant?"

Mitch's eyes grew colder as he phrased his answer using the same code as his caller. "You know that I would prefer to acquire the Icon for my own collection."

There was a significant pause before the caller replied, "I understand, but there are certain conditions you must agree to before I can offer you a contract." He cleared his throat.

"The most compelling of which is that you not bid privately on the Icon."

"Your terms are less than attractive."

"Agreed, but I am also instructed to tell you that the terms are binding only for the duration of the contract. Does that sound more appealing?"

Mitch's lips twitched into a quick, mirthless smile. "Very."

The relief in the caller's voice was obvious. "I was hoping you would agree. A ticket has already been purchased with your usual carrier—all you have to do is call to confirm the reservation at Orly and pack a bag. I'll meet you at the airport tomorrow. And, teach? Thanks."

Mitch slowly replaced the telephone receiver, fighting the hatred and anger that flooded his veins. He retrieved his glass, emptied the remainder of his drink into the sink in the wet bar, then carefully washed and dried the crystal tumbler. The mundane task had the hoped-for calming effect. After placing the tumbler with its mates, he reached for the telephone and dialed the airline at Orly. Within a minute he had confirmed his reservation on the three-o'clock flight with the cheerful clerk. He broke the connection and then dialed a second number. The answering voice was feminine and thick with sleep.

"I'll be out of the country for a while, Maureen," Mitch told his employee without preamble. "You know how to leave a message for me in case anything urgent happens. All the electronic alarms will be activated upon my departure."

"Understood. *Bon voyage.*"

Mitch returned the receiver to its cradle without replying. He left the library and walked quickly through the spacious foyer and up the curved staircase that led to the second floor, which had been extensively remodeled to provide each bedroom with a private bath. The six bedrooms to the left of the central staircase were used exclusively by those who employed Mitch and his staff. The six bedrooms to the right of the staircase were used by the staff when they were in residence.

Pausing on the landing, Mitch surveyed the two wings, familiarity allowing him to ignore the ceiling-mounted cameras, which, when in operation, displayed the length of the hallway on a screen in an observation station located in the reinforced basement of the château.

The silence, Mitch thought, was notably oppressive tonight. Although he was a man accustomed to living alone, the château nonetheless seemed particularly empty at a time like this, when his employees had returned to their own homes after an assignment had been completed. Now, at the age of forty-one, Mitch regarded his five-year-old business as an unqualified success, a success, unfortunately, that reflected the times. Being a security consultant in a world grown increasingly insecure had proven lucrative—his employees were well paid, and, as did any good corporation, he provided pension plans and benefits for everyone. The only difference between his business and other, more public industries was that he and his staff often placed themselves between their clients and the source of physical danger. The clients were highly appreciative of such services and more than willing to pay a substantial fee for the danger to Mitch and his people.

Mitch turned right and entered the room at the end of the hall. Here, too, a camera was mounted from the ceiling; like its hall cousin, it was not in operation. Flipping on the light, he went to the antique wardrobe and pulled from it a suitcase. In less than ten minutes he had packed clothing and shaving articles. He retraced his steps to the first floor and opened the front door.

Entering one of the closets that flanked the front door, he touched a part of the molding inside that activated a trapdoor, which swung open to reveal a recessed area two by three feet in dimension. The electronic panel now displayed consisted of two rows of ten red-lit buttons and a numerical keypad. Mitch entered a code on the pad, pressed each of the buttons in sequence, then entered a second code on the pad. The buttons immediately began to blink, a signal that the various pressure and heat-sensitive alarms in the château were now armed. These alarms were passive in nature; when triggered, they would make the devil's own noise and relay the alarm to the local police, but would not inflict bodily injury on an intruder. The aggressive alarms, located behind a second trapdoor in the closet, were used only when the château was occupied. Only one light—that of the front-door alarm—remained unblinking when he closed the panel, took a down vest from a hanger and left the closet. When he closed the front door behind him, its electronic lock fell into place and the final light on the panel began to blink.

Mitch walked across the crushed rock, horseshoe drive to the converted carriage house. Inside was a gray Mercedes. He tossed his bag onto the back seat, slid under the steering wheel and started the engine. The engine purred with leashed power, and Mitch smiled. The Mercedes was more than a simple sedan; its body was armored and the windows were bulletproof. A former client had once commented that riding in the Mercedes was wonderful if one happened to enjoy being hermetically sealed away from the world. It was a security precaution that Mitch now took for granted.

The Mercedes rolled onto the driveway and stopped. Mitch took what appeared to be a calculator from the glove compartment and entered a series of numbers. The garage door rolled downward; when it stopped, he pressed the Enter button on the calculator to arm the security alarms for the converted carriage house. The main road was at the end of the mile-long drive, and when Mitch reached that intersection, he stopped the car and walked a few feet into the trees. There he located a small, metal post. Bending, he reached around to the back of the post until he found a small toggle switch. He pressed the switch and returned to the car. Now the explosive charges and pressure plates in the forest were deactivated. With the château empty, the last thing he wanted was for some unfortunate hiker to get lost, meander through the forest in hope of finding the main road and get blown up for his trouble.

Mitch drove to Paris, left his car in the private garage that he rented by the month and took a cab to Orly Airport. It was midnight by the time he had paid for the cab and entered the terminal. Bypassing the Air France counter, he went instead to one of the lounges and nursed three drinks until two o'clock. He paid his tab, left a generous tip, then stood in line at the counter to claim his ticket. The clerk looked at him sharply, and her tone was scolding as she told him that they preferred passengers on transatlantic flights to check in at least an hour and a half before departure. Mitch said nothing, simply accepted his ticket and baggage claim tag and walked to the departure gate. One of the precautions he relentlessly drilled into his clients was the convenient targets travelers presented to terrorists at airports. He advised them to limit their visibility when waiting to board a flight, and he followed his own advice. He walked at a leisurely pace, arriving at the departure gate just as his flight was boarding.

One of the pleasures of flights such as this one was that few people had the energy to make conversation. Mitch stowed his vest in the overhead compartment and then folded his length into the seat. The man next to him in the first-class area was asleep almost as soon as the plane reached cruising altitude. Mitch reclined his seat and closed his eyes. Now, at last, he could surrender to the sweeping hatred the unexpected phone call had unleashed. It was a simple matter for his mind to conjure up an image of the Russian Icon.

Mitch's jaw clenched at the code name. *Icon* was Aleksandr Fedoryshyn, a known KGB agent. Six years had passed since he had last seen Fedoryshyn, six years since the meeting in a quiet Vienna park that had left Mitch with a bullet in his stomach and a dead partner.

Fierce green eyes snapped open when Mitch felt a blanket being placed over him.

"I thought you might be cold," the stewardess informed him with an inviting smile. This tall, well-built man with fascinating green eyes had attracted her attention during boarding. It was going to be a quiet flight across the Atlantic, and she hoped to find a way to work her address and phone number into any conversation they might have. "I didn't mean to wake you."

"You didn't." His tone was as hostile as his eyes and put a swift end to the stewardess' planning. "As long as you're here, you can bring me a mineral water."

The stewardess' smile dimmed, and she turned quickly to attend to another passenger. Mitch lit a cigarette and, when the stewardess returned a few moments later, he gave her a curt nod as he accepted the drink. Removing a small bottle of aspirin from his shirt pocket, he shook three tablets into his hand and downed them with a large swallow of water. He'd been getting a lot of headaches lately; Maureen, his employee and, once upon a time, his bed partner, had been urging him to see a doctor. He hadn't, of course. He trusted doctors about as much as he trusted the hierarchy of the Central Intelligence Agency.

As the plane left the French coastline behind, Mitch's thoughts returned to Fedoryshyn. Six years ago the Russian had been working for Directorate K of the KGB—the directorate that deals with the penetration of foreign intelligence organizations—and Mitch had been employed by the CIA, stationed in Vienna. His assignment had been simple enough: follow his counterpart, Fedoryshyn, in an effort to determine which organizations might be compromised. He and his partner, Jim Groves, had done so, and in the end reached the inescapable conclusion that it was the CIA itself that had been penetrated.

Jim had had a source within the Soviet delegation in Vienna, and at his request, the source had investigated Fedoryshyn and found the proof Mitch and Jim needed in order to take their suspicions to their chief of station. Because of the urgency of the information, instead of using the usual dead-drop, Jim had arranged a meeting with his source in order to receive the information.

They had waited in that quiet park for over an hour, Jim sitting on one of the benches surrounding the pond while

Mitch took advantage of the shadows directly across the pond from his partner. Jim's source had arrived, and, behind him, Fedoryshyn; the source had unknowingly led an assassin to his Agency control officer. Fedoryshyn had calmly killed the two men and removed a thick envelope from the dead Soviet's coat before Mitch had been able to react to the assassinations by drawing his handgun and shooting at the killer. Fedoryshyn had returned the fire with nearly fatal accuracy, badly wounding Mitch, and only the unexpected arrival of a group of students had prevented the Russian from finishing the job. Mitch had been whisked out of Vienna by the CIA and had spent his convalescence planning Fedoryshyn's death.

By the time Mitch was well enough to return to duty, the Russian had been transferred from Vienna to Moscow and, until now, he had remained safely within the borders of the Soviet Union. Mitch crushed out his cigarette and leaned back in his seat. It seemed reasonable to conclude that he had been asked to return to Langley because he was the only CIA officer who had had contact with Fedoryshyn and lived to tell about it. The Agency needed to pick his brain, learn everything that he remembered about the Russian, and was willing to pay for the privilege, provided he left Fedoryshyn alone while he was acting as a consultant to the Agency. Once his contract was up, however, Mitch could do as he pleased. The thought was enough to bring a genuine smile to his lips.

Mitch Carlisle believed in the biblical code of an eye for an eye. He would deal with Fedoryshyn in his own way and in his own time.

Greg Talbott patiently awaited Mitch's arrival at the gate. Clad informally in jeans, sweatshirt and jacket, a half smile on his boyish face, Greg looked more like a Boy Scout than a CIA agent. Nothing about him signified that he was anything but a friend or relative here to meet a plane; he had been trained to blend into his surroundings so well that no one would look at him twice. It was an invaluable trick, one of many he had learned from Mitch Carlisle before the older man had left the Agency.

The CIA frowned on his association with Mitch—Carlisle had left the Agency after a blowup with the deputy director regarding the existence of a mole within the Agency— but since Mitch had made quite a name for himself within the counterterrorist community in Europe, it was expedient for the CIA to allow the association to continue. Mitch would have nothing to do with the CIA itself, but he was loyal to his friends, such as Greg, the man he had helped train.

Mitch came through the gate. Greg straightened and allowed his smile to stretch into a grin as Mitch came to a halt in front of him. "Welcome home, teach. How was the flight?"

Mitch raised an eyebrow. "Quiet."

Greg laughed and extended his hand. "It's good to see you."

Not even Mitch could resist Greg's blatant charm. He smiled and shook the other man's hand. "Let's get my suitcase and then I'll see how much pull you have with the customs people."

"Am I going to need influence?" Greg asked as they made their way to the baggage claim area.

The quiet note of concern in Greg's voice drew another smile from Mitch. "Relax, kid—there's nothing in my suitcase that shouldn't be there."

Half an hour later they were in Greg's car, heading out of Washington. Mitch lit a cigarette and studied the flow of traffic through the nation's capital. "Okay, fill me in."

Greg glanced quickly at his friend and then returned his attention to the road. "You and I have to get a few things straight before I update you. First, I'm the one who suggested you be brought in on this—the deputy director only agreed because I convinced him that having you here in the flesh would be more helpful than simply reading your old reports on Fedoryshyn."

"What do you want, a percentage of my salary?" Mitch joked. "Look, kid, I'm grateful—"

"I don't want your gratitude," Greg replied steadily. "I happen to be the official liaison officer between the FBI and the Agency, and if Fedoryshyn mysteriously disappears or turns up dead in an alley, I'm the one who's going to catch the fallout. I want your word that you won't touch the Russian while he's in the States."

Mitch stared at his protégé's profile. "I agreed to that stipulation over the phone."

"And I know how badly you want Fedoryshyn. I only hope you don't want him badly enough to betray a friend."

"I see." Mitch drew a deep breath. "Okay. I won't touch him in the States. When I take him, there won't be anything to connect him to the FBI or you. Good enough?"

"Good enough," Greg echoed. "Second, the FBI doesn't know that you're a consultant. They think you're still a case officer, directly employed by the Agency. You aren't to do anything to make them think differently. Agreed?"

"Agreed," Mitch replied, a sardonic smile twisting his mouth.

"And last, please don't alienate the FBI."

"Now, why would I do that?" Mitch demanded, silently amused by the beseeching quality of Greg's request.

"The FBI agent I'm working with is young and strictly by-the-book. But he's a nice guy and he tries hard."

"So?"

Greg looked at his former mentor. "So, I've watched you take people apart verbally, and it's not a pretty sight. All the information we've received thus far has been courtesy of the FBI—don't kill the goose that lays golden eggs. Deal?"

"I'll handle him with kid gloves," Mitch vowed, a hand over his heart.

"See, that's the problem. I don't want you to 'handle' him—I want you to cooperate with him."

Mitch chuckled. "Different words, same result."

"That's what worries me." Greg shook his head and signaled for the off ramp labeled CIA-Langley.

Chapter 2

"Minnesota?" Mitch narrowed his eyes against the smoke from his cigarette and regarded the FBI agent across the table from him. They were in a small, windowless room that held one round table, four chairs and a counter along one wall, on which reposed a coffee maker. "What the hell is Fedoryshyn doing in Minnesota?"

"As of next Friday, he will be giving a series of lectures at Llewellyn College in Minneapolis on the abuses of power during the Stalin era in the Soviet Union." Special Agent Keith Johnson shuffled the papers in one of his many folders and closed the cover. It was ten o'clock Friday morning on the East Coast, and he had just stepped off the plane from Minneapolis two hours ago, after twelve hours of following Aleksandr Fedoryshyn from the tea given in his honor through his guided tour of the city. He was hungry, tired, suffering from jet lag and feeling harassed by the endless stream of questions Mitch threw at him.

"Right. And I'm queen of the May," Mitch snapped. "Why did you people approve his visa? The man is a known KGB agent."

"Was," Special Agent Johnson pointed out. "We have no evidence to indicate he is still a member of that organization."

"Evidence," Mitch growled. "I'll give you evidence, you little—"

"Mitch," Greg broke in before his former mentor said something that would alienate the FBI man. "Keith is just doing his job."

"What exactly is his job?" Mitch demanded. "Setting up guided tours for the KGB?"

Greg sighed heavily. "According to the information given on his visa application, Fedoryshyn is a college history professor. You know he isn't, I suspect he isn't, but State has to have proof in order to pull his visa."

"There are procedures to be followed," Keith concurred. "And unfortunately, until we have evidence to the contrary, the man is simply a visiting professor."

"Dare I ask why you don't simply pull him in and question him?" Mitch asked sarcastically.

"We have no *legitimate* reason to do so," Johnson replied. "If we did what you're suggesting, we could create a major diplomatic incident, and we at the FBI would just as soon avoid that."

"Fine," Mitch grated out. "We'll do this the hard way. Let's pretend, just for the sake of argument, that Fedoryshyn *is* KGB. Tell me what is going on in Minneapolis that would interest him."

"That's a rather broad question," Johnson began nervously. "Minneapolis has several large computer and ordnance firms, almost all of which hold government contracts—defense contracts—of one sort or another. These firms do software and hardware design, as well as the actual manufacturing of defense products."

Mitch nodded. "That would seem to be a good starting point. I assume you have a team following Fedoryshyn."

"Of course."

The contemptuous note in Johnson's reply almost brought a smile to Mitch's face. "Good. Now, what about the college where Fedoryshyn is supposedly lecturing?"

"What about it?"

"Special Agent Johnson, we are playing a game of 'what if,'" Mitch intoned with exaggerated patience. "We have already ruled out one of the reasons for Fedoryshyn's presence in the Midwest, assuming he is still a member of the KGB—acting as security for a Soviet delegation. That leaves us with the second reason—espionage. Now, you have brilliantly outlined the technology available in Minneapolis. If he is indeed meeting someone from the defense industry, I would like to discover why he chose to use Llewellyn College as a cover story rather than keep the meeting with his contact covert."

"We—that is, I—have no idea."

Mitch sighed and crushed out his cigarette. "Just tell me about the college, Johnson."

Special Agent Johnson reached for another folder. "Llewellyn College is a small, private college which has an enviable reputation of academic achievement in all of its departments. Its liberal arts program—"

"Johnson," Mitch interrupted, "I'm not interested in whether or not the music department has discovered that Mozart was a fraud who took credit for someone else's work, and neither is Fedoryshyn. What about Llewellyn's science departments?"

"Those departments also have excellent reputations. Several, in fact, have applied for and received government research grants."

Mitch paused in the act of lighting another cigarette. "What kind of grants—what are they for?"

The FBI agent paged through the file. "Nothing spectacular—rather run-of-the-mill, I would say. Two ecology professors are researching the environmental impact of landfill sites as they pertain to the aquifers that supply most of the water to the state. A biologist is studying the effect of cigarette smoke on rats' sex lives." He peered over the top of the report and gave Mitch a meaningful look. Mitch grinned mirthlessly and finished lighting his cigarette. "And a physicist received a grant three years ago to develop a ceramic superconductor."

"I don't know much about superconductors," Mitch admitted. "Is it something our Soviet friend might be interested in?"

Keith shrugged as he hastily skimmed the summary in the file. "The grant was financed by the Defense Department. The most immediate use of a superconductor would be in high-speed computers, and that may be anywhere from three to five years in the future. Further down the road, theoretically, you understand, a superconductor might be used to float trains on magnetic cushions or be used in power lines that can meet tripled electric demands with superconductor cables." He looked up from the file. "However, as I said, the uses are purely speculative. The scientists have yet to come up with a superconductor that functions without being supercooled to incredible degrees." He closed the file. "And this particular team has published its findings in scientific journals. Anything Fedoryshyn might be interested in, he could pick up by reading."

Mitch rose and walked to the counter to pour more coffee into his mug. "Okay," he said, resuming his seat. "From what you've told us, it's my guess that Fedoryshyn is using the college as a cover. Whatever he's after is going to come from one of the businesses. Agreed?"

Special Agent Johnson and Greg both nodded.

"There is one more thing," Keith said to Mitch. "You're the only one around who has any kind of experience with Fedoryshyn, and my supervisor wants you in Minneapolis. In fact, he's probably talking to your deputy director right now. Does that present a problem for you? Any backlog that you can't clear up or hand off to someone else?"

Mitch's eyes glowed with green fire. "If the deputy director approves, I'm all yours."

*   *   *

Brenna Hawthorne, professor of history at Llewellyn College, stepped out of the history chairman's office and quietly closed the door behind her. Her cheeks were pink, lines were etched between her brows—a result of the past hour's argument—and her eyes sparkled angrily. Bradley Jackson, the history department chairman, made uncomfortably aware of what would happen to his department if alumni donations made to it were sharply curtailed, had agreed with Coach William "Bull" Miller and the athletic director that one of Brenna's students, Jake Larken, had no need of a tutor. Larken's grade for the quarter, Brenna had been informed, would undoubtedly be low, but it *would* meet the academic eligibility requirement that would allow him to participate in the upcoming playoffs.

She had lost the battle, Brenna thought as she pushed her glasses to the top of her head and massaged the ache that had begun in the middle of her forehead, but it was Jake who had lost the war. She didn't enjoy failing any student, but Jake had found his way into her heart. The freshman tackle had come to Llewellyn on a football scholarship and enrolled in the introductory history class Brenna was teaching. Thus far he had failed every test and quiz she had given. Concerned, she had gone back over his test papers and come to the conclusion that Jake was not stupid, but that he simply didn't read well enough to do the assigned work. When she had asked Jake to stay after class a week ago, Brenna had suggested that he take an incomplete for the class and hire a reading tutor.

Jake had agreed—the athletic scholarship was his only chance to earn a college degree—and yesterday he had informed Coach Miller of his plans. Within an hour the athletic director had called Bradley Jackson and demanded a meeting with Brenna and Coach Miller. The result was that Jake's academic future had been neatly sacrificed for Llewellyn's football season. At the moment, Brenna wasn't certain who she hated more: herself, Jackson or Coach Miller.

"Professor Hawthorne?"

Brenna pulled her thoughts away from the disastrous meeting and summoned a wan smile for the department's general secretary. "What is it, Penny?"

The secretary looked distinctly uncomfortable. "There are two men waiting for you in your office. Police."

"Police," Brenna echoed. When Penny merely nodded, she asked, "Did they say what they wanted?"

"No, Professor, only that they wanted to speak with you. They were very insistent," Penny blurted out. "They wanted to wait here, but I knew Professor Jackson wouldn't approve, so I showed them to your office. I just didn't know what else to do."

Brenna sighed. "It's all right, Penny. Thanks for the warning." She marched out of the reception area and headed for her second-floor office.

Meredith Hall was a square building, four stories high, which housed the history and archaeology departments. Constructed in two concentric squares, the inner square held classrooms, labs and lecture halls while the outer square contained faculty offices. The department chairmen's offices were on the first floor. Brenna entered one of the four corner stairwells just at the end of eight-o'clock classes. In moments she was clinging to the banister to keep from being crushed underfoot as students stampeded to their next class. When she reached the hallway leading to the faculty offices, she gave a quick sigh of relief. The students seemed to be getting younger, taller and quicker with every passing year; more and more, the flow of traffic in the narrow corridors and stairwells resembled an obstacle course.

Her office door was open, and the two men waiting inside both stood as Brenna entered. They weren't in uniform, which meant, she assumed, they were detectives. "Professor Hawthorne?"

"That's me," she answered, closing the door and gesturing them back to their chairs. Her office was small, barely large enough for her desk, swivel chair and the plastic chairs the police presently occupied. Murmuring "Pardon me," she stepped over her guests' feet and seated herself behind the desk.

"We have a few questions to ask you," the older of the two began.

"No doubt, but if you don't mind, I'd like to see some identification before we go any further." Both men reached into their jacket pockets and produced their badges and picture identification. Brenna flipped her glasses back onto her nose and studied the photographs before nodding and settling back into her chair. "Okay, Inspector, what can I do for you?"

"You are acquainted with Professor Mark Prescott," the older man replied as he replaced his badge.

"Yes, he's a friend of mine," Brenna acknowledged, puzzled. Mark, a physicist, was part of Llewellyn's staff, and they had dated for the past three months. "Has something happened to him?"

"When did you last see him?" the younger man, a sergeant according to his identification, asked.

"Last night."

"What time?"

Brenna frowned. "Around five-thirty, I guess. We attended a faculty tea given for a guest lecturer here at the college. Why?"

"Have you had any other contact with Professor Prescott since then? Has he called you since last night?" the inspector pressed.

"No." Brenna's puzzlement was changing rapidly to concern. "Look, would you mind telling me what this is all about?"

"Did Prescott say anything about leaving Minneapolis, maybe taking a long weekend?"

Brenna shook her head. "We had planned to go out last night, but Mark had to cancel—he said he would call me today and we would decide...." Her voice trailed off. "Has something happened to Mark?"

"What reason did he give?" the sergeant queried. When she looked at him in confusion, he clarified, "Why did Professor Prescott cancel your date?"

"He said there was a problem in the lab—a problem with one of the tests they were running on the superconductor he's developing. He was going back to the lab to work." Brenna watched the sergeant record this answer, as he had all the others, in a small black notebook, and a shiver ran down her spine. "Will one of you *please* tell me what's happened?" she asked, feeling her palms grow slick with perspiration.

"Professor Prescott has disappeared," the inspector said softly, watching the color leave her face at his words. "And from what we've been able to learn, you appear to be the last person to have seen him." He offered Brenna an apologetic smile. "We really do need to talk further with you, Professor. Do you have any classes this afternoon?"

"Just one," Brenna answered, her voice small and breathless, her blue eyes filled with disbelief.

"Would it be possible for you to arrange for a substitute? Our questions really can't wait."

By the time Brenna turned into the driveway of her Victorian-style home, it was five o'clock. She had spent the afternoon at the police station, answering endless questions put to her by a succession of polite but insistent detectives. She told them everything she knew about Mark Prescott, which, judging from their expressions, was very little indeed. She and Mark had shared a passion for animal rights, old movies and pasta, but beyond that they had little in common. What she knew about his work, and his private life, could be put in a thimble. Mark had explained his superconductor project to her once, or tried to; her eyes had glazed over five minutes into his monologue, just as his had done when she had described the court politics of Elizabeth I. After that debacle, they had tacitly agreed not to discuss their respective fields except in the most general terms. Odd, but until the police had questioned her, she had not realized how superficial her relationship with Mark had been. Now she did.

The garage was set far back behind the house, and, when it and the house had been built, had been a carriage house. Brian, her ex-husband, had replaced the original double doors with the modern one-piece door for security. Brenna had lifted the garage door and was returning to her car when she finally noticed the two pickup trucks parked in front of her house. The vehicles were noticeably out of place in the quiet cul-de-sac, and the sight of them worried her. Instead of parking the car in the garage, she left it idling in the driveway and started up the sidewalk to the back door of her house. She was within six feet of the entrance when the storm door swung open and a smiling, burly man emerged.

The screech Brenna emitted startled him, and his smile disappeared momentarily. It was back within seconds. "Hiya, Doc. What's the matter? Did I scare you?"

Brenna's gloved hand fell away from her throat. "George! I completely forgot about you."

"You did? Your neighbor had the key, just like you said." He hefted the wooden toolbox he carried and grinned. "We're just picking up—be out of your hair in fifteen minutes or so." He edged around her and started down the driveway.

Walking back to her car, Brenna watched as he carried the toolbox to one of the pickups that bore the legend We Do Renew on its side. Between her argument with Coach Miller and the news that Mark had disappeared, Brenna had indeed forgotten that George and his firm were to start the remodeling work on her kitchen today.

She was juggling a stack of midterm papers and a bulging briefcase while trying to lower and lock the garage door when George made his return trip to the house.

"I thought once you taught college, you didn't have homework," he joked, hurrying forward to take her briefcase and lock the garage door for her. "Listen, I don't want you to worry when you see the kitchen," he continued as he held open the back door of the house. "It don't look like much now, but in another month it'll be beautiful. Trust me.''

It was a good thing she had been warned, Brenna thought when she stepped into the kitchen. The room was in the process of being gutted. Two of the four walls bore white scars where counters and cupboards had once been; the refrigerator, microwave, dishwasher and stove had been pulled away from the walls and stood forlornly next to a butcherblock island in the middle of the floor. Next to them was a tarpaulin-covered mass that George's four employees walked around in order to carry their equipment back to the pickups. The wall that had once separated the kitchen from a small walk-in pantry was now minus its plaster, and the laths stood out like bones.

''We put your dishes and stuff in boxes and covered them with the tarp,'' George explained, setting her briefcase on the stove while Brenna placed the midterm test booklets on the one remaining countertop. ''The wall decorations and wind chimes we packed and put down in the basement. Your table and chairs are down there, too. Also, all your appliances except the dishwasher still work,'' he said reassuringly, pointing to the thick, orange extension cords that looked like life-support equipment as they snaked across the linoleum to wall outlets. ''In a week or so we're going to have to clear the kitchen, but we're trying to keep the room usable until then.''

Brenna felt like crying. ''How long did you say the remodeling is going to take?''

''Four weeks—six at the outside.'' George peered down at her, his ever-present smile slipping. ''I warned you it was going to be a mess.''

''I know, George,'' Brenna sighed. ''I guess I just didn't expect it to be so—'' she gestured helplessly ''—drastic.''

''Doc, by New Year's Eve, this is all going to seem like a bad dream.'' He turned away to pick up a crowbar.

''It already does,'' she mumbled under her breath. ''Did you have any trouble?'' she asked when George straightened.

"Nah. The messiest part is taking down the pantry walls, replacing the plumbing and ripping up this flooring." He glanced once more around the devastation, nodding in satisfaction. "We'll be back Monday, Doc."

With a wan smile, Brenna walked him to the back door and locked it after him. Then she walked slowly through the disaster that had once been a kitchen as she stripped off her gloves. Propped against one wall was her bulletin board, and with a sigh she crouched in front of it and sorted through the various papers pinned to it. Finally, buried under a notice from the city regarding recycling efforts, she found the note she had written to herself about the remodeling project. Tugging it from its hiding place, she read the reminder: "George & co. Friday, 11/23, 9 a.m. Marcia will open house."

Marcia Thompson, her friend and neighbor, lived directly across the street and had volunteered to let George and his demolition derby into the house for the duration of the remodeling. Brenna sighed again and crumpled the note in her fist. She might be absentminded, but she wouldn't need the note to herself now that she would be living with the mayhem created by George and his happy band.

Locating the wastebasket, Brenna tossed the note into it and then pushed through one of two swinging doors in the kitchen that led, respectively, into the central hall and formal dining room. She hung her coat on the oak coat tree next to the front door and placed her boots alongside it before trudging upstairs to her bedroom.

When she opened the door, half a dozen voices howled their welcome. Reclining on the bed, chair and mirrored vanity were the six cats she had acquired either through her own efforts or by chance. Last weekend the number of her menagerie had been ten, but she had managed to find good homes for four of her housemates. Brenna silently blessed Marcia for having the foresight to keep the cats separated from the workmen. Sitting on the edge of the bed, she scratched the ears of the feline closest to her. A moment later a large, gray, battle-scarred tom leaped lightly into her lap and demanded equal time.

"Hello, Jasper," Brenna murmured, stroking the soft, thick fur and receiving a satisfied purr for her efforts. "And how was your day?"

When Jasper curled up in a ball on her lap, she lifted the phone on the bedside table and punched in a phone number as familiar to her as her own. "Hello, Marcia," she sighed when her friend answered. "Sit down. You won't believe what's happened."

Saturday afternoon was sunny and cold, and found Mitch and Greg sitting at desks in the Minneapolis FBI office, going over files that had been compiled on the different defense projects being developed in the Twin Cities area. They had been at the chore since early morning, taking time only for a quick lunch.

Special Agent Keith Johnson had been working with them until half an hour ago, when he was called into his supervisor's office next door for a meeting. Mitch tossed the last folder aside and rose, stretching to work out the kinks in his muscles.

"What do you think?" Greg asked, picking up the discarded folder.

"I think there is the possibility of hundreds of leaks," Mitch said bluntly. "But nothing I've read tells me who, what or where."

Greg nodded in agreement. "Our best bet seems to be tailing Fedoryshyn with the hope that he'll lead us to the leak."

Mitch reached for the aspirin bottle sitting next to his coffee cup and shook three tablets into his hand. "Which will also be an exercise in futility, unless Aleksei has lost his touch. Which I doubt." He washed the tablets down with cold coffee, grimacing.

"So what do you want to do?"

"What I'd like to do is pump our Russian friend full of so many drugs that he'd confess to sinking the Titanic,"

Mitch growled. "Unfortunately I don't think our FBI friends would take too kindly to that approach."

"Neither would the deputy director," Greg reminded him.

Mitch pulled out a cigarette and lit it. "Which means we wait and hope that the surveillance and phone taps turn up something." He paused as the door opened to admit Keith. "Welcome back. I'd ask if you have any good news, but the look on your face says it all."

Keith Johnson quietly closed the door and shoved his hands into his trouser pockets. "I just came from a meeting with the Minneapolis police," he began.

Mitch raised an eyebrow, but said nothing as he waited for the young man to continue.

"Is there a problem?" Greg asked.

"Possibly." He leaned against the door, his eyes fixed on the pile of folders. "The Bureau's assistance has been requested to investigate a disappearance."

"That's a little out of your jurisdiction, isn't it?" Mitch inquired. "Unless the disappearance is a kidnapping?"

"There is that possibility," Keith admitted. "But the police are calling the incident a disappearance. We're being brought in because of the victim's connection with the government." His gaze shifted to Mitch. "Professor Mark Prescott has disappeared. Literally. It's like the earth opened up and swallowed the man."

"Prescott," Mitch repeated. "The physicist, right? The one developing a superconductor?"

Keith nodded. "And to make matters worse, Prescott's research team has discovered that the lab files and documentation on the superconductor that were kept in Prescott's office have disappeared. And so has the ceramic material they were testing. Also, when the research team tried to recover the project data from Prescott's personal computer, they found that the files no longer exist—someone has completely erased the computer's memory."

Mitch momentarily hushed the little voice that was screaming for attention, telling him that this was what the

Russian was after. "I thought all this superconductor stuff was theoretical."

"It is, at least I thought so. According to Prescott's colleagues, however, they came up with the formula in early September, manufactured the ceramic by midmonth and were testing by the end of the month."

"And," Greg prodded.

"And—" Keith drew the word out "—all the test results have been positive. Better than anyone hoped, in fact. The ceramic conducted electricity at temperatures up to and including seventy-two degrees."

"I thought these ceramic conductors had to be super-cooled?" Mitch put in, recalling Keith's original briefing.

Keith met the older man's gaze stoically. "So did the members of the rest of the scientific community. Only Prescott and his staff knew differently."

Mitch's little voice began screaming again, and this time he listened to it as his cold, impassive eyes slid to Greg. "Bingo."

Mark Prescott's town house was located in one of the upwardly mobile suburbs south of Minneapolis. The small yards were cookie-cutter perfect and nearly identically landscaped. The cars in the driveways were European imports, mute testaments to their owners' successful careers. Mitch yanked the yellow plastic tape, stenciled with the words Police Barricade, Do Not Cross, away from the front door and stepped inside the small split foyer, Keith and Greg right behind him.

The police had searched both Prescott's home and office yesterday, but the FBI had opened its own investigation and would conduct its search and gather evidence in its own way. The three men had decided to go through the town house first, as it was probably the more pristine of the two scenes. Mitch climbed the six steps leading to the upper floor.

All the drapes were open, and winter sunlight dappled the gray carpet. From his viewpoint on the landing, Mitch could see the living room, dining room, kitchen and the hallway that he assumed led to the bedrooms. What struck Mitch first was the perfection of the rooms. Even with the previous search, the town house retained the neat appearance that a home assumes when the owner has gone on vacation. He walked through the upper floor, noting the coffee grinder and pasta machine, which stood on the kitchen counters. A quick check of the bathroom revealed an electric razor, toothpaste and cologne; in the bedroom the bed was made and three pieces of luggage reposed on the floor of the closet. There were a minimum of empty hangers in the closet, indicating that wherever Prescott had gone, he had taken little, if any, clothing with him.

Mitch took the two half-flights of steps that brought him to the lower level of the town house. Again, the family room, half bath and laundry room were tidy. Nothing indicated a struggle, let alone a kidnapping. He crouched in front of the stereo system, which took up the length of the common wall between Prescott's town house and the one next door. The sound system was relatively new, as were most of the compact discs he found in the storage unit. Again, he could find nothing to indicate foul play. On his way back to the upper level, he opened the door leading to the garage. As the police report had indicated, Prescott's car was missing.

"Anything?" Greg asked as he and Keith searched through the kitchen cabinets.

"Nothing of interest," Mitch replied, opening the refrigerator and examining the contents. He took a carton of milk from the shelf, opened it and sniffed tentatively. The milk hadn't soured.

Keith closed the final cupboard. "Everything we've found—or not found—indicates that Prescott didn't plan on leaving. The police came to the same conclusion."

Mitch pulled out one of the dining room chairs and folded himself into it. "On the other hand, if I wanted to disappear, this is exactly the way I'd leave my home." He stared thoughtfully out the French doors that led to a small deck. "Did the local police check Prescott's bank accounts?"

Keith nodded. "They also found his checkbook, savings passbook and safe-deposit box key. The last check was written to the gas company. If Prescott planned all this, he would have taken his money with him."

"Prescott's assets are now frozen?" was Mitch's next question.

"As of noon yesterday," Keith confirmed. "The police have also supplied us with a copy of their investigation."

"Good. I want to look at that after we've seen Prescott's office." Mitch rose and started for the stairs.

"Why search Prescott's office?" Keith asked, starting after the older man. "There's nothing to be found."

"That's the point." Mitch's voice floated back to the two men. "You can tell as much by what you don't find as by what you do."

By ten o'clock Saturday night, the FBI had completed its search of Mark Prescott's laboratory and office. Mitch, Keith and Greg were seated at one end of an oval table in a conference room, the cardboard containers of their take-out dinner scattered like flotsam across the highly polished oak tabletop. Mitch tossed the police report he had been reading into the growing pile of folders in the middle of the table and got up to stretch his legs.

"What's your opinion?" Keith asked, drawing a weary hand over his face.

Mitch watched the headlights of the traffic weave through the brightly lit Minneapolis streets. "Fedoryshyn hasn't gone anywhere today?"

"We've had a team staked out across the street from his apartment, and another team in the apartment next to his. He hasn't stepped foot outside the building."

"You have a tap on his phone and more in the apartment itself?" Greg queried. At Keith's nod, the CIA man shook his head. "If Prescott is his contact, Fedoryshyn is playing it very cool."

"He's not the type to come apart under stress," Mitch reminded the other two men.

"Hell," Keith suddenly burst out. "We can't be sure he *did* come here to meet Prescott. There is every reason to believe that Prescott's disappearance is just a coincidence."

"No, there's no coincidence—Prescott's the one," Mitch said with quiet certainty.

"How can you be sure?" Keith demanded. "Just this morning you were positive Fedoryshyn's contact was someone in the business community! Read the reports the police compiled after talking to Prescott's friends and colleagues. The man did nothing, *nothing,* out of the usual during the last few months. Don't you think that if he had sold this superconductor for a small fortune there would have been some indication of it?"

Mitch spun the flywheel on his battered, stainless-steel lighter, absently studying his reflection in the window. "You're assuming that our physicist is a fine, upstanding citizen. I'm working from the assumption that he's anything but."

"Why Prescott?" Keith insisted again. "Why not one of the hundreds of people who are working in the defense section?"

"A couple of reasons." Mitch turned and gave Keith a brief, humorless smile. "One—defense projects are highly compartmentalized and its workers, with a very few exceptions, don't have access to every step of whatever project they're working on. One guy might write the software for the electronic sensors on a radar-guided missile, but he won't know about the hardware design of the radar itself. The same goes for the other defense projects in your files. Accessibility is the key, and your average worker just doesn't have it."

"Which leads us to two—Prescott had accessibility to every aspect of the superconductor development, and he kept the compiled lab notes and all definitive documentation in his office. The only other key to his office is the master key the janitor carries. Now, I find it rather difficult to believe that the janitor took the hard copies of the documentation *and* erased the computer memory, don't you?"

"Three—Fedoryshyn arrives and, according to the police report, Prescott breaks a date with his girlfriend in order to work late in the lab, claiming there is a problem with the ceramic. But when the police question the other people on his team, not one of them knows anything about this supposed problem. I don't believe in coincidence. Do you?"

"But Prescott's home and office were so...neat," Keith argued. "And what about his bank accounts? Wouldn't he at least have taken his money with him if he planned to disappear?"

"It depends on how much Fedoryshyn is paying," Mitch said casually. "The selling price of a superconductor probably makes the balance in Prescott's bank accounts look like chicken feed."

"Everything you say makes sense," Keith fretted, "but it's all circumstantial."

"Agreed."

Silence descended as each man considered Mitch's logic. Greg sipped at his coffee and frowned up at the recessed lighting. "Let's say you're right," he said at last. "How do we know Prescott hasn't passed the information to Fedoryshyn already?" He hunted through the pile of manila folders until he found the one he wanted. "Here, he and the Russian were introduced at the faculty tea welcoming Fedoryshyn. He could have passed Fedoryshyn the documentation after the tea."

"Except that Fedoryshyn left with the chairman of the history department," Keith put in. "And we started surveillance at the tea—a team has been tailing him since Thursday afternoon. If he met Prescott, we would have seen it."

A pleased gleam entered Mitch's eyes. "Which means..."

"That Prescott is still somewhere in the city," Keith said at last, a smile creeping across his face.

"Possibly," Mitch hedged. "Or he might be long gone, waiting in Mexico or the Cayman Islands for someone else to make the delivery."

Greg immediately understood his friend's reasoning. "A middleman. But who?"

"A likely candidate is that professor Prescott's been dating." Mitch flipped open the folder he had recently discarded. "Brenna Hawthorne."

"As I remember the police report, she was just as surprised as anyone over Prescott's disappearance." Greg took the folder from under Mitch's hand. "Look, they've only been dating for two or three months."

"If I were Prescott," Mitch speculated, "I wouldn't risk showing myself after my clever disappearing act, so I'd need someone to act as go-between. Someone uninvolved with the project itself—like a history professor, who, coincidentally, happens to have access to Aleksei Fedoryshyn on a daily basis."

"It makes sense," Keith breathed. "It's circumstantial as hell, but it sure does make sense."

"I suggest you start a second stakeout, at the Hawthorne house." Mitch crushed out his cigarette. "I also suggest that you compile a dossier on the history professor—I'll bet it makes fascinating reading."

Chapter 3

Sitting in the van parked at the T-shaped intersection formed by Brenna Hawthorne's cul-de-sac and the cross street, Mitch Carlisle sipped coffee from a disposable cup and glanced at his watch when the lights in the Hawthorne house went on.

"Six o'clock in the morning," he muttered, entering the time in the log they kept. "What do you suppose she's doing?"

"Probably making Thanksgiving dinner," Greg replied. He stretched as much as the cramped quarters of the van's driver's seat allowed. Twisting around to look at Mitch, who was seated in one of the captain's chairs in the rear of the van, he added, "Or did you forget what day it is?"

Mitch rubbed his eyes. He had forgotten; living outside of the States for ten years, surrounded primarily by foreigners, tended to allow a man to forget national holidays. "I guess I did."

"Maybe you should think about coming home."

"My business, in case you've forgotten, is in Europe."

"So move it here," Greg suggested amiably. "There are plenty of American corporations that would be happy to pay you to train their employees."

"It's been too long," Mitch mused more to himself than Greg as he stared out of the smoked-glass window at the snow-covered expanse of lawns with their thrusting spires of frosted evergreens. "Besides, there's nothing here for me, not anymore."

Greg didn't reply. He knew that Mitch's parents had died years earlier, before Mitch had joined the CIA, and his brother shortly thereafter. Mitch had told Greg about his family just five months ago, when the two of them had visited some of the sleazier bars in Paris and proceeded to drink themselves blind. It was that job that had set Mitch off, Greg realized now. Mitch had been hired by an old acquaintance, Seth Winter, to teach the Dateline News staff how to protect itself when a terrorist group called the Freedom Brigade had threatened, then kidnapped Seth's star reporter, Cassandra Blake.

Mitch had handled the terrorist threat well enough; it was when the entire affair was over and he had watched Seth and Cassandra cling to one another that a state that Greg could only term depression settled over Mitch. They had gone on a three-day binge that Greg could recall only with difficulty, but he did remember Mitch saying that he envied Winter. Sober, Mitch would never admit that he had said such a thing, but Greg knew how ruthless a life his friend led. There was no gentleness in his life and, with the exception of Greg, no one that he truly called a friend. Women— well, Greg shrugged inwardly, women were a convenience for Mitch Carlisle, a tool to be used as he would a gun or a garrote. Nothing in Mitch's life was permanent, with the possible exception of the French château that he had blackmailed from the Company and now used as the base for his business.

"I wonder if she's having company today," Greg asked out loud, his thoughts turning to his parents' home in Pennsylvania. If Fedoryshyn had stayed in the Soviet

Union, he would be there now, playing with the nieces and nephews his siblings seemed to provide on a regular basis.

"I doubt it," Mitch replied to Greg's question. "According to the file Keith compiled, her parents are dead and her brother lives in another state. The only family she has here is her ex-husband, and since he's living with another woman, I don't think he's going to show up."

Their shift ended at eight, when a two-man team in another van relieved them. Greg drove them back to the hotel, where they had breakfast before returning to their room. Greg fell asleep immediately, but Mitch was tense from the eight-hour vigil and the coffee he had drunk. Sleep eluded him and eventually he rose and padded silently into the outer room of their suite.

Retrieving a manila folder from an end table, his eyes lingered for a moment on the leather case that contained the badge and picture identification proclaiming him to be Special Agent Carlisle of the FBI. Greg had an identical wallet, and both were courtesy of Langley, not the FBI. In fact, the FBI was unaware of their phony identification. Between watching Fedoryshyn and Prescott's colleagues and searching the Twin Cities area for some clue as to Prescott's whereabouts, the FBI resources were stretched thin, and the special-agent-in-charge considered watching the Hawthorne woman a waste of time. But Mitch, with Greg backing him, had insisted, so the two of them had been assigned the midnight-to-eight shift of the stakeout. Their identification would keep them out of trouble with the local police—in the event such a problem arose—but technically they had no power at all. They were CIA, and the CIA's legal jurisdiction was outside of the United States. Keith's superior had even refused to issue the CIA men weapons, but that was hardly a problem. Greg had made another phone call and, within twenty-four hours, he and Mitch were legally armed with .38 revolvers. Not Mitch's weapon of choice, but they were better than nothing.

Now Mitch found a chair in the darkened room, turned on the lamp beside him and began rereading the dossier compiled by the FBI on the Hawthorne woman. "Brenna Elizabeth Hawthorne, née Sanders. Age: thirty-five. Occupation: professor of history, Llewellyn College. Marital Status: divorced. Education Background..."

He closed his burning eyes. He had the entire file memorized, but he found it hard to reconcile all the facts so neatly printed out on the buff-colored pages to the faraway look and half smile she wore in the black-and-white picture attached to the folder.

She had been a model student academically; in her field she was considered one of the new, emerging geniuses. On the other hand, she had such a devil of a time balancing her checkbook that her bank no longer sent her overdraft notices. One of the bank officers had discovered several years ago that Brenna considered such notices junk mail and simply threw them away. Now, whenever she came dangerously close to overdrawing her account, the officer called her and suggested she put some money into checking. Fortunately for Brenna, her teaching salary was amply supplemented by income from a trust fund established years ago by her parents. Brenna always thanked the bank officer graciously and transferred the funds. Unless she had forgotten to make a note of it, in which case he had to remind her again.

Notes. Mitch skimmed down the page until he found the paragraph he wanted. The woman constantly made notes to herself, and not just about such things as doctor appointments, like normal people. She had to write a note to remind herself to go grocery shopping! How could anyone not remember there was no food in the house, Mitch wondered. It came as no surprise that her marriage had ended in divorce.

He flipped a few more pages until he came to her arrest record and shook his head in disgust. She couldn't remember to buy a quart of milk, but she never forgot to attend a demonstration when the cause was dear to her. Her first arrest had been during her freshman year at college. She had been participating in a protest against the Vietnam War; the protest had got out of hand and the police moved in and hauled everyone off to jail. She was charged with disturbing the peace, had pleaded guilty and got off with a small fine.

In graduate school she became involved in protesting the killing of baby snow seals. She and three friends had found out that one of the fashion industry's biggest furriers was returning from a buying trip in which the white, baby-seal skins figured prominently, and had flown to New York to meet him. They had accosted the poor soul at Kennedy Airport and an argument ensued. When the man justifiably shoved them aside and tried to walk away, Brenna opened her voluminous shoulder bag and threw the contents at him. The contents had been balloons, filled with liquid vegetable oil laced with red dye, that burst upon contact. The group had been charged with assault and battery. Again, Brenna and her friends had pleaded guilty, agreed to pay replacement costs for the furrier's clothing and flown back home.

The next escapade had occurred while she was working on her doctorate. There was a well-known medical research facility attached to the medical school at the university she was attending, and it was common knowledge that unclaimed animals were purchased from the city pound and used for experimentation. Brenna's group had broken into the research building and kidnapped—or animal-napped—the creatures. The scientists had come to work the next morning to discover all their experiments gone. It had taken a little longer for the police to track down the group this time, but eventually seven people were arrested, including Brenna. This time, however, Brenna used the media hype surrounding the event to her advantage. By the time her trial date arrived, the papers had given appalling accounts of what went on in the laboratories, along with pictures of experiments that were under way and photographs of the animals that had been saved from such a fate.

The day of her trial there was a demonstration under way in front of the courthouse steps, calling for the release of

Brenna and her cohorts. Public opinion had been firmly, fiercely behind the suspects. This time, however, when they pleaded guilty, they were sentenced to ten days in the county workhouse, to be served on consecutive weekends. By the time Brenna and her friends had served their sentence, they had all the other inmates writing letters to their congressmen on everything from banning nuclear testing to wildlife conservation.

Mitch covered his eyes with his free hand and shook his head. The woman was a nut, certifiable. But he couldn't prevent a smile when he imagined the seven activists handing out pens and paper during their weekends at the workhouse.

The next entry, however, wiped away the smile. Professor Hawthorne had met Professor Prescott at an animal rights meeting in August, and they had dated routinely right up until his disappearance. Mitch tossed the folder aside, turned off the lamp and made his way back to the bedroom. His last thought before falling asleep was that Brenna Hawthorne had flouted the law often enough in her past. Would she quibble at selling her country's technological secrets to a rival?

Brenna rose early Thanksgiving morning, washed her hair and showered, then, dressed in bathrobe and slippers, hurried downstairs into the disaster area that George insisted upon referring to as her kitchen. The cats followed, and sat flanking the refrigerator, their tails neatly curled around their paws as she went through the ritual of making coffee. Once the coffee maker was started, the cats began an atonal cry that indicated it was now their turn to be fed. Brenna frowned at them as she opened the refrigerator and removed the thawed turkey from the bottom shelf.

"Come on, guys, it's Thanksgiving. In six hours you're going to stuff yourself on turkey and dressing. Can't you wait?"

The cats, obviously, could not think beyond the moment. Resigned, Brenna flipped back a corner of the tarp and located the box containing the cat food. The last of the cupboards and counters had disappeared two days ago, and out of consideration for the upcoming holiday, George and his crew had left standing two sets of sawhorses with plywood stretched over them as work areas for her and had postponed removing the kitchen sink until next week. Brenna had unearthed two vinyl tablecloths to place over the plywood so her makeshift counters were at least clean.

Once her housemates were busy eating, she turned her attention to preparing the meal, but her thoughts strayed, as they often did, to Mark's disappearance. What could have happened to him? she wondered for perhaps the hundredth time since last Friday. People in her world simply did not vanish into thin air, leaving behind a mystery for the police to solve. The police had hinted at a possible drug connection, but Brenna had dismissed it at once. Mark had been a health fanatic; he ran ten miles every day and was a staunch vegetarian. Drugs had no place in his life. Brenna sighed heavily and turned her thoughts back to preparing the meal.

In half an hour the turkey was stuffed and baking in the oven, and Brenna was carefully setting a place at the cherry dining room table with her good crystal and china. The cats ignored her now, turning their attention to the wind chimes that hung in every room of the house. There were wind chimes in the enclosed front porch, as well, and in the summer, between the light breezes and the cats' fascination with moving objects, her home echoed with sound. Crystal, a pure white cat with incredibly green eyes, leaped to the top of the china hutch and batted playfully at the metal wind chime resembling birds in flight that hung in the corner.

Returning to the kitchen, Brenna poured herself a second cup of coffee and then walked through the central hall to the family room. She and Jasper spent the morning curled on the plush sectional couch, watching the Thanksgiving Day Parade on television. When the parade ended, Brenna dressed in jeans and a sweatshirt and put the finishing touches on the meal. At midafternoon, she and the cats shared the meal she had prepared. In light of the special occasion, she allowed the cats to eat in the dining room, and they took their meal in front of the china hutch, eating from paper plates decorated with a large, colorful turkey. Once the dishes were washed and put away, Brenna returned to the family room to review the proposal one of her doctoral candidates had submitted while Jasper slept beside her.

By eleven Brenna was ready for bed. Jasper and Crystal followed her through the nightly routine of checking the locks on the doors and turning out the lights on the first floor. Upstairs the six cats claimed their various sleeping areas in the master suite and adjoining bath while Brenna changed into her nightgown.

It was while Brenna was brushing her teeth that the phone rang. After hastily spitting toothpaste into the sink, she hurried into the bedroom and accidentally stepped on Hobo, a huge black tom who had lost part of his ears to frostbite, in the process. Hobo yowled, Brenna slipped on an area rug as she tried to avoid squashing him with her other foot and fell flat on her bottom while Hobo ran beneath the bed for protection and hissed at her. She grabbed at the phone and was just in time to hear the click of the caller disconnecting. Swearing, she rose and rubbed her abused posterior as she returned to the bathroom.

When she crawled into the king-size bed, Jasper, Hobo and Crystal joined her. Hobo had apparently forgiven her, for he padded up from the foot of the bed and butted her hand, demanding affection. Brenna stroked him with one hand while Jasper, stalking up to the empty pillow, curled into a tight ball and proceeded to purr into her ear. Crystal was snuggled into the area behind her knees. Brenna smiled drowsily; it was nice to share the bed, even if her companion—or companions—were feline. She fell asleep to the drone of Jasper's contented, rumbling purr.

Hours later Brenna awoke with a start. Strange. Usually she slept like the dead. Groggily she turned her head to look around. The room was quiet, faintly lit by the streetlight that illuminated the closed miniblinds. All seemed in order, but she couldn't shake the feeling that something had changed while she slept. Easing a hand out from under the covers, she felt for Jasper's comforting shape. He wasn't there, and upon further exploration, she discovered Crystal and Hobo were gone, as well. Ridiculously the hair on the back of her neck prickled in alarm.

She struggled upright, frowning in the darkness. "Jasper," she whispered. There was no answering meow. He must have knocked something over during his nocturnal wandering, Brenna decided, and the sound had wakened her. That perfectly logical explanation soothed her, and she released her pent-up breath with a soft puff of air. She was just snuggling back under the comforter when she heard a soft thunk from the first floor.

"Honestly, Jasper," she muttered in exasperation. Throwing back the covers, she groped her way across the room and out into the hallway. "I thought cats had perfect night vision."

Halfway down the steps she heard Jasper's distinct growl of displeasure, followed by a long, drawn-out feline hiss that she recognized as Hobo's. Brenna froze. The doorway of her first-floor office was just to the left of the staircase, and now she could see a beam of light sweep across the room. It stopped when it reached the foyer and landed on a quivering, irate ball of fur. Jasper growled again, his tail switching ominously in the yellow glare.

The chill nighttime air of the house couldn't compare to the cold that suddenly emanated from the very center of Brenna's bones. Someone was in her house! It seemed to take an eternity before the beam of light moved on, leaving the hissing feline in shadow, and when it did, Brenna was aware of the precariousness of her position. Her first thought was to get out of the house, but that was impossible. In order to reach either the front or back door, she had to pass by the office, in plain sight of the burglar. Her only hope was to get back to her bedroom and call the police. She placed a shaking hand on the banister and cautiously backed her way up the stairs, her eyes glued to the office door and that horrible, flickering light.

The hardwood floor beneath her feet had been one of the selling points of the house, but now Brenna was painfully aware that some of the boards squeaked and groaned whenever pressure was put on them. When she reached the landing without mishap, she almost sobbed in relief, but stifled the betraying sound by grinding her back teeth together. She continued backing across the landing until the office door was out of sight. Then she turned and, with exquisite care, made her way down the hall. It seemed to take forever to reach the bedroom, but then she was there, using one hand to guide herself around the bed so she didn't stumble. She found the phone and gave a quick prayer of thanks for the dial that lit up when she lifted the receiver.

She punched in the three numbers of the emergency line and waited for the call to go through, her eyes watching the bedroom doorway. What she would do if the burglar decided to investigate the second floor, Brenna didn't know. She could jump out of the window, she supposed wildly, provided the man didn't hear the sound such an action would cause, and the snow should cushion her fall sufficiently... Her terrified thoughts were brought up short by the voice answering her call.

"Please," she replied in a whisper, praying the anonymous man on the other end of the line could hear her. "There's someone in my house." She swallowed back another sob when the man asked a question. "Yes, right now, downstairs. Please, send someone— Wait!" She took the receiver away from her ear, listening. Did she hear a footstep on the stairs, or was it only the sound of her own heartbeat? Something fell heavily on the floor—a book, Brenna guessed—and she started to breathe again. The intruder was still on the first floor.

"Miss? Miss?" The voice was urgent.

"Yes, I'm here." She couldn't control the wild tremor in her voice.

"Give me your address."

Brenna did so, her fingers gripping the receiver so tightly that the joints ached.

"I'll have a car there in less than five minutes," the man assured her. "Now, listen to me. Where are you?"

"In my bedroom." She could barely force the words past lips that seemed frozen.

"Exactly where is your bedroom?"

"Upstairs," she whispered. "The first door to the left of the staircase."

"Close the door and lock it if you can, then wait for the police to get there. Do you hear me?"

"Yes."

"*Do not* leave the room and *don't* hang up. I want you to talk to me. Do you understand?"

"Yes." Her answer was little more than a thin thread of sound. She laid the receiver on the mattress and cautiously edged around the bed until she reached the door. She could hear Jasper and Hobo downstairs, still growling and hissing at the intruder, and her heart turned over. If only the cats had followed her back to the bedroom. Tears welled in her eyes as she eased the door shut. There was no lock, and she certainly couldn't risk dragging the small bedroom chair across the room to brace the door. Trembling, she retraced her steps to the phone.

"Miss?"

"Yes, I'm here. The door's closed."

"Okay. Now, talk to me. Tell me what you do for a living."

"Oh, God!" Her heart was threatening to beat its way out of her chest. "I—I can't."

"All right," the voice said calmly. "Then I'll do the talking. You just say something once in a while so I know you're still there."

The operator talked continually in that same self-possessed tone, but Brenna didn't know what he was saying. All her attention was fixed on the white porcelain knob on the bedroom door.

* * *

"Must be an accident," Greg Talbott observed from the driver's seat of the van when he caught sight of flashing rotary lights in the rearview mirror. Oddly enough, he did not hear a siren. He took another sip of coffee and watched the vehicle approach. "Ever think of changing professions?" he asked idly as the vehicle came close enough to be identified as a police car. "When I was a kid—what the hell?"

The police car had cut its emergency lights and turned sharply, slewing around the corner into the cul-de-sac. In the distance Greg could see a second police car rushing to join the first. "Mitch—" he said warily.

He didn't have to continue. Mitch, seated in the back of the van, was watching the first vehicle skid to a stop in front of the Hawthorne house. From what he could see, the house was dark, but the first uniformed policeman hit the ground at a dead run before the car had shuddered to a complete stop. His partner followed a moment later, just as the second police unit cleared the intersection. "Christ! Get us over there!" The cellular phone buzzed, and he grabbed the receiver as Greg started the engine and pulled a U-turn in the middle of the street. "What," he barked.

"This is the police dispatcher. We've got a possible break-in at your position."

"I can see that," Mitch snarled, bracing himself as the van slid on a patch of ice. "Thanks for the warning. Do me a favor and let your guys know we're coming in." He practically threw the receiver back onto the handset. Five days of boredom and now this! The way his luck was running, one of the locals would shoot him before he had a chance to show his bogus identification.

By the time he and Greg jumped out of the van, two policemen had taken up positions on either side of the front door, and a third was working his way around the corner of the house. Mitch put one foot on the sidewalk and froze when a fourth uniformed man popped up from behind the open door of the second police car and brought his gun to

bear on his chest. Mitch slowly raised his hands. "We're
FBI."

The gun barrel didn't waver. "On the ground," came the
order. "Facedown."

"Damn it," Mitch argued. "Didn't you hear me? We're
with the FBI. We've been staked out here for five days."

"Good for you. Now, you drop to the ground, facedown, and stay there and we won't have any problems."

Swearing, Mitch obeyed and sensed rather than saw Greg
follow suit. Only then did the policeman approach. The guy
was good, Mitch had to admit. He frisked Greg first, handcuffed him, flipped him onto his back and finished his
search for concealed weapons. Then he turned his attention to Mitch.

"Okay, FBI." He grabbed Mitch by the back of the collar and hauled him to his feet to complete the weapons
check. Stepping carefully out of Mitch's reach, he said,
"Let's see some ID."

Mitch carefully withdrew the leather wallet containing his
badge from his shirt pocket and handed it over. "Satisfied?"

The cop compared the picture to the man in front of him
and finally nodded. He returned the wallet to Mitch. "Okay,
Carlisle. Here's the keys to the cuffs. You can turn your
partner loose, but you both stay here until I say otherwise."

"You should be inside by now," Mitch pointed out.
"There's a woman in there—"

"She's the one who called us. My partner is looking for
a way in right now," the cop shot back. "So, FBI, if you
want to help, you and your buddy stay right here while I join
my partner." He started toward the house and then turned.
"I suppose you have a weapon or two stashed in the van?"
Mitch answered in the affirmative. "Just be sure of your
target before you start shooting. And you better display
those badges—there's more backup on the way." With that
final admonition, he circled the house in the opposite
direction of his partner while Mitch freed Greg's wrists.

"Happy guy," Greg commented as he stepped into the side door of the van. He withdrew two pistols in shoulder holsters from beneath one of the rear captain's chairs and handed one to Mitch.

Mitch checked the cylinder, shoved his arms through the webbing of the holster, then retrieved his jacket from the van. Turning the wallet inside out, he slid it into a jacket pocket so the badge was visible. Greg did the same. Then there was nothing left for them to do but wait. The two men at the front door had not moved by the time a third police unit arrived. Mitch greeted the two men, identified himself and unabashedly listened in when one of the cops at the back of the house called in to report they had found an open window and were going in. In spite of the cold, Mitch broke out into a sweat. This was taking too long. If Fedoryshyn had been in the house, he had had ample opportunity to escape. The radio crackled again.

"The first floor's clear. Opening the front door now."

The policemen at the front went in one at a time, leapfrogging one another. Mitch shifted uneasily and felt his shirt sticking to his chest.

"One room left on the second floor," the radio hissed. "Get ready."

Mitch started forward, only to have his arm grabbed by the policeman who had remained with the car. "It's our operation. Stay put."

Waiting for the report, one puzzling question after another flashed through Mitch's mind. If Brenna Hawthorne was acting as a go-between, why had she called the police? Had the Russian decided, for whatever reason, to eliminate the go-between? If so, the only possible link between Prescott and Fedoryshyn was gone. The Company would demand that he and Greg fly back to Langley; he might never get another shot at the Russian.

"Okay, we've got her. Start a search of the perimeter."

Greg was moving before the end of the report, Mitch right behind him. One of the policemen met them at the front door.

"Where is she?" Greg demanded as the man began throwing switches, illuminating the interior of the house.

"Upstairs, to the left." The cop inclined his head toward the weapons the two men carried. "Better put those away—she's pretty upset."

They holstered their pistols and climbed the steps. "Should have bugged the house," Mitch growled. "We could have had Fedoryshyn."

Greg threw him a searching look. "If it *was* Fedoryshyn."

Brenna was seated on a small upholstered chair in one corner of the bedroom, answering the policeman's questions in a voice as white as her face, but she looked up when the two men entered the room. She had found time to throw on a robe, Mitch noted, but her feet were bare and her toes were curling and uncurling against the icy floor. If she questioned their lack of uniform, her expression did not show it. Her gaze slid over them and returned to the officer questioning her. As she spoke, her fingers stroked the two cats huddled in her lap.

"Go outside and see if the police have found anything," Mitch told Greg in a soft voice. "Then call Johnson and tell him what happened." Greg left and Mitch studied the room while listening to the policeman's questions.

The bedroom didn't seem to fit the woman described in the dossier, Mitch decided. The walls were pale blue, the windows covered with miniblinds and frilled, floral priscillas. On the floor at the foot of the bed was an oval rug patterned in royal blue and cream. All of the furniture was cherry, including the four-poster bed and the glass-doored bookcase occupying one wall. Somehow he had expected her furnishings to be modern.

And the photograph and description in her dossier didn't do her justice, either, Mitch thought as his gaze came to rest on Brenna. For one thing, her waist-length hair wasn't red; it was a deep auburn that trapped light, turning it into dark fire. Her heart-shaped face was chalk white now, her eyes standing out like twin sapphires, but not even her pallor could detract from the fine, aristocratic molding of her cheekbones and nose. And her mouth—the inquisitive gaze now leveled on him turned Mitch's thoughts to the matter at hand.

Somewhat recovered from the initial shock of the break-in, Brenna frowned at the man lounging against her bedroom door. "Exactly who are you?"

Mitch pulled the wallet from his pocket and came forward so that she could examine both the badge and picture identification. "FBI, Professor Hawthorne."

The bleak explanation set off all sorts of internal alarms, but she hid her reaction by examining his badge. His identification card read Mitchell Carlisle. She sat back in the chair and lifted her eyes to his face. She had always thought that the FBI had a dress-and-appearance code—if so, this man would not fit easily into such a correct atmosphere. His black-and-white-checked flannel shirt, open at the neck, was tucked into jeans, and his feet were inappropriately encased in leather running shoes. Rich, gold hair brushed the collar of his jacket; the same lush color was duplicated in the heavy stubble of his beard.

She lingered over her examination, noting his height, well over six feet, and the supple muscles that rippled against the denim fabric of his jeans. All in all, she thought, he looked more like a rock star than an FBI agent. Her eyes met his once again and moved no farther. His eyes were a sharp, piercing green, the color of a fine emerald. Eyes were supposedly the windows of the soul, Brenna mused, but wherever this man's soul resided, no trace of it would be found in those vivid emerald depths. His eyes were cold and hard, reflecting nothing but the artificial lighting of the bedroom. Brenna shivered in reaction to his impersonal regard. Instinct told her that the danger posed by the intruder was nothing compared to the leashed menace she sensed in this man. "I don't imagine you people have now taken to investigating break-ins?" Her attempt at levity was lost on the man.

"I'm Special Agent Mitch Carlisle, Professor. My partner and I have a few questions we'd like to ask you regarding the disappearance of Mark Prescott."

· "I see." To hide the fact that her hands were trembling, Brenna shooed the cats from her lap, then returned her attention to the uniformed policeman. "Do you have any further questions, Officer?"

"No, Ms. Hawthorne. If you find anything missing, please make a list and turn it in at the station."

"Yes, I will." Brenna rose and offered her hand to the officer before he left the room. "If you don't mind, Agent Carlisle, I'd like to get dressed before I answer any more questions."

"Of course. I'll wait downstairs."

By the time Mitch descended the stairs, under the hostile eyes of the two large cats who sat on the second-floor landing like twin guardians, Greg and the police had returned. "What did you find?" Mitch asked his partner.

"We found a set of footprints," Greg replied as he pulled off his gloves. "It looks like the intruder parked his car one street over and cut through the back of the lots."

"He jimmied the lock on one of the dining room windows," one of the police officers added. "That's how he got in. The kitchen door is unlocked, so I imagine he got out that way just before we arrived. We've dusted the window, door and office furniture for prints, but my guess is the guy is a professional and wore gloves. We're checking the other street now, in case anyone saw him, but at this hour, during a holiday..." He shrugged. "It's doubtful there will be any witnesses."

Brenna had paused on the bottom step to listen to the policeman. Now she stepped down into the foyer. "Thank you for everything," she said, escorting the remaining three policemen to the door. "And thank you for arriving so quickly."

"I don't think you were in any danger," one of the officers assured her. "It looks like the guy took off when he heard you moving around upstairs. Just to be on the safe side, though, you better change the locks on your doors. And have that window fixed.''

"I will. Thank you again." She watched the officers return to their cars and then closed the door and studied the two men who remained in her home. To Mitch, she said, "I imagine this gentleman is also with the FBI?"

Mitch nodded. "This is Special Agent Greg Talbott."

Brenna inclined her head. "Agent Talbott." Her gaze swung back to Mitch. "I'd like to make some coffee before answering your questions."

"Fine," Mitch agreed. "Greg and I could both do with a cup," he added with what Brenna considered a large dose of presumptive arrogance before wandering into her office.

"Can I help?" Greg offered as Brenna started by him.

"No." Brenna smiled at him. "But you could look around down here for Jasper."

"Jasper?"

"He's a gray tomcat," she explained. "It was Jasper's hissing that warned me someone was in the house."

Greg grinned. "I'll find him."

Mitch, seated comfortably on an antique swivel chair, opened the third drawer of the rolltop desk in Brenna's office. For a nut, her desk was remarkably well organized. There were no loose papers; all her papers—be they monographs, notes or lectures—were in neatly labeled folders and the folders themselves were alphabetized and filed in the four-drawer wooden filing cabinet standing beside the desk. Computer manuals in their cardboard cases marched in a row across the back of the desk, and a cordless telephone and accompanying handset sat atop the filing cabinet. Even the pencils in the top drawer of the desk were sharpened to fine points. For some reason, he found that comical.

Brenna appeared from the kitchen, where Hobo was currently hiding under the tarp, and watched the man going through her desk for several moments before speaking. "Find anything interesting?"

Mitch swiveled to face her. "Not yet." Her sweatshirt bore the plea Kill A Mosquito, Save A Minnesotan, and he

almost laughed aloud at the unexpected display of humor.
Almost.

"Meaning you think you will?"

"Meaning I don't know," he said quietly.

Brenna shoved her hands into the back pockets of her
jeans. "I think you're supposed to have a search warrant
before going through my possessions, aren't you?" His eyes
flashed, their cold, cameralike appearance briefly replaced
by something more human. The display of emotion lasted
for only a second before the dispassionate gaze returned.
She picked up a copy of Shakespeare's complete works that
had fallen to the floor and returned it to the bookshelf before turning and heading back to the kitchen. She glanced
into the living room as she passed by and saw Agent Talbott peering behind furniture and calling, "Here, kitty
kitty," in a coaxing tone. Her hand had just come to rest on
the swinging door to the kitchen when Mitch's voice halted
her.

"Son of a—"

The startled shout was throttled into an inarticulate cry of
anger and brought both Brenna and Greg into the office at
a run. Mitch stood in front of the tall bookcase, struggling
unsuccessfully to remove an outraged mass of gray fur from
the back of his neck. Several vivid, physically impossible
curses followed the first.

"You've found Jasper!" Brenna hurried across the room
and reached up to grab the cat.

"Ouch, damn it! Watch out—he's got his claws in my
neck."

"Be quiet, you're scaring him," Brenna ordered, trying
to get a hand under Jasper's paws in order to force him to
retract his claws.

"I'm scaring *him*—"

"Bend down so I can see what I'm doing." Mitch complied, but not without uttering several vile threats that en-
dangered eight of Jasper's nine lives. "There." She lifted the
cat away from the man and hugged the tom tightly. Jasper

immediately calmed and started purring. "Where did you find him?"

The cold green eyes were glittering with emotion now, and Brenna wasn't certain she cared for the change. Mitch gave the cat a malevolent look and dabbed at his wounds with a handkerchief. "He was waiting on top of your bookcase apparently, the little assassin."

"Brave Jasper," Brenna cooed, her fingers moving soothingly through the gray fur. "Ready to defend me to the death."

"*I* wasn't threatening you," Mitch felt obliged to point out.

The look Brenna gave him made Mitch wish he'd kept his mouth shut. Someone had already broken into her home, and just seconds ago she had caught him going through her desk. If anyone had a right to feel threatened, it was probably Brenna Hawthorne.

"Cats are excellent judges of character, Agent Carlisle." She nuzzled her cheek against the cat and was rewarded by the rasp of his tongue. She hid her smile in Jasper's fur. Nothing like a few scratches to put her on an even footing with Agent Carlisle. "Come along, Jasper, I'm going to give you a huge saucer of cream." She walked out of the office and called over her shoulder, "The coffee is ready, if anyone is interested."

In the kitchen she set the cat on the floor, took a carton of cream from the refrigerator and poured a generous amount into a plastic bowl. As the cream heated in the microwave, she poured coffee and handed a cup to each of the men. The microwave buzzed and she removed the bowl and placed it on the floor for Jasper. The cat meowed his appreciation and promptly ignored everyone in favor of his reward.

Mitch surveyed the shambles of the kitchen without comment, but the look he exchanged with Greg spoke volumes. "Remodeling?" he questioned amiably, aware that their meeting had been less than auspicious thus far.

"No, I'm into performance art," Brenna replied airily. Picking up her cup, she led the men into the dining room. "Now, then," she began as she took the chair at one end of the oval table, "would you mind explaining why your questions couldn't be answered at a more reasonable time? Like sunrise?"

Mitch took one of the ashtrays residing on the china hutch and slid into the chair at the opposite end of the table. "You're a . . . friend of Mark Prescott's."

Brenna watched him light the unfiltered cigarette. "Agent Carlisle, please don't make the mistake of thinking that I am so shaken by what has happened this evening that I can't think clearly. I am, for instance, most curious about your presence here."

His gaze met hers across the length of the table. This wasn't Brenna Hawthorne the absentminded professor facing him, or Brenna Hawthorne the animal rights activist. This was a self-possessed, intelligent woman who, due to her experience with the law, probably would not take anything he said at face value. He flipped his lighter closed. "We've been assigned to watch your house, Professor—that's how we arrived on the scene so quickly."

Brenna nodded, as if the admission did not particularly surprise her. Inwardly she was shaking. "I see. And why have you been watching my home?"

"Not just the house," Mitch clarified. "We've been following you."

"Because of Mark?" She phrased it as a question, but she had the sinking feeling that her life was about to become very complicated.

"Yes." Mitch exhaled. "Do you know about the project Mark Prescott was working on?"

"Only in the most general terms. Mark and his team are developing a superconductor." She sipped her coffee, her eyes never wavering from his. What exactly did he want from her? "But you already know that much—the grant Mark received, and why he received it, is hardly a secret on campus."

"We're aware of that," Greg put in, hoping to dispel some of the tension in the room.

"Yes, I thought you might be," Brenna said with a small smile.

"What do you know about Prescott?" Mitch persisted, as if Greg hadn't spoken.

Brenna lifted her hands in helpless gesture. "We dated for a few months. I like him."

"The two of you were...close?"

He made it sound indecent, Brenna thought. "I suppose so."

"What did you talk about?"

She shook her head in disbelief. "What does anyone talk about? Current events, politics, the weather—"

"Work?" When Brenna nodded hesitantly, Mitch added, "How much did he tell you about his job, his research?"

"Not a great deal. He's a physicist, a little out of my field. We discussed our careers in general terms. I could no more understand the intricacies of what Mark did than he could comprehend the vagaries of Elizabethan politics."

Mitch watched her closely, searching for some indication that she was lying. "Have you seen or heard from Prescott since his disappearance?"

Brenna set her coffee cup down with a sharp clink. "No, Agent Carlisle, I have not. *If* I had, I would have contacted the police."

"Really?"

His reply was edged with a patent disbelief that triggered Brenna's temper. "Yes, really." She rose and glared across the table at Mitch. "As pleasant as this has been, I think it's time you...gentlemen...leave."

Greg immediately came to his feet. Only Mitch remained seated, his long frame slouched insolently in his chair. "Did you know that all the documentation relating to the super-conductor, as well as the ceramic material itself, has disappeared from Prescott's lab?"

"Fascinating," Brenna commented acidly.

"I think so," Mitch calmly replied. "Prescott's ceramic, I understand, is a technological breakthrough. It is also highly marketable and would, I imagine, turn a nice profit for its seller."

Brenna threw up her hands. "I'm afraid I'm rather slow at two in the morning. What are you talking about?"

Mitch rose slowly, a predatory light in his eyes. "It's called technological espionage, Professor Hawthorne, and it's a very lucrative business."

"Make your point," Brenna snapped.

"The point," Greg broke in before Mitch could speak, "is that we suspect that Mark Prescott planned to illegally market the formula for the superconductor."

Brenna snorted. "That's absurd. Mark is one of the most law-abiding people I know." She folded her arms across her chest and stared at Greg. "Next you're going to tell me that you suspect Mark was selling the formula to some foreign power."

"That's exactly right, Professor," Mitch said as he ground out his cigarette.

Stunned, Brenna watched Special Agent Carlisle come around the table and halt directly in front of her.

"So, as you can see," Mitch said in a quiet, detached voice, "we can't allow you to end the interview quite yet."

It seemed to Brenna that it took hours for her to gather her scattered thoughts. "Do you realize how ludicrous your suspicions are?" she asked at last. "Mark wouldn't—" She stopped abruptly, one hand going out to steady herself against the back of a chair. Just last week, when the police had questioned her, she had realized how superficial her relationship with Mark had been. In all honesty, she couldn't be sure that the FBI's suspicions were misplaced.

Brenna looked at the younger of the two men; it would be easier to question him than his older, harder, partner. "Am I under suspicion, as well?" she asked in a small voice.

Greg hesitated for a fraction of a second, then nodded. "You were dating Prescott, and you have access to the man we believe is Prescott's contact. Aleksandr Fedoryshyn."

"Fedoryshyn? Aleksei Fedoryshyn?" Brenna stared at him in disbelief. "He's a professor of history and a guest lecturer at Llewellyn College. I met him last week at a faculty tea given for him and found him absolutely charming. The thought of Aleksei being a spy is ludicrous!"

"Are you certain?"

The question came from Carlisle, and Brenna forced herself to meet his stony gaze. "Yes, I'm certain. Bradley Jackson, the history department chairman, has been working on this series since last spring."

"But when did you learn *who* would be coming to Llewellyn," Mitch insisted.

"When fall quarter began." Brenna frowned, thinking. "No, that's not right." Momentarily forgetting her uninvited guests, and the fear that had darted through her when she had been told she was an FBI suspect, she left the dining room and walked down the hall to her office.

Mitch rolled his eyes and motioned to Greg to follow her.

"Jackson told us the name at one of the weekly faculty meetings...." She lifted her briefcase onto the desk and began digging through it until she found the notebook she used when making notes during faculty meetings. Taking her glasses from the desktop, she opened the notebook and paged through the pale green, lined sheets. "August twenty-first...Vittorio Camaretti...oh, that was interesting." She smiled up at Greg. "The history and archaeology departments pooled their resources and invited Camaretti here for a month—he's a well-known archaeologist," she informed the younger man when he looked at her quizzically. "The Science Museum had a display of Caesarean artifacts and it seemed logical to take advantage of the display and have a series of workshops." Her eyes took on a faraway look. "The Romans are quite maligned, you know. I will grant you that they did steal a great deal of their culture from other societies, but they did have a way of incorporating their ill-gotten gains to the benefit of all...Caesarea actually has several levels to it, archaeologically speaking—"

"Professor, if we could get back to the matter at hand," Mitch inquired impatiently.

Brenna blinked at him, momentarily disoriented. "Oh, of course." A large measure of her original fear returned at the look on his face. She bent over the notebook again, frowning. "Here, September twenty-eighth, we discussed a Soviet lecturer—no name was given, just the university, his speciality and possible dates for next spring." She hurriedly turned several pages. "October thirty-first, Halloween. Jackson was told that Professor Aleksandr Fedoryshyn would be available earlier, in the November-December time frame, and he leaped at the opportunity." Pushing the glasses onto the top of her head, she gave Agent Carlisle a smug look. "You see, your suspicions were wrong. We were given the name nearly a month ago."

Mitch leaned a shoulder against the wall. "How convenient. According to Prescott's colleagues, the ceramic formula was discovered in late September and testing was begun immediately. That allows more than a month for Prescott to make contact with his buyer and arrange delivery—which, by the way, can be a time-consuming process—and for your history department to be informed as to the lecturer's identity." He raised a skeptical eyebrow. "A little too coincidental, wouldn't you say?"

Brenna sighed and closed the notebook. "Somehow I don't think my opinion matters. You'll believe whatever you please—up to and including the absurd notion that I am some sort of middleman."

"Which you aren't, of course," Mitch commented softly, sarcastically.

Brenna's head came up with a snap. "I think I've had enough for one night," she replied tightly. "I want you both out of my house. Now."

Mitch came away from the wall. "If you're as innocent as you claim, I assume you won't object if we search your house."

"I certainly will," Brenna parried, her temper rising. "You can suspect me all you want, put me at the top of your list if it will make you feel any better, but I won't have you pawing through my home!''

"Of course.'' Mitch smiled. "I can understand an upstanding citizen such as yourself wanting us to comply fully with the letter of the law. Agent Talbott and I will leave—'' the smile disappeared, leaving in its place a grim, implacable expression "—and we'll be back in thirty minutes with a court-ordered search warrant. Fair enough?''

"Thank you for offering me a choice in the matter,'' Brenna mocked, rising. "If you'll wait here, I have a phone call to make.'' She was halfway to the family room when she realized she was being followed. A glance over her shoulder showed Special Agent Carlisle barely two steps behind. Actually, stalking more accurately described his silent, intense pursuit. Grimacing, she marched straight to the phone sitting on the wet bar. "Wouldn't you rather listen in on the office extension?'' she inquired when he came to a halt beside the bar.

"You're calling your lawyer, right? I wouldn't dream of violating lawyer-client confidentiality,'' he replied easily, lighting a cigarette while she dialed.

"Now, why don't I believe that?'' she muttered just before her call was answered. "Hello, Tony, it's Brenna. Yes, I know what time it is, and no, I haven't been arrested again,'' she groaned when her lawyer asked the obvious question for a late-night phone call. "Just listen.''

Mitch watched Brenna through narrowed eyes, noting the way she nervously twisted the cord in her free hand while she explained what was happening.

Brenna fell silent, listening to Tony's less than comforting recommendation, and a minute later offered the receiver to the intense man beside her. "He wants to talk to you,'' she said blandly.

Mitch took the receiver, identified himself and didn't have a chance to say another word, because Brenna's lawyer immediately enlightened him as to the generosity of his client's pending actions. For a man just roused from a sound sleep, Mitch decided, the lawyer was remarkably quick-witted.

When the lawyer was finished, Mitch was allowed to say "I understand," and no more before the connection was broken.

Mitch replaced the receiver and turned back to Brenna. "You're going to cooperate."

"To a certain point," she agreed, annoyed by the advice Tony had given her. "You can search my home and the garage, but I am to receive a receipt for anything you remove from the property."

"So I was told," Mitch said dryly.

"If you don't mind, I'd rather not watch you paw through my things," Brenna told him coldly. "I'll be in my bedroom, unless you have any objections."

"No objections, but I will remove the telephone. With your permission," he added at the flash of anger in her eyes.

"Be my guest," Brenna ground out and led the way to her bedroom.

When Mitch returned to the office, the trim blue phone in one hand, Greg shook his head. "I'm not sure Johnson is going to approve of this," he said quietly.

Mitch shrugged. "She gave her permission, with her lawyer's approval, I might add." He set the disconnected phone on the desk. "But you better call Johnson again and tell him what's going on. And ask him for some more men—this is a big house."

Chapter 4

Like a naughty child, Brenna shut herself in her bedroom in self-imposed isolation. She heard the arrival of the other agents in the early-morning hours, heard the sounds of the search being conducted, and a chill settled in her heart. The FBI was in her home, searching for evidence of technological espionage, and the thought was a sobering one indeed. If the FBI's suspicions about Mark were correct, his disappearance was no longer a mystery. He was probably sitting on some tropical island working on his tan while the FBI was tearing her home apart. She hoped. The alternative explanation was that he had met with foul play, and that theory was even more discomforting than the first.

Brenna paced the confines of her room, seeking to draw a logical conclusion from an illogical situation. She didn't for a minute believe that Professor Fedoryshyn was guilty of anything except being the wrong nationality in the wrong place at the wrong time; after all, it would be a simple matter to check his credentials. But what was truly frightening was that she could understand how the FBI might believe that she was involved with whatever fate had befallen Mark.

She knew so little about Mark, really, but to a suspicious man like Mitch Carlisle, her inability to answer his questions probably sounded like evasions.

As if summoned by her thoughts, there was a knock on her door and Mitch Carlisle stepped into the room before she could answer.

"We've finished with the basement and first floor," he said when she whirled around to face him. "I thought you might like to go downstairs while we work up here."

Startled, Brenna hesitantly glanced around her bedroom and adjoining bath. The thought of strangers examining her most personal possessions made her feel ill. Drawing a deep breath, she started for the door.

"Does this house have an attic?" Mitch asked when she was in front of him.

"Yes, but I don't store anything there," she replied softly, her mind still lingering on the invasion of her privacy.

"We'll want to look at it anyway."

Brenna sighed. "I thought you might." Shaking her head at his tenacity, she led the way to the last bedroom on the right.

Mitch followed, then came to a sudden stop when he entered the room. The bedroom had been converted into what, years earlier, would have been called a music room, and sunlight flooded through the windows. A spinet sat against the wall on his right, while the wall in front of him contained built-in oak shelves that held row after row of sheet music. But what held his attention was the dainty, double-banked harpsichord positioned squarely on a rose-and-cream Persian rug in the middle of the room. He walked forward slowly and reached out to touch the scrolled music stand, then slide away thc keyboard covers. The delicate sound of plucked strings echoed delightfully through the room when he depressed several keys.

The sound made Brenna pause in the act of opening the door that led to the attic and turn back to the room. "Please be careful with that," she requested, walking back to him. "It's very delicate."

Mitch barely glanced at her before his eyes were drawn back to the harpsichord. "I know." He gingerly settled his weight on the small, padded bench and deftly ran his right hand through a two-octave scale on the top keyboard.

Brenna stared at the sight of his large masculine hand caressing the keys. "Do you play?"

"The piano," he answered, his attention centered on the keyboard. "But not in years." His left hand hovered over the bottom keyboard, and he executed a series of major and minor scales with both hands that belied his earlier words.

Why he would lie about his obvious skill puzzled Brenna, but she was in no position to push for an answer.

"Where did you find this?"

"I didn't," she answered in a hushed voice. "It found me—or rather, the graduate student who was building it found me." His hands lifted from the keys, and she found herself the object of that intense, green stare. "It was part of his doctoral dissertation," she explained. "He didn't realize how expensive the project would be. When he did, he started looking around for a financial backer. Luckily I heard about his project before someone else volunteered to foot the bill. He ended up with his doctorate and I got a harpsichord." Smiling, she ran a loving hand over the curved side.

"Do you play?" Mitch asked impulsively.

"It depends on who you ask," Brenna replied, an impish quality creeping into her smile. "I think I do, but my former teacher doesn't agree with that assessment."

Her smile intrigued him. He studied the generous, sensual curve of her bottom lip and felt something stir deep within him. She had an infinitely kissable mouth, one that made a man want to test the innate promise there in the most primitive manner possible. And the absurdity of that desire reminded him where he was and why. He rose and slid the hinged wood covers over the keyboards. "Let's see the attic," he ordered.

Brenna's smile flickered and died at his abrupt manner. His stare had held her immobile, afraid that the slightest movement would ruin the unexpected rapport between them. If Agent Carlisle had sensed the rapport, however, he was obviously unaffected by it. "Over there." She indicated the open door with a flick of her hand. "Enjoy yourself."

Mitch let her go without another word, ignoring the regret he felt at destroying the momentary bond that had existed between them. She's a suspect, remember, he taunted himself. You ought to—you argued the point with Johnson when he raised holy hell over what he considered a premature—if not illegal—search of the premises. Mitch drew a hand over his face and headed for the attic stairs. He located the light switch and flipped it on before climbing the steps. As Brenna had said, the attic was empty. If anything was hidden up here, it was behind yard upon yard of fiberglass insulation sandwiched between the beams. He descended the stairs and turned off the light. They would need gloves and masks before they disturbed the fiberglass.

He left the music room without glancing at the harpsichord.

"We found nothing," Keith Johnson said patiently. He, Mitch and Greg were standing in the conference room in the Bureau's office in downtown Minneapolis. The winter sun had set quickly, and now the blinds had been drawn and the harsh fluorescent lighting activated.

"That doesn't mean she isn't involved with Prescott," Mitch commented idly.

Keith sighed. "I agree, that's why I convinced the special-agent-in-charge to allow the search, but right now all we have against either Prescott or the Hawthorne woman are suspicions. We have no proof, Carlisle." He fixed the older man with an intent stare. "And demanding to search her home was, at best, foolish—at worst, you've violated her constitutional rights."

"She agreed to the search."

"I'm certain her lawyer could prove duress if he set his mind to it," Keith replied.

Mitch lit a cigarette. "I may have made a mistake," he conceded at last. "But no permanent damage has been done—all that's changed is that she now knows she's under surveillance."

"Not any longer," Keith said. "The special-agent-in-charge is discontinuing surveillance on Brenna Hawthorne until evidence is found that, one, Prescott is selling the ceramic formula to Fedoryshyn, and two, the Hawthorne woman is involved."

Greg swore softly and shoved his hands into his trouser pockets. "I think that's a mistake."

Johnson shrugged. "Mistake or not, that's the word."

"If it's a matter of manpower, Mitch and I will work one-man shifts," Greg offered.

"That's not the point." Keith shook his head. "Right now we don't have enough evidence to charge Brenna Hawthorne with jaywalking, let alone espionage, and I don't want her lawyer filing charges of harassment against the Bureau. As of this moment, you two are off the case."

"I suppose that means Greg and I get to cool our heels in the office until Prescott is found," Mitch commented coldly.

"No, that means that you and Mr. Talbott are officially detached from the FBI," Keith answered. "It is felt that you overstepped your authority. Your deputy director has ordered that you fly back to D.C. as soon as you can book a flight." He started toward the hallway, then stopped and turned to face the two men. "And by the way, the police who responded to Ms. Hawthorne's call last night said that two FBI men were on the scene within minutes. The police chief called this morning and apologized for having handcuffed Special Agent Talbott. A word to the wise, gentlemen—the Bureau takes a very dim view of counterfeit identification and people who impersonate Bureau agents." He smiled. "Working with you has proved . . . interesting. Have a nice flight." He turned and left the conference room.

Greg and Mitch looked at one another in silence for several moments.

"Well, that's that," Greg said dejectedly. "We tried."

Mitch crushed out his cigarette and reached for his jacket. "Come on, I'll buy you dinner."

They found a small, quiet restaurant a few blocks from the FBI office. After ordering their meal, they settled back with their drinks.

"What do you plan to do now?" Mitch asked, savoring the twelve-year-old Scotch he had requested.

"Go back to Langley, what else?" Greg sighed. "I think we really blew this one, teach. If Brenna Hawthorne is involved, she isn't going to go within a mile of Fedoryshyn now." He finished his drink and indicated to the waitress that he wanted another. "What about you? Back to Paris?"

"Not quite yet."

The detached tone of Mitch's voice brought a frown to Greg's face. "Teach, don't even think about staying here," he began warningly.

"I'm a free agent," Mitch stated, then waited until the waitress had deposited Greg's drink and departed before adding, "It might be interesting to monitor some history courses at Llewellyn."

"If the Bureau catches you—"

"How are they going to catch me? They aren't even planning to keep Hawthorne under surveillance, remember?" Mitch smiled coldly. "And even if the Bureau finds out, what can they do? I'm a private citizen, not affiliated with any government agency. The worst that can happen is Hawthorne's lawyer slapping me with a nuisance suit." Determination glinted in his green eyes.

Greg had seen that look often enough to know that further argument would be useless, but he was responsible for bringing Mitch within striking distance of Fedoryshyn. "I can't let you keep the badge or pistol," hc said apologetically. "And I can't stay with you. Langley will have me monitoring bird calls on Guam if I disobey a direct order."

"That's the nice thing about owning your own company—no one can give you orders." Mitch chuckled. "Don't worry—the equipment goes back with you. I won't need it."

Pushing his glass to the side, Greg leaned forward. "Teach, go back to Paris. Let the Bureau handle whatever is going to happen here." The friendly warmth in Mitch's eyes disappeared, and Greg knew that he had finally discovered the boundaries Mitch placed on their relationship.

"My contract with the Company is concluded," he said forbiddingly. "There won't be any evidence to connect me to you, the Company or the Bureau. Now it's time for you to live up to your part of our deal and walk away so I can take Icon."

"Part of the deal also included you not doing anything to the Icon here in the States," Greg reminded him, risking their friendship because his gut told him that Mitch's quest for vengeance would somehow turn out horribly wrong. "You promised," he persisted when Mitch simply stared at him. "Mitch, you gave me your word."

Mitch lit a cigarette and examined his protégé through a cloud of smoke. "I lied."

The admission told Greg more about Mitch's feelings toward Fedoryshyn than any conversation would have revealed. It also scared the hell out of him. Mitch was a hard, sometimes cruel man, but he could always be counted on to be brutally honest. Right now he was clearly out for revenge and determined to go it alone, without the benefit of the support system he would have had if the Icon had appeared somewhere in Western Europe. Leaning back in his chair, Greg smiled at the older man. "I have an incredible amount of leave built up. I think I'll send the equipment back to Langley by special courier and spend a few weeks exploring the winter activities in Minneapolis."

"I don't need an Agency watchdog," Mitch growled.

Greg gave his friend an exasperated look. "I don't plan to play watchdog, but even you can't be in two places at the same time. You stick with the pretty professor and I'll keep an eye on our Russian friend."

"I don't need—" Mitch began stubbornly.

"You need a friend," Greg interrupted heatedly. "And whether you like it or not, that's what I am." He smiled suddenly. "Come on, teach, it'll be like old times. We made a great team."

Mitch frowned, torn between accepting the help he knew he would need and placing his friend in jeopardy. "If the Agency finds out, it could mean your job."

Greg grinned. "Who's going to tell? Not me." He lifted his glass. "Well?"

Mitch hesitated, then touched his glass to Greg's. "I hope you know what you're doing."

"Funny, I was about to say the same thing."

Except for a brief expedition to the grocery store on Saturday, Brenna spent the weekend grading midterm exams at her dining room table and trying to recover from the shock of being an FBI suspect in technological espionage. Given her involvement with various movements, Brenna had always wondered if the FBI had a file on her. Now she no longer had to wonder. None of her arrests, or subsequent trials, had intimidated her, but involvement on a federal level was a whole other matter.

Tony had called late Saturday evening to inform her that the FBI was removing the surveillance on her until further notice. The news was cold comfort, but Brenna gladly embraced it. She was a college professor, not a trench-coated spy, and thankfully the FBI had reached the same conclusion. Her life could resume its normal routine.

Still, as she drove to Llewellyn on Monday morning, she found herself checking the traffic to see if another motorist paid her unwarranted attention. By the time she swung into her assigned parking place and pulled her purse, briefcase and an armful of papers from the passenger seat, she was certain that the FBI had told Tony the truth. She hurried through the cold, returning the greetings of students and colleagues she encountered on her way to Meredith Hall.

Behind the wheel of his rented compact car—his preferred vehicle, a Mercedes, would draw too much attention, he had decided—Mitch watched Brenna Hawthorne gather up a staggering amount of paperwork and walk briskly along the shoveled sidewalk. He smiled tightly, recalling her obvious efforts at trying to spot a tail on the freeway. Escaping her attention had been a simple exercise. He had remained behind her and frequently switched lanes, dropping in and out of sight of her rearview mirrors. By the time she was on the exit ramp, she had stopped worrying about being followed and he was one car behind her.

Mitch extricated himself from the confines of the car and started after his quarry. Within moments he was engulfed in the pedestrian traffic on campus. He was grateful for the energetic pace Brenna set—Minneapolis was a good thirty degrees colder than Paris in November—but after seeing two students skid and fall on patches of ice, he slowed his pursuit. Nothing like a forty-one-year-old man with a broken leg to draw attention. When Brenna Hawthorne became aware of him, he wanted the moment to be of his own choosing.

Meredith Hall greeted him with an embrace of warm air. He watched Brenna disappear toward the faculty offices, then stepped out of the flow of traffic to unzip his jacket and pull a folded piece of paper out of his shirt pocket. The Hawthorne file had contained a list of her present class and room assignments; Special Agent Johnson hadn't realized that Mitch had made a copy of the entire file. Mitch glanced first at the paper and then at the stainless-steel watch on his wrist. Her first class would start in twenty minutes. He started to reach for a cigarette, then caught sight of the sign, lettered in bloodred ink, that smoking was strictly prohibited except in designated areas. He tapped the cigarette back into its pack and went in search of a coffee machine.

At precisely eight-fifty, Brenna stepped into the brightly lit lecture hall. She was greeted with scattered applause, and a few wolf whistles. These she acknowledged, respectively, with a regal wave of her hand and a fierce scowl. Her glasses resided on the top of her head and her arms were full of blue test booklets.

Climbing the two steps to the raised dais, she dropped the booklets onto a long table and carried a three-ring notebook to the podium. "Thank you, thank you." Her voice, amplified by the microphone, carried to the back of the lecture hall. "Obviously three days of mother's cooking and clean clothes have worked miracles, but I must tell you that flattery will in no way affect the grade on your midterm."

Laughter greeted her rejoinder, and she smiled at the sea of eager young faces. "We will break five minutes early today so that you can reclaim your test papers—those of you who used a pseudonym will need to see me after class."

More laughter, and Mitch, in his position in the back row, slid a little lower in the padded seat and narrowed his eyes at the slight figure behind the podium. She sure as hell didn't *act* like a stuffy college professor, he thought, and she didn't look like one, either, except for the way her hair was piled at the top of her head in a style that was curiously old-fashioned. The royal blue blouse she wore was made of some shimmery fabric, and a cream-colored cardigan was draped around her shoulders. Hidden now were the cream-colored, pleated trousers that had nipped her slender waist and clung to the rounded outline of her hips and derriere when she had momentarily turned her back on the tiered lecture hall.

"At any rate, welcome back," Brenna said, flipping her glasses onto her nose and opening her notebook. "I'm sure you all remember that we have just dealt with the Mediter-ranean cradle of civilization, up to and including the Ro-man Empire. For the rest of the quarter, we're going to study the fall of Rome, the rise and influence of the Cath-olic Christian church and the rise of Islam. Aside from the chapters in your textbooks, there is a supplemental reading list of three books you must peruse." Brenna's announce-ment was greeted with groans. She pulled her glasses down to the tip of her nose and looked over the top of the frames at the class. "Those of you hoping for a passing grade will want to make note of the titles."

All that was heard until Brenna spoke again was the rus-tling of paper as the students opened their notebooks. Mitch was amazed at the discipline this group of over one hundred eighteen-year-olds displayed. He wondered idly if they responded this way to all their instructors, and knew instinctively they did not. Brenna Hawthorne, certified nut, rescuer of animals and espionage suspect, held this class in the palm of her hand. And she kept them there for the next fifty minutes. When, as she had promised, she ended the class five minutes early, the students swarmed from their seats to besiege the dais, and Mitch rose and left the lecture hall.

Following Brenna proved absurdly easy, Mitch discovered during the course of the week. Of the five classes she taught, three were held in the lecture hall, and he sat through all of these. The other two were graduate courses, held in a classroom that had a capacity of thirty. Brenna might overlook him in a lecture hall, but not in that setting. These two Mitch avoided, passing by the open classroom door only to make certain that Brenna was there at the beginning of class.

On her lunch hour Brenna usually walked the block to the student union and took a table either by herself or with a colleague or two from the history department. Mitch stationed himself at a table halfway across the room—in the smoking section, since Minneapolis was quite stringent about its indoor air quality—and kept a close eye on his prey. After lunch she returned to Meredith Hall, taught her last two classes of the day, kept office hours until five, then went home. Her schedule deviated only on Wednesday, when she taught a night class in medieval English history. On that evening she did not return home until ten o'clock.

Every evening he followed Brenna home and parked at the intersection of the cul-de-sac to watch her house. While he ate sandwiches purchased at noon at the union and washed them down with chilled soda—one nice thing about Minnesota in winter was that he was never caught with lukewarm soda to drink—he wondered how she filled her evenings. He had considered planting a bug or two in her house, but had discovered that doing so would prove nearly impossible. He would have to avoid the remodelers, which meant getting into the house on Wednesday evening while Brenna was still on campus, but unfortunately her neighbors came and went at all hours. His forged identification might be enough to convince curious neighbors that his reason for being inside the house was legitimate, but Brenna would then know she was still a suspect, and he couldn't take that risk.

Greg had been as good as his word. He had called Langley and requested a three-week leave of absence. The deputy director had agreed, and Greg had returned the badges and weapons to Langley by special courier. Not that they had remained unarmed for long. Mitch had a worldwide network of contacts, including the States, and by Sunday evening he possessed two .45 automatic pistols and two sets of forged identification. Greg had been less than pleased by both acquisitions; he had taken the automatic but refused to use the papers identifying him as an FBI agent. Like Mitch, Greg would follow the Russian and try to blend in with the crowd on campus; unlike Mitch, he had a better chance of successfully doing so because of his relative youth.

Dual surveillance had its drawbacks, particularly when they were virtually living out of their cars and dared not maintain radio contact in case their transmissions were picked up by the authorities. Sleep was caught at odd moments; Mitch dozed during Brenna's lectures and while watching her house at night. Greg's schedule was much the same. Prearranged meetings were almost impossible under their present circumstances. They had to maintain twenty-four-hour surveillance on their subjects and avoid any FBI stakeouts at the same time. Still, he and Greg needed to be able to get in touch with each other at a moment's notice without losing track of their subjects for an extended period of time. Mitch solved that problem by the use of cellular phones and remote pagers. The cellular phones were installed in both cars and would be removed before the cars were returned to the rental company.

Mitch's greatest fear was that one night Fedoryshyn and Hawthorne would be able to manage a clandestine meeting because either one or both their guards had fallen asleep.

Mitch was living on strong black coffee, caffeinated soda and sheer nerves. So was Greg.

By Friday Mitch was almost convinced that his suspicions about Brenna had been unfounded. As usual, he followed her to the union for lunch and watched while she read over what were undoubtedly the notes for her next class. Tailing Brenna Hawthorne was getting him nowhere fast, he thought to himself as he ate what was supposed to be a cheeseburger and drank coffee. Mitch had allowed Greg to tail Fedoryshyn because he felt his normal iron control slip at the thought of following the Russian. If he had to maintain daily contact with Fedoryshyn, Mitch wasn't sure what his reaction would be, but he was afraid he might simply kill the man in front of God and any number of witnesses. It was the thought of witnesses and the need to prove Fedoryshyn a spy that kept the Russian safe, not any scruples Mitch had about exacting vengeance.

He pushed the remains of his meal away and reached for the aspirin bottle in his shirt. He had just swallowed three tablets when he saw Brenna rise as two men approached her table. He didn't recognize the shorter, rotund man, but the taller, blond man was unforgettable. Ice seemed to replace the blood in his veins as Mitch watched Aleksandr Fedoryshyn capture Brenna's outstretched hand in both of his. She smiled warmly, gesturing for the two men to join her, and Mitch found it hard to breathe.

Fumbling for a cigarette, he saw that his hands were shaking. Jesus, Carlisle, you're falling apart, he told himself caustically. But not even castigating himself for his reactions steadied his nerves. For years his fantasy of vengeance had ruled his life, his emotions, burning away every other passion with its coruscating flame. No matter how involved he became in his counterterrorist business, the thirst for vengeance had never abated, but had merely been pushed to a corner of his mind while he dealt with teaching the newest batch of executives how to protect themselves from terrorist attacks. He had no family, no friends—unless he counted Greg—and no lover. His was a solitary ex-

istence, one he had chosen deliberately, and he suddenly
realized how empty his life would be once he had disposed
of Fedoryshyn and revenge was no longer his constant
companion.

Brenna Hawthorne rose, and Fedoryshyn was on his feet
immediately, holding her coat for her and talking rapidly.
She laughed and nodded, and Mitch put aside his unwelcome introspection when the two of them started out of the
cafeteria. He stubbed out his cigarette, grabbed his backpack and followed, pulling on his jacket as he went.

At five o'clock Mitch was stationed at the side entrance
to Meredith Hall—the one Brenna always used, since it was
closest to her office—trying to blend into the ever-
diminishing campus population by rummaging through his
backpack. When ten minutes had gone by with no sign of
Brenna, he went in search of his absentminded professor.

He found her with no trouble—she was standing in the
midst of several men he recognized from her classes as
graduate students, her briefcase in one hand and her huge
purse slung over the opposite shoulder. Both she and the
students were wearing their coats and, judging by the anxious looks they alternately directed at the stairway and their
watches, they were waiting for someone to join them. Mitch
waited, as well, stationing himself at a corner so that he
could duck out of sight if Brenna looked his way. Her attention, however, was all for her students. When the lag-
gard finally arrived, Brenna said something in a soft voice
that made him duck his head in embarrassment and then led
her flock out of the building and across the campus to the
music/theater building.

Mitch followed, keeping Brenna's auburn head in sight.
After he entered the building, his eyes were drawn to the
large sandwich board standing squarely in the two-story
foyer. Fedoryshyn's picture and name came into focus, as
did the notice that refreshments would be served during in-
termission, and Mitch finally understood the reason for the
exodus. Brenna was accompanying her students to the Russian's lecture. As he followed Brenna and her group into the

recital-hall/theater, he caught sight of Greg lounging in a chair in the back row. Their eyes met, but neither man acknowledged the other. Mitch found a seat two rows behind Brenna and her students. The theater, with its capacity of two thousand nearly met, vibrated with the noise generated by the audience.

The lights overhead dimmed, the stage lights came up and Aleksandr Fedoryshyn strode through a side door across the stage to the podium to the sound of applause. He nodded, beamed his thanks and bent toward the microphone to begin his lecture.

Whatever Fedoryshyn said was lost on Mitch; he simply slouched in the comfortable seat, absorbing the accented cadence of the Russian's voice, and tried to ignore the little voice whispering in his ear, telling him what an ideal target Fedoryshyn, blinded by the stage lights, presented.

Aleksei's lecture series was open to the faculty and students from two other private, metropolitan colleges under a reciprocal credit agreement, but Brenna hadn't expected this full-capacity audience. Half an hour into the lecture, she shifted restively and glanced around to see if her reaction was mirrored by anyone else in the audience. Aleksei's discourse tonight pertained to the purges and agricultural collectivization in the 1930s. She was familiar enough with these events to realize their far-reaching effects, and had been prepared to be fascinated by the lecture. Instead, she was being treated to a stale recitation of facts and dated party dogma. She had also come to the unpleasant conclusion that some of the "facts" he was spouting were a sanitized version of the events.

And to make matters worse, she was definitely having a problem following Aleksei's train of thought, but everyone she saw—her graduate class included—seemed enthralled by the presentation. She found Aleksei's style almost fatally boring, which to her was as great a sin as inaccuracy. History was a brilliant panorama that shaped the present and future, not simply a parroting of dates and numbers! If

Aleksei was a typical Soviet professor, she pitied the Soviet students.

Frowning, Brenna returned her attention to the stage and tried to concentrate on what Aleksei was saying. Russian history wasn't her field, but she was determined to find something of interest in this lecture. Fifteen minutes later, Brenna had lost her concentration again and she noticed one of the other history professors—whose field *was* Russian history—sneaking a look at his watch. She gave a little sigh of relief. At least she wasn't the only one whose attention was wandering!

When the time for the break finally arrived, after two hours of listening to Aleksei drone on and on, Brenna was toying with the idea of sneaking home. When Aleksei and Bradley Jackson had dropped by her table during lunch, it had been to invite her, along with several other members of the department, to Aleksei's apartment after the lecture. Now she wasn't sure she was up to smiling politely and telling him how much she had enjoyed the lecture. Deciding to see the lecture through to the end and forgo the party, Brenna rose, grabbed her purse and joined the crush of humanity in the aisle to make her way to the foyer and the refreshment stand.

Someone rudely elbowed past her, and Brenna felt herself falling to the side. Encased within a high-heeled pump, her foot turned one way, her ankle the other and she was dumped unceremoniously into a row of seats.

Only the seat she landed on wasn't empty. Strong arms came around her, halting the slide that would have ended in an undignified sprawl on the floor. The handsome, blond man looked just as startled as she felt, and she started to form an apology, but the words died when she met his cold, green stare.

"You—" Brenna began, only to be brought up short when his hands bit into her upper arms.

"Not here, Professor," he murmured in a voice so low that only she could hear. He steadied her, pushing her upright as he also rose. "The guy must have been in training for the roller derby," he joked for the benefit of their audience.

"You okay, Professor Hawthorne?" one of her students asked.

Brenna turned and managed a smile. "Just fine. Go on— I'll catch up with you."

"Let me buy you a drink, Professor," Mitch said, edging her back into the aisle, one hand wrapped securely around her arm.

The crush abated somewhat in the foyer, and Mitch steered her toward an unoccupied corner.

"I thought you were going to buy me a drink, Agent Carlisle," Brenna said tartly, twisting her arm out of his grasp and trying to rub some feeling back into it.

"No need to stand on formalities," he replied with a cold smile. "Call me Mitch."

"I can think of several things to call you," she hissed. "'Mitch' isn't on the list."

"I don't doubt it, but let's keep this civil, shall we?"

"Right." Brenna matched his smile with an icy one of her own. "My lawyer was informed that I was no longer under surveillance."

"A misunderstanding."

"Really?" She brushed aside a tendril of hair that had escaped the bun and glared up at him. "It's my guess that you're a trifle overzealous in pursuit of your duties. Let's just call Tony, shall we, and see what he has to say about this?" She started by him and was immediately brought up short when he reclaimed possession of her arm.

"Let's not," he said softly.

Menace radiated from him, sending a shiver of alarm up Brenna's spine. "You have no right—" she began shakily.

Mitch felt the tremor and relaxed slightly. "Professor, I'm a very determined man and you're in a very untenable position. I'm sure that if we discuss this rationally, we can reach an . . . accommodation."

The foyer was rapidly filling with people, and Brenna was forced to move back into the corner. "I don't want to reach an accommodation, Agent Carlisle," she told him angrily. "I want you out of my life—permanently."

"That can be accomplished, with a little cooperation on your part." Mitch bent toward her and caught a faint whiff of her perfume. Roses underlined with musk. An old-fashioned scent that suited a woman who played the harpsichord.

"Cooperation," Brenna echoed in patent disbelief. "How dare you bulldoze your way into my life and then calmly expect me to cooperate?" Her last word emerged on a burst of air. She shrugged out of his grasp a second time and faced him, a spitting kitten unafraid of the larger lion that stood motionless in front of her. "I'm going to call your supervisor, or whatever his title is, and demand that you stop harassing me."

He couldn't allow that. Mitch almost reached for her, but thought better of the idea. Physical coercion brought out her temper, and he wanted Brenna thoroughly intimidated rather than angry when he started lying through his teeth. "I've been following you all week, Professor. Just me, no other agents." He nodded when those sapphire eyes of hers widened in surprise.

"That's right—I've even gone so far as to attend your lectures, unobtrusively, of course. And out of consideration for your position, I haven't invaded your two graduate-level classes. If you insist upon going to the special-agent-in-charge, my inconspicuous surveillance is going to be nothing but a memory. He'll assign so many agents to you that every time you step foot outside of your house, you'll look like you're leading a damn parade." He raised an inquiring eyebrow. "Is that what you want, Professor Hawthorne?"

A sick feeling rose in Brenna's stomach at his words. Bradley Jackson would have a stroke at the sight of FBI agents invading Meredith Hall. "You know it isn't," she finally replied, her eyes looking anywhere but at him.

Mitch barely managed to control a victorious smile. She'd swallowed without question the lies he'd uttered so authoritatively. Now all he had to do was reel her in. "I have to tell you, the consensus at the office is that your involvement with Prescott was innocent." Her incredibly blue eyes met his, and he saw hope flash in their depths. Being an FBI suspect could end her academic career and she knew it. He felt a brief flicker of regret at threatening her, but ruthlessly crushed it. Brenna Hawthorne and her career weren't important. Nailing Fedoryshyn was.

"I *am* innocent," she whispered fiercely. "How many times do I have to say that before you're convinced?"

In his book she was still the most viable suspect, but Mitch kept his thoughts to himself. Let her believe the lies. "Actions speak louder than words," he said slowly.

Brenna shook her head, confused. "If I knew something—anything!—I would tell you, but I don't. What more do you want from me?"

"I need a pretext for being on campus, and for being around Aleksandr Fedoryshyn."

Brenna shrugged. "You haven't encountered any problems this week, have you?"

"No, but it's only a matter of time." He watched her intently. "I'm a little old to be a student."

That was the truth, Brenna thought. The man was on the wrong side of forty; she was sure of it. "If you want access to Aleksei, I can introduce you to the professors who teach Russian history. I'm certain they—"

"Professor, I don't want to broadcast my presence," Mitch informed her dryly. "You can provide me with the necessary access."

"Well, I can't introduce you as one of my doctoral candidates," she retorted. "You couldn't withstand the scrutiny of my other grad students. And the same problems arise if you assume the identity of a history professor," she continued, blissfully unaware of his suspicions regarding her innocence.

She had an angel's face and a devious mind, Mitch thought as he watched her sort through the problem he presented. If she could think along the lines of establishing a suitable cover identity for him, she could certainly pull off the delivery of Prescott's formula to Fedoryshyn.

"I have a solution," Mitch offered when they had stood in silence for several moments. "Care to hear it?"

Brenna raised her eyes to his face. "Oh, I'm all ears, Agent Carlisle," she murmured with saccharine sweetness.

Mitch stepped closer, forcing her to retreat until her back was literally to the wall. His voice was soft, but held a cutting edge when he spoke. "Hello, Cousin Brenna. I'm so glad you invited me to spend the holidays." His lips twisted into a genuine smile as she stared at him in stricken silence.

Chapter 5

For a day that had begun beautifully, Friday had definitely taken a turn for the worse, Brenna thought as she looked out at the well-lit cul-de-sac from the bay window of her home office. Sighing, she allowed the drape to fall back into place and resumed pacing the first floor of the house. It was eleven o'clock, and in the past hour she had discovered that awaiting Agent Mitch Carlisle's arrival held all the charm of anticipating a case of frostbite.

Reaching the living room, she turned on the stereo and perched nervously on one of the two sofas, which faced each other across a wide, low oak coffee table. Familiar Christmas songs floated from the tall speakers that occupied the two exterior corners of the room, but neither the music nor the tranquil blue-and-gray color scheme of the room's decor did anything to alleviate her anxiety. The FBI, in the form of Mitch Carlisle, was about to take total control of her existence. The quiet, serene life she had made for herself was shattering, and she was ill-equipped to handle the complications Mark had—however inadvertently—brought upon her.

She still found it difficult to believe she had actually agreed to have Carlisle move into her home. How was she going to explain him to the neighbors in general, and Marcia in particular? She certainly couldn't tell her friends the truth, that she was providing Carlisle with his "cover," and she was certain Marcia wouldn't fall for the cliché of a long-lost cousin suddenly appearing out of nowhere. Brenna frowned. Agent Carlisle hadn't seemed worried about the feasibility of the cliché; he had been too busy hinting at how bad her noncooperation would look to the government.

Brenna's gaze came to rest on the cordless telephone that had somehow found its way from her office to one of the shelves of the entertainment center. She should call Tony, let him know that she was cooperating with the government. Her lawyer would undoubtedly be pleased that she was finally aiding the law instead of discovering new ways to break it. She shook her head, horrified at how easily she had become a suspect.

The FBI's theory about the superconductor linked her to Mark and his disappearance, and she had no way to disprove that theory. By Carlisle's logic, since she couldn't produce the formula for the superconductor, she was hiding it. And if she did produce the formula, it would prove that she was Mark's accomplice. She was trapped; the only possibility of exoneration lay in either Mark's return or the discovery of the formula in someone else's possession. Until such a time, there was nothing anyone, including a lawyer, could do for her. After several arrests, she knew her rights as well as any attorney. She could take care of herself, unless the FBI actually arrested her for espionage. No, Brenna decided as she heard a car in her driveway, she wouldn't call Tony unless she was actually taken into custody.

Telling herself to remain calm, that she had nothing to fear, Brenna rose and walked into the kitchen, the cats following her. The knock on the back door came just as she switched on the sole light fixture that had yet to fall victim to the remodeling, and in spite of her resolve, her heart crashed against her rib cage. After wiping her damp palms against her corduroy skirt, she turned the dead-bolt lock and opened the door. Mitch Carlisle stood on the doorstep, a suitcase in one hand and a backpack slung over the opposite shoulder.

"Hello, Professor." Mitch's eyes swept over her, noting her unnaturally stiff carriage and the tension that fairly vibrated through her.

"Agent Carlisle." Brenna looked away from the cool assessment in his gaze. "Come in."

Mitch entered and dropped his luggage on the floor, but prevented her from closing the door by the simple act of laying his hand against the wood. "Is there room in your garage?"

"Room?" Brenna frowned at him.

"Is there room in your garage for my car? I would prefer it out of sight."

And you with it, Brenna thought, but she merely nodded. "The key is in my purse. Wait here." Turning, she hurried down the center hall to the foyer, where her purse hung on the coat tree.

Mitch shoved his hands into his jacket pockets and eyed the six cats who had arrayed themselves in a semicircle around Brenna's feet and now regarded him with varying degrees of feline condescension. One of the cats, the huge gray tom who had attacked him the week before, laid back his ears and directed an ominous hiss at him.

"Keep it up and I'll turn you into violin strings," he replied in a baritone rumble. When the tom hissed again, Mitch smiled threateningly, then looked up to find Brenna standing in the doorway, watching the exchange. He started to explain why he was talking to a cat, then decided to forgo the attempt. *He* wasn't sure why he was talking to the cat.

"It's this one," Brenna said, separating a small green key from the others on the ring. "Park on the right." He left, the door closing quietly behind him, and she bent to pet Jasper. "He's going to be here a while, boy. It might be best

not to antagonize him." Jasper gave a throaty meow and
stalked from the room.

Hoping that keeping her hands occupied would lessen the
anxiety that had gripped her since falling into Carlisle's lap,
Brenna began preparing the coffee maker for the morning.
Water had been measured into the reservoir, and she was in
the midst of filling the basket with coffee when Mitch returned. She paused, the measuring spoon suspended between the coffee and the basket, and watched him throw the
dead bolt. The sound seemed to reverberate through the
room.

Mitch sauntered over to the sheet of plywood Brenna was
still using as a counter and dropped the key ring onto it. The
noise made her start, and he felt a brief flare of regret. He
needed her cooperation and his tactics in obtaining it had
been less than fair, but he truly felt that in this case the end
justified the means. Now he was here, about to take up
temporary residence in her home. It was time to switch
strategy and change her grudging consent to act as his cover
into willing compliance. "Do you lose a lot of keys?"

Brenna swallowed nervously. He was standing a good two
feet away, but he was still too close for her peace of mind.
"Occasionally. Why?"

"Except for your car keys, all the other keys are either
different colors or have different-colored circles painted on
them." He kept his eyes on the key ring and maintained the
distance between them, making his posture and attitude as
nonthreatening as possible as he shrugged out of his jacket
and dropped it onto the plywood.

"Yes, well, I kept forgetting what key went in what lock,
so I worked out a color-code system." Her eyes were drawn
to the holster that was now visible. The straps that supported the leather looped around both shoulders, and another strap circled his body and kept the holster tight against
the left side of his chest. Clipped to his belt was what appeared to be a remote pager. She nervously wet her dry lips
with the tip of her tongue and dipped the measuring spoon
she held back into the coffee can.

Mitch idly sorted through the keys. "Green for the garage because they both start with *g*?"

"No, because the lawn mower is stored there and the lawn is green." She was unaware of the astounded look Mitch gave her because she suddenly realized that she had forgotten how much coffee she had already measured out. With an inward shrug she added two more spoonfuls and slid the basket into place.

There was a certain twisted logic to that, Mitch admitted. Pointing to a key with a large white circle painted on it, he ventured, "This would be for the front door of the house, then, since your house is white?"

She shook her head, relaxed enough now to offer him a tentative smile. "Actually that's for the house across the street. Marcia has a key for my house and I have one for hers. That way we're never locked out of our homes, unless of course the other person happens to be gone, and then we have to either call for a locksmith or break a window." She paused, thinking. "Of course, if I lose my key ring, I won't be able to get home since I won't have my car keys, either. It's really a dilemma, isn't it? If you follow the progression far enough, you will eventually need spare keys for spare keys for—"

"Wait." Mitch held up his hand in a gesture for silence. "Your neighbor's house is brown. Why the white circle?"

"Because her bedroom set is white."

"That makes perfect sense," he murmured. He was beginning to regret opening this line of questioning. In a louder voice he asked, "What color is *your* house key?"

Brenna moved a step closer to him and picked out a black key. "That's for the back door. Black/back—it rhymes."

"Of course."

"And this one—" she pointed to a bright blue key "—is for the front door."

He considered the logic of that for nearly a minute before admitting defeat. "Why blue?"

"I like the color." She smiled and watched as he fumbled in his shirt pocket and withdrew a bottle of aspirin. "Headache?" she asked sympathetically.

He firmly resisted the urge to say yes and explain exactly what had given it to him. Instead, he settled for nodding his head. "Could I have a glass of water?"

Brenna pulled a glass from one of the boxes, filled it with water and handed it to him, then watched while he swallowed the three tablets he had shaken out. Somehow the headache made him seem less threatening. "When did you eat last?"

"The same time you did—at noon, in the union." He placed his glass in the sink.

"You might feel better if you had something in your stomach." She walked to the refrigerator and pulled open the door to the freezer.

Following, Mitch peered over her shoulder into the compartment. The freezer held three trays of ice cubes. He sighed inwardly.

Glancing at him, Brenna saw the disappointed look on his face. She closed the freezer and opened the refrigerator door. The top shelf held a carton of milk, juice and a container of yogurt; the second held several cans of soda. The next shelf was occupied by a bag of apples. The door shelves held various condiments and a tray of eggs.

"Is this your normal diet?" Mitch asked in the deepening silence.

"I wasn't expecting company," Brenna explained, uncomfortably aware of the contemptuous light glowing in the green eyes that studied her.

"It doesn't matter." He reached past her to claim an apple.

Brenna took a can of soda for herself and closed the refrigerator door. Unearthing another glass, she poured the soda into it, then added several ice cubes while Mitch meticulously washed and dried his apple.

Looking up, he found Brenna's sapphire gaze resting on him. "Don't worry about it, Professor. I don't expect you to treat me like a houseguest."

Brenna's hand tightened around the glass. "Exactly how *am* I supposed to treat you?" she asked in a hushed voice. "This is all quite new to me, I'm afraid. I've never lived with an FBI agent before." When the implication of her last statement hit her, a blush crept across her cheeks.

Mitch was fascinated by the way her cheeks pinkened. He hadn't even noticed the innuendo in her words until she blushed and lowered her eyes. Her puritanical reaction was astonishing. "We do have a few things to discuss, don't we?" When she hesitantly raised her eyes to his, he offered her a smile that had always reassured his clients in the past. "First of all, I'll try to have as little impact on your life as possible."

That sounded completely impossible, in light of the fact that he would be living in her home, but Brenna refrained from commenting.

"Secondly," he continued when she remained silent, "don't worry about introducing me as your cousin. I have found—" He caught his error as soon as the words had been said. "That is, the Bureau has had great success using this ploy." He bit into the apple and chewed thoughtfully for several moments. Swallowing, he added, "People tend to accept familial relationships without too many questions."

"I hope so," she said softly.

"Worried about your reputation, Professor?" He took a large bite out of the apple.

"Yes," she answered bluntly, studying the contents of her glass. "I had a devil of a time convincing Marcia that you and the people you had ransacking my house last Friday were actually remodelers."

Mitch grunted. "Why didn't you simply tell her the truth?"

Brenna looked up at him, appalled. "Tell my best friend that the FBI was searching my home? You're obviously not as intelligent as I thought you were."

"What's a best friend for?"

"Agent Carlisle, coming under suspicion of espionage is not something one broadcasts."

"Embarrassed?"

Brenna drew quick rein on her temper, but sparks of fury lingered in the depths of her eyes. His snide tone tempered the fear that had been riding her since encountering him at the lecture. "No, I'm not embarrassed. But as you so gallantly pointed out earlier this evening, this particular allegation could very easily ruin my career. The situation would be laughable, if it wasn't so potentially dangerous."

Tossing the apple core in the wastebasket, Mitch walked back to the refrigerator and removed a can of soda for himself. "Prove me and my suspicions wrong," he returned, punctuating the challenge with the pop of opening the soda can.

"I won't have to," she told him haughtily. "Time will vindicate me. My only concern is that my life—and reputation—remain intact despite your intrusion." She turned on her heel and stalked from the kitchen, the cats gamboling after her.

His resolution to treat Brenna Hawthorne more kindly went up in smoke when she absentmindedly turned off the kitchen light as she passed the switch. Scowling, Mitch stuffed her key ring into his pocket, slammed open the swinging kitchen door with the palm of his free hand and followed her to the living room, where she and three of the cats occupied one of the sofas. Another cat sat atop the stereo, its gold eyes staring hypnotically at the glass wind chime suspended a mere two feet above the cabinet. "You've been arrested several times, Professor," he stated, settling into the sofa on the opposite side of the coffee table from the one she occupied. "I think it's a little late in the game to be worried about your reputation!"

"What does that have to do with anything?" she demanded as he lit a cigarette, then tossed the pack and lighter onto the coffee table.

"If the neighbors are inclined to gossip, you've already given them plenty of ammunition." He gave her a fierce, satisfied smile and settled back into the cushions.

"You really are a hateful man," Brenna observed.

"I'm not here to win a popularity contest."

"Obviously!" Brenna set her glass down on a crystal coaster with a sharp clink. The man irritated her to no end—when he wasn't busy intimidating her. "There is a difference between knowingly committing an illegal act in order to defend a moral position and espionage. The two are hardly related!"

"I disagree. Break one law and it becomes easier to break another," Mitch stated bluntly. "The law is black and white, not varying shades of gray."

"The law—as you well know—is in a constant state of flux," she replied, warming to the argument. The challenge of a philosophical debate made it possible to forget that the man across from her thought her guilty of espionage. "We honor the first Continental Congress, but they, in fact, were guilty of treason. When I have broken laws, it was because I firmly believed in the higher moral purpose of the act."

"Terrorists use the same reasoning to justify murdering defenseless hostages." When she paled under the import of his words, Mitch smiled coldly and added, "You live in an ivory tower, Professor. I'm sure you and your friends sit around and debate serving a 'higher moral purpose' for hours, but none of you have the vaguest idea what that really means. You stay in your safe little academic world, experiencing reality through newspapers and scholarly tomes." The cold smile vanished, and he looked at her with an expression of open scorn. "When was the last time you put something other than your reputation at risk for a cause, Professor? What have you ever laid on the line besides a few hundred dollars for a fine or weekends in county jail?"

Brenna gaped at him. "I do what I can, Agent Carlisle. And for your information, putting my reputation on the line is quite a risk in my world. If it weren't, you wouldn't be sitting here now, enjoying my cooperation. I would have told you to go to hell when you suggested that I act as your cover story."

In spite of himself, Mitch admired the courage it took for her to argue with him. "It would probably be best," he drawled, "if we stop this discussion before it ends in bloodshed."

Understanding his reasoning, Brenna bit back a reply and said, "Agreed. Where's your partner, by the way?"

"Greg Talbott?"

She nodded. "Right, Agent Talbott. The teddy bear who looks like he moves small mountains for a living."

"Observant, aren't we?" He found Brenna's description annoying, particularly because the analogy was so accurate in describing Greg's compact, wrestler's body. "Greg has been reassigned."

"To a different part of this investigation or to a new case?"

"To a new case," he answered impatiently. The small lie was justifiable, he decided, in order to protect Greg and his career in case Brenna Hawthorne ever took it into her head to contact the local FBI office. "Are you done playing twenty questions?"

Hearing the annoyance in his voice, Brenna's lips twitched in a effort to control her smile. Turning this man's tactics on him was rather enjoyable. "Not as much fun answering questions as asking them, is it?"

Mitch ignored both the question and the smug note in her voice. "Look, Brenna, we're going to be spending a lot of time together. Let's make it easy on both of us, okay?"

"Okay," she responded brightly. She was beginning to understand how this man operated. He called her "Professor" when he was about to use coercion to gain her cooperation; he used her name when he wanted her willing compliance. A tiny smile toyed with the corners of her mouth. If this was the game he wanted to play, she would oblige. "It's been a long day, Agent Carlisle," she said delicately. "So in the spirit of . . . cooperation . . . I'll show you to your room."

She was slipping out of his control, Mitch thought uneasily as he returned to the kitchen to retrieve his suitcase and backpack and then followed her up the stairs. While he hadn't wanted her so frightened that she was unable to function normally, her present level of impertinence was unacceptable. The woman simply tended to forget that she was afraid of him. He was going to have to do something about her attitude, but suddenly he wasn't sure what approach to take.

Her wild mood swings were not unexpected; he had had clients who either ignored or made light of any threats they received. The trick to keeping those clients alive and safe had lain in driving home the danger, forcing them to see themselves as the terrorists did. Patience, he counseled himself. Patience and reassurance had always proven effective when dealing with a client who had steadfastly refused to confront the precariousness of his position. The same strategy should work on Brenna Hawthorne.

His room was at the opposite end of the hall from the master suite, Mitch noted wryly, and was done in unobtrusive shades of beige accented with blue. The room was comfortably appointed with a double bed, bureau, an armchair upholstered in royal blue and a single lamp sitting on the nightstand. A set of copper wind chimes hung in one corner. Brenna opened the small closet to withdraw a set of linens from the shelf.

"I'll let you make up your own bed," she said casually, dropping the sheets onto the beige comforter as she watched the man lounging in the doorway.

Mitch caught her arm when she started by him. "In the spirit of cooperation," he said mockingly, "it's only fair to tell you that, in case you have any thoughts about contacting Fedoryshyn or Prescott once I'm safely tucked in for the night, the Bureau has a tap on your phone and a team watching your house."

Brenna glanced at the hand gripping her arm and then lifted her gaze to his face. "You really should see someone about that paranoia," she managed lightly, although his warning had caused her stomach to sink into the vicinity of her knees.

"Paranoia keeps me alive, Professor."

"Then you have my sympathy, Agent Carlisle," she told him in a soft voice. "May I go now?"

Mitch released her arm and watched from the doorway as she entered her bedroom. The cats followed and Brenna, after casting him a last, troubled look, quietly closed the door behind them.

It was an exceptionally loud, high-pitched whine that brought Mitch awake with a start the following morning. He didn't recognize the sound immediately, but he did react to the internal alarms it set off. Instinct told him that a red-headed history professor was not responsible for the noise. Not bothering with the jeans he had flung across the chair upon retiring, he snatched the automatic from its holster and raced out of the bedroom to the stairs. He was three steps from the foyer when Brenna came into sight.

Clad in jeans and a soft, yellow sweater, Brenna put one hand on the newel post and stopped dead at the apparition on her staircase. Her face went white at the sight of the automatic pistol he held in both hands, then just as abruptly flooded with color when her eyes flickered to the exposed, hair-roughened expanse of chest. She found both sights equally disturbing.

"I—I'm sorry," she squeaked, trying to find something other than the scantily clad FBI man to look at. Her gaze ran down the hard, muscled length of his legs and came to rest on the first step of the staircase. "I guess I should have told you last night that the carpenters would be here at eight."

Mitch drew a deep, calming breath and flipped the safety catch of his weapon on. "That would have been nice," he agreed, lowering the automatic so that the barrel pointed at the step. "Your remodelers are working weekends?"

"Just Saturdays," she answered, annoyed to find that her gaze had curiously returned to his chest. It was, she decided shakily, a very nice chest. The pelt of hair covering it was the same entrancing shade of gold as his beard and formed a rough triangle that arrowed down across his stomach and disappeared into the waistband of the white bikini shorts he wore.

And he obviously didn't have a modest bone in his rather large body, she thought when he simply stood there, watching her. Grimly she pulled her eyes, and thoughts, away from the man towering over her.

Her reactions to his present state were interesting, Mitch thought wryly, and remarkably unsophisticated given her age and marital status. "I apologize for my unorthodox appearance." He almost smiled when she gave a jerky nod but didn't look at him. "Did you want something?"

The low purr in his words surprised Mitch as much as it did Brenna. He wasn't given to double entendres or sensual allusions in his dealings with women, nor had he ever considered crossing the invisible but very real boundary between his professional duty and his private interest. Interest? He mused, suddenly struck by the vulnerability he sensed in her. No, he wasn't interested in Brenna Hawthorne except as she pertained to Fedoryshyn, he told himself bracingly. And she was about as vulnerable as a lioness, he thought, remembering her temper and the way she pulled herself together to face his allegations.

"N-no," Brenna said in that same high-pitched voice. Swallowing convulsively, she continued, "I can't offer you breakfast or lunch, I'm afraid—we're in the process of dismantling what remains of my kitchen. But there's a thermos of coffee in the dining room," she tacked on in a louder voice when the high-pitched whine started again.

Mitch recognized the whine now; someone using an electric saw. "Thanks."

Brenna nodded and started back to the kitchen without looking at him again. The sight of the skeletal room was a welcome change from the overpowering masculinity that had assaulted her senses. With a grim resolve, she picked up another packing box and carried it down the narrow stair-case into the basement.

The kitchen, Mitch saw twenty minutes later when he had shaved, showered and dressed, was in its death throes. The plywood counter had disappeared completely, while the re-frigerator and a two-burner hot plate now stood forlornly in the dining room. Two men were in the process of remov-ing the sink and its cabinet while another workman was finishing the task of sawing away the exposed laths of what once had been, Mitch assumed, a pantry. A burly, grinning man was attacking the floor covering with obvious relish, and Brenna was struggling to lift a packing carton from the center of the room. Her hair had been casually pinned to the top of her head, and several auburn wisps now trailed along her neck.

"Need some help?" Mitch offered when their eyes met.

"I can manage, thanks," she puffed, heading for the basement stairs. For some strange reason, she instinctively felt that allowing him to help in any way would result in his slipping into her private life, and the last thing she wanted was to have Agent Carlisle any more entangled in her life than he already was!

Her wishes, however, were not going to be taken into consideration, Brenna discovered upon her return to the kitchen. Agent Carlisle was folding down the top sections of one box in preparation for its removal. He wore a red-and-black checked flannel shirt with his jeans, and though she was certain he was armed, try as she might, she could see no evidence of either the shoulder holster or weapon.

"You must be the cousin Doc was telling me about," the burly man called to Mitch from his position across the room.

Mitch looked up and met what was apparently an ever-present grin with a smile of his own. "That's right. Mitch Carlisle."

"I'm George Weston, owner of We Do Renew," George offered blithely. "Sorry about the mess, but the Doc didn't tell me she was having company over the holidays."

"My visit was unexpected," Mitch explained, raising an eyebrow at Brenna as she approached and tugged at the box in his possession. "Let go, Cousin Brenna," he advised mildly. "The least I can do in exchange for room and board is carry these things to the basement."

"The very least," Brenna ground out, relinquishing her hold.

Smiling, Mitch easily lifted the box onto one shoulder and carried it down to the basement. Within minutes, the remaining four boxes had met the same fate, and Mitch was talking with George while the older man worked on the linoleum.

"I'm glad you're here," George was saying when Brenna returned from the dining room with a cup of coffee. "Somebody broke in a week ago, you know."

"So Brenna said," Mitch replied, lighting a cigarette.

"We fixed the window for her, and she had a locksmith out a few days later, but there's nothing quite like having a man around to discourage prowlers."

"George, you know better than that," Brenna exclaimed, shocked. "Just because Ag er, Mitch," she hurriedly amended. "Mitch's presence doesn't constitute safety." That was the truth, she thought vehemently. She had felt threatened since meeting the man!

George shook his salt-and-pepper head in disagreement. "Too many crazies around nowadays," he pronounced solemnly, exchanging a man-to-man look with Mitch. "A woman alone is a perfect target."

"Excuse me," Brenna huffed, unable to control her outrage at the condescension permeating the air. "This target has some errands to run." She turned on her heel and executed as graceful an exit as possible.

She was shoving her arms into her coat when Mitch sauntered out of the kitchen. "Going somewhere?" he asked.

"I am going out," she informed him loftily, snatching her purse from the coat tree. "The cats are out of food."

"So are you," he pointed out, noting that his jacket had been moved from the kitchen to one of the pegs on the coat tree.

Brenna closed her eyes and counted to ten. "I will also pick up human food at the grocery store," she conceded, investigating the depths of her purse. "I'm sure George will keep you suitably entertained in my absence."

"George really upset you, didn't he," he commented idly.

"Yes, he did," she replied in disgust, looking up just long enough to glare at him. "I fail to see what he thinks you could have done that I didn't." She stalked into her office and wrenched open the top drawer of her desk.

"He thinks I would have protected you," Mitch said, following her.

"Well, we both know how wrong *that* assumption is," Brenna snorted as she pulled her checkbook out of the drawer and closed it with a controlled slam.

"Do we?"

Brenna raised her eyes to the man standing in the doorway, and her fingers tightened around the checkbook. Something swirled in the emerald depths of Mitch's eyes, something that raised the hair on the back of her neck. "Yes," she whispered, "we do."

Mitch lifted the cigarette to his hard mouth and exhaled slowly. "I would have protected you," he said at last.

Why did she believe him? Brenna wondered fleetingly. He constituted the main danger in her life, so why was she suddenly, intuitively certain that he would protect her? She started to voice that question, only to be brought up short by the summons of the telephone. She automatically reached for the portable handset on her desk, then remembered that she had left it in the living room. She stepped around the barrier his body presented and hurried down the hall.

"Hello," she answered breathlessly.

There was a slight hesitation on the other end of the line. "Mitch Carlisle, please."

"Yes, just a minute." Brenna carried the phone back to her office and handed it to Mitch. "For you. Leave it on the desk when you're finished."

"Carlisle. Just a minute." Mitch covered the mouthpiece with one hand. "You're not going anywhere, Brenna, not without me. This won't take long."

She could object, but it wouldn't do her any good, Brenna realized. Nodding, she left Mitch to his conversation and went in search of her key ring. It had been left in the kitchen last night, so maybe George or one of his men had moved it. As soon as she found her keys, she was leaving, with or without her appointed watchdog.

When she was out of hearing, Mitch brought the receiver back to his ear. "Sorry, Greg. What's going on?"

"He's in a cab heading for downtown Minneapolis," Greg answered. "I'm three vehicles back from the other surveillance car."

"Stay on him," Mitch instructed. "For the next hour or so you can reach me on the car phone or the pager. I'll call once we're back at the house."

"Do you think the Icon has a meet arranged with your pigeon?"

They had agreed upon the generic term *pigeon* to identify Brenna, and Mitch found himself smiling when he considered what the pigeon's reaction would be to the label. Greg's excited inquiry, however, erased the flash of humor. "Anything's possible," he told his friend. "Don't lose the Icon."

"Trust me, teach."

"If I didn't, you wouldn't be here," Mitch replied more sharply than he had intended. "One more thing. The pigeon thinks you're out of the picture, so let's keep it that way." When no reply was forthcoming, he demanded, "Did you hear me?"

"I heard you," Greg answered, understanding the protection Mitch was trying to provide him. "Thanks, teach. I'll be in touch."

Mitch collapsed the antenna and returned the receiver to the handset on the desk. The day had not begun on an auspicious note, he thought, lifting his jacket from the hall coat tree as he passed by on his way to the kitchen. He needed coffee and food before he confronted anything else.

"The Doc's in the basement," George volunteered when Mitch entered the kitchen. "She thinks her keys may have ended up in one of the storage boxes."

Waving his thanks, Mitch descended the stairs and found Brenna kneeling on the concrete floor, searching through the first of several boxes that had been stacked in front of her kitchen table and chairs. "Come on, Brenna, I'm going to buy you breakfast."

"In a minute." Brenna didn't bother looking up. "My key ring is down here somewhere."

"I have your keys," he informed her, going down on one knee beside her.

"You . . ." She frowned at him. "Why? How?"

"I took them last night when you stormed out of the kitchen." Her hands had stilled at his words, so he began to repack the box with quick, efficient moves.

Brenna considered the admission for several moments. "May I have them back?"

Mitch carefully replaced a cut-glass serving bowl and closed the box before answering. "You don't need them."

"I most certainly do," she argued.

Rising, he closed a hand around her arm and hauled her to her feet. "No, Brenna, you don't," he insisted blandly, seeing the sudden wariness in her eyes. "I'll open any doors that need opening."

"I see." And she did. It had never occurred to her before just how significant her key ring was. Without it she could not use her car, get into her office in Meredith Hall or unlock her own front door. She was well and truly caught in Agent Carlisle's net. Cautiously she pulled her arm free. "I suppose allowing me to drive my car is out of the question?"

"For the time being."

"Well, then, I have no alternative but to accept your breakfast invitation," she said, avoiding his eyes as she adjusted the strap of her purse over her shoulder.

He had no reason to feel guilty, Mitch told himself bracingly as she preceded him up the stairs and out to the garage. If she was innocent of any involvement with Fedoryshyn, his presence would be, at most, an inconvenience, one that she would soon forget once he was gone.

Mitch was in the process of backing his car out of the garage when a pickup pulled into the driveway, blocking his path. In seconds, his right hand had opened both his jacket and his shirt and was gripping the butt of the pistol riding securely in its leather harness. He relaxed only when he saw Brenna smile at the woman stepping out of the pickup.

"Good, you're ready," Marcia declared as she jumped lightly onto the driveway. "My four rug rats are busy terrorizing a new sitter, and Ted and I have the entire day free."

"Ready," Brenna echoed, trying frantically to remember what she was supposed to be ready for.

Marcia threw up her hands in a theatrical gesture of despair. A fitting gesture, Brenna thought, since she was an actress with the repertory Guthrie Theater. "We're going tree-hunting today, remember? We decided that this year we were going to cut our own trees instead of settling for those needle-dropping fire hazards that are precut...." Her words trailed off at the sight of the man who had unfolded himself from the compact car and was now stalking toward them. "Oh, my, Brenna, not bad at all!"

Determinedly Brenna fought the blush that threatened and smiled thinly at her friend's avid expression. She was dimly aware of Ted swinging out of the driver's side of the pickup as Mitch approached.

"Is this someone I should get to know?" Marcia murmured sotto voce, a delightful gleam in her brown eyes.

"My cousin." Brenna forced the lie through gritted teeth. "Mitch, come meet my neighbors." She performed the introductions with alacrity, desperately hoping that she could get herself and Mitch away from Marcia before the other woman asked any pointed questions.

"Cousins," Marcia sighed as she studied Mitch. "What a pity."

"I beg your pardon?" Mitch frowned at the statuesque, irrepressible brunette who had been eyeing him with open fascination.

Marcia chuckled. "Sorry, Mitch, but for a minute there I had hopes of Brenna being interested in something other than dead conquerors and kings."

"Marcia," Ted said reprovingly, "stop teasing her."

"Oh, Brenna doesn't mind," Marcia said breezily. "He's family, after all, and everyone knows I've been matchmaking for Brenna since the divorce."

"Really?" Something close to amusement sparkled in the normally impassive green eyes as Mitch glanced at Brenna. "Had any luck?"

"No." The single word was laced with disgust. "You know Brenna—all she does is work."

"About those trees," Brenna put in, hoping to distract Marcia from her favorite topic.

Marcia dealt with the distraction by ignoring it. "And she's so incredibly picky. I'd about given up hope until she started seeing that scientist, Mark what's-his-name." She shrugged. "Of course, then *he* up and disappeared. Not that that was such a great loss. Did the police ever find out what happened to him?" This last question was directed at Brenna.

"Not yet—"

"Well, personally, I never cared for the man."

"Honey," Ted groaned, "I don't think Mitch is interested in your opinion of Mark Prescott."

Ted's intervention was also disregarded. "I ask you, would you trust a man who ran ten miles a day, was a vegetarian and didn't have a single bad habit?"

"Sounds suspicious to me," Mitch agreed, grinning.

It was time to take control of the rapidly deteriorating situation Brenna decided desperately. "I think the two of you had better go to the tree farm without me," she began firmly. "George is back with his munchkins and there's nothing in my kitchen but a ceiling, a floor and four walls. We haven't even had breakfast yet—"

"Neither have we. Scraping cereal and bananas off the floor after the kids have eaten has a tendency to depress one's appetite. We grown-ups can stop along the way to the tree farm and have brunch," Marcia suggested. "Unless you had something else planned for your cousin?"

"Mitch is rather tired—"

"Sounds like fun," Brenna's "cousin" disagreed.

Pasting a sympathetic smile on her face, Brenna fixed her houseguest with a steely look. "Don't be silly, Mitch, you don't even have winter boots with you. You're simply not equipped to go tromping through the snow."

"Ted has an extra pair, don't you, Ted," Marcia countered.

"Give it up, Brenna, and surrender gracefully," Ted sighed. "You know what Marcia's like when she gets an idea into her head, and she's bound and determined to go out and murder an evergreen this year."

"It's not just me," Marcia protested. "Brenna and I decided this together." She smiled at Mitch. "It is up to you, though. If you'd rather not go along, we won't force you."

"Want to bet," Brenna murmured.

Fifteen minutes later she was sitting in Mitch's car, her eyes fixed grimly on the pickup they were following. The situation was intolerable, but short of telling Marcia the truth, there was nothing Brenna could do to short-circuit her outgoing friend's efforts to make Mitch feel welcome. Laboring under the misconception that Mitch was family, Marcia would continue to be her normal garrulous self, and God knew what else she would innocently tell Mitch about Brenna's private life.

The thought made her cringe, and she slanted a look at her companion. Mitch was talking softly into the car phone and she sighed inwardly. It would have been easier to accept the FBI surveillance if Greg Talbott had been assigned to watch her instead of Mitch. Greg, she felt, would at least have given her the benefit of the doubt regarding the superconductor, not merely assumed her guilt, as Mitch had. There was an inexorable quality about Mitch's devotion to duty that was almost frightening. He had decided, she sensed, that her guilt or innocence in this matter was immaterial, just as she herself was. His only concern was to bring Mark and whoever he was dealing with to justice.

She felt Mitch's gaze fall on her when he returned the receiver to the cradle, but she was in no mood to extend even a pretense of courtesy to him. She folded her arms across her chest and studied the freeway traffic.

Mitch allowed the small display of feminine displeasure to continue until he followed the pickup into the parking lot of a restaurant. He pulled into a parking space some distance from the pickup and left the engine idling when he turned to face his captive. "You have two options," he stated in a calm, deadly tone when she continued to stare stonily out the window. "Either go along with the charade, which means acting normally, or I'll tell your friends the truth right now."

The threat brought Brenna's gaze to him with a snap of her head. "You wouldn't," she finally managed to say. "You won't risk—what's the phrase?—blowing your cover. Not after all the trouble you've gone to."

"You think not?" he challenged silkily. "Your friends, while a little different, seem trustworthy. I'm sure I could guarantee their silence until this business is finished."

A quick glance over his shoulder showed Brenna that Ted and Marcia were out of the pickup and walking toward the car. He had cornered her—again. "With very little effort, I could really come to hate you, Agent Carlisle. All right," she capitulated, her hands clenched into two fists of indignation when he shrugged and reached for the door handle. "Just don't drag Ted or Marcia any further into this mess. Agreed?"

Another dart of guilt speared through Mitch at her submission. He had hoped that threats would no longer be necessary to gain her cooperation, but Brenna was fighting his presence in her life every step of the way. They were clearly engaged in a contest of wills, a contest he dared not lose. "Agreed." He cut the engine with a swift, ruthless motion of his wrist and climbed out of the car.

By four in the afternoon, Brenna was cradling a glass of wine in her hands and considering the scene in her living room. Ted and Mitch were attempting to force the spruce tree to stand proudly in its holder while she and Marcia, mostly Marcia, called out instructions. The cats, released from their confinement in her bedroom, prowled around the new addition with overwhelming curiosity glinting in their eyes.

A large platter of cheese, meat and crackers lay on the low coffee table, along with two bottles of cabernet. The food had been purchased on their return route home, and Ted and Marcia had declared their desire to help Brenna arrange the two trees she had selected. The platter was as much a temptation to the cats as the trees—she had already tapped Jasper's nose when he had tried to sample the selection.

Her eyes fell on Mitch, lying on his side beneath the tree. He was working the screws on the stand while Ted held the tree in place. He was really very good at blending in with his surroundings, Brenna thought as she took a sip of wine. He had played the part of visiting cousin with such authenticity that the Thompsons had accepted him completely, right down to buying his story of being a carpenter. Brenna had nearly choked when Ted had asked if Mitch could help him install a new front door, but Mitch had taken it all in stride. He had talked about such things as shimming the frame and hanging the door to plumb, so perhaps he really did know something about carpentry.

"How's that?"

Mitch's voice, muffled by the tree and the fact that he was talking into the carpet, drew Brenna back to the present. "Just fine," she replied, setting aside her glass to pick up the plastic pitcher of water she had placed on the floor. "Get out from under there so I can water the poor thing."

One of Mitch's hands thrust itself out from under a low-hanging limb. "Just hand me the pitcher," he said in a commanding tone. "There's no sense in you crawling around down here when I'm already bent like a pretzel."

Hateful man, Brenna thought as she walked to the tree. For just a moment she considered the relative merits of dumping the contents of the pitcher over him, but she discarded the idea when he turned his head and fixed her with an impatient glare. Shrugging, she handed him the pitcher and walked back to her seat.

"Do you think he's too old for my sister?" Marcia asked, reaching for another cracker.

The question was outrageous, even from Marcia. "It depends on what she wants him for, I suppose," Brenna said lightly.

Marcia chuckled. "You know what I mean. Mitch isn't engaged or otherwise 'involved,' is he?"

Now that, Brenna decided with a sinking feeling in the pit of her stomach, was a very good question. If Mitch had a wife or girlfriend waiting somewhere, just what lengths was he willing to go to in order to pull off his cover story? A horrifying vision of Marcia's past matchmaking attempts floated through Brenna's mind. She was going to have to protect Marcia from herself. "He's seeing someone, I think," she said at last.

"Mmm, he would be."

Brenna couldn't help but smile at her friend's obvious disappointment. "Sorry."

Marcia grinned. "That's okay. I still have you."

"Not everyone wants to be married," she felt obliged to point out.

"Don't be silly," Marcia disagreed with an airy wave of her hand. "Everyone wants to be happy."

"The two are not necessarily compatible."

"They are with the right partner," Marcia insisted, smiling at her husband as he settled at her feet.

"Matchmaking again?" Ted asked as he popped a cheese-topped cracker into his mouth.

"She was trying for my cousin, but I cut her off at the pass," Brenna volunteered.

Instead of seating himself on one of the couches, Mitch availed himself of the space on the floor next to Brenna's feet. "Thanks, cuz, I appreciate your efforts."

When she frowned down at him, he gave her an easy smile that told her to relax. *He's playing his part,* Brenna told herself, *and I had best do the same.*

An hour later Brenna watched her friends hurry across the street. Tonight, with the help of their four sons, Ted and Marcia would put up their own tree and decorate the house. This was Brenna's second Christmas alone since her divorce, and she missed sharing with someone the intimacy of unpacking the various ornaments and decorations. Sighing, she closed the front door and firmly locked it before returning to the living room to clean up the remains of the snack.

Mitch was one step ahead of her. He met her in the doorway, carrying the serving platter and stemmed glasses. "Where are we going to wash these?" he asked, shaking his head when she reached for the platter.

"The basement laundry tub, I suppose," Brenna said thoughtfully. "They may as well be with the rest of the kitchen." She picked up the empty wine bottles and trailed him to the basement, pausing only to drop the bottles in the trash can that occupied her ruined kitchen.

The basement had been turned into a warren of passages by the relocation of packing boxes and kitchen appliances, and Brenna carefully negotiated her way toward the laundry area. It took several minutes for her to locate the box that held her dish soap and kitchen towels, but when she did, she turned to Mitch with a shaky smile. Now that her friends were gone, she felt uncomfortable allowing him to do the things any normal houseguest would. "You don't have to bother—"

"It's no bother," Mitch replied with a trace of his earlier impatience. "I'm here."

She couldn't very well argue with that! Brenna handed him a towel and drew water into the double laundry tub. "I want to thank you for today," she said when the silence stretching between them threatened to become unbearable.

"Thank me for what?"

Brenna swallowed nervously. "For... playing your part so well, I guess. Do you really know how to install a new door?"

"Yes, I really do," he replied, obviously amused by her disbelief. He rinsed the four glasses and carefully dried them. "And as far as playing my part is concerned, it was easy. Your friends aren't the suspicious sort."

"No, they aren't," she agreed quietly, spending more time than was necessary washing the platter. "They won't be watched, will they? Because of today?"

Mitch leaned against the tub and frowned down at her. "I don't understand."

"Ted and Marcia aren't under suspicion because they're my friends, are they?" she asked, lifting worried eyes to meet his gaze. "They really don't know anything about Mark or superconductors."

Her anxious expression brought a return of the guilt he had felt earlier in the day. "No, they won't be placed under surveillance," he answered, rescuing the ceramic platter from her death grip. "I can guarantee that."

Brenna gave a sigh of relief and smiled her thanks. If she ignored this morning's threat, Mitch had lived up to his promise to have as little impact on her life as possible.

Well, damn! Mitch swore silently at himself as he dried the platter. The first rule of successful interrogation required taking advantage of any weakness displayed by the suspect. Had he lied, indicated that she had placed the Thompsons in a precarious position, Brenna might have cracked and admitted her part in Prescott's scheme. Instead, he had taken one look at those huge sapphire eyes and fallen all over himself to reassure her. Hell!

Brenna drained the sink and carefully rinsed out the last of the soap suds. Since both trees were up, one in the living room and the other in the family room, she should really bring out the tree ornaments, Brenna thought as she dried her hands. And as long as she was getting those four boxes, it wouldn't hurt to carry the others upstairs, either, particularly since George was planning to lay the kitchen floor on Monday, which meant no traffic would be allowed until the following morning.

"These go upstairs, right?" Mitch queried, placing the four glasses on the platter.

"On the china hutch," Brenna replied absently, starting off in the opposite direction from the steps.

"Where are you going?" Mitch called, frowning.

"I'll be right up."

"That's not what I asked." When Brenna didn't answer, he shook his head. Obviously she was off on a tangent again. Shrugging, he walked through the mess created by the remodelers and climbed to the first floor. At least he didn't have to worry about his suspect. There were no exits from the basement, nor was there a phone.

He was flipping through her compact disc and record collection when he caught sight of Brenna staggering through the center hall under the weight of a very large cardboard box. Intrigued, he followed and nearly ran her down when she hurried back through the family room doorway. Automatically he reached out to steady her when she rebounded off his chest, and was startled by the tiny gasp she gave when his hands closed around her shoulders.

"Sorry," he growled, aware of the tremor rippling through her.

"M-my fault," she stammered, backing hurriedly away when the touch of his hands seemed to burn through her sweater. "Next time I'll yell 'fore.'"

Mitch's gaze flicked around the casually appointed room. Unlike the rest of the house, this room held no antiques or area rugs. Instead, the floor was covered by dark green wall-to-wall carpeting, and seating was provided by a pastel yellow sectional arranged around a television set. A wet bar and four high-backed stools took up one wall. A built-in bookcase lined another wall, while an octagon game table and chairs sat by the front window of the room. Like the other rooms, this one, too, had a gentle, welcoming quality to it that he found unaccountably soothing. A musical ringing came from a corner, where one of the cats sat on a console table, batting at a set of butterfly wind chimes.

Brenna followed his look, wondering what was so out of place that it would hold his interest. When she saw his stare come to rest on Athena, the black-haired Persian mix she had rescued from a shelter two years ago, she bit her lip. The man obviously didn't care for her choice of pets, as witnessed by the way he had threatened Jasper last night.

Had he really barged into her life only last night? Brenna thought wonderingly. Somehow it seemed much longer. And she didn't doubt it would feel like forever before Mitch Carlisle removed himself from her life with the same alacrity with which he had entered it.

Mitch stepped around Brenna in order to examine the bedraggled box she had placed in the area between the sectional and the game table. One of the top flaps had been torn off, and the corners were reinforced with what looked to be silver duct tape. On the side, written in big, red, block letters were the words Christmas, Box 1.

"I assume this means you're planning to decorate," he said finally.

Nodding, Brenna edged toward the doorway. "As long as the trees are up..." He turned, the green gaze freezing both her words and actions.

"How many boxes do you have?"

"Eight, I think." She thought back, trying to remember precisely how many boxes she had packed in January. "Maybe one or two more. Brian would know." They had each carried a box, and they had made *how* many trips down the narrow stairs? Three, certainly, and then the fourth time Brian had nearly tripped over Hobo....

Emerald green eyes narrowed at her. "Brian Hawthorne? Your ex-husband? What does he have to do with it?"

The question made her lose count. "He dropped by to pick up some books he had forgotten when he moved out. I was taking down the decorations, and one thing just sort of led to another." Where had she been? Oh, yes, four trips and then how many more?

The thought of her ex-husband performing such homey little tasks, as if the divorce hadn't changed their relationship, inexplicably irritated him. "Does he do that often?"

She lost count again and gave up on the mental exercise. "Put away my storage boxes?"

"Drop by," he clarified in a subdued growl that made her eyes widen.

"Of course," she replied, as if it were the most natural thing in the world. "We're friends."

"You're divorced," he informed her repressively.

"What does that have to do with anything?" she demanded in return, confused by his annoyance.

"Most people," Mitch said in a tone that Greg would have interpreted to mean that he was hanging onto his patience by a thread, "don't continue to see their former spouses."

Brenna shrugged. "We do."

"So I see." Fishing a cigarette out of his pocket, he lit it and wondered why the hell he was pushing the issue. Her relationship with Brian Hawthorne had no bearing in the part she may be playing in the Prescott affair. He had no business prowling through this part of her life and he knew it, but he couldn't rid himself of the suspicion that Brenna was being used by her ex-husband.

It wasn't until he forcefully reminded himself that he was acting the part of FBI agent that Mitch was able to suppress his curiosity and redirect their conversation to a less personal note. "I'll give you a hand with the rest of the boxes."

"You don't have to bother—"

"Professor," he interrupted testily, "I've already been bothered today and I don't plan to spend the rest of the evening watching you drag these damn boxes around. Let's get them upstairs and get back to some semblance of a normal routine."

The command in his voice caused Brenna to raise a placating hand. "Whatever you say, Agent Carlisle."

The phone call came at three in the morning. Roused from a sound sleep, Brenna reached for the bedside phone and mumbled a sleepy greeting into the receiver.

"Where is the formula?"

"What?" Frowning, Brenna levered herself up on one elbow.

"The formula, Professor Hawthorne. I mean to have it," came the muffled, faintly menacing voice.

The bedside lamp snapped on, and squinting against the unexpected intrusion, Brenna saw Mitch standing next to the bed. He silently mouthed the question, "Who is it?"

With a slight shake of her head, she returned her attention to the phone. "I don't know what you mean." Her voice still sounded sleepy, but her mind had come fully alert.

"I don't play games," the harsh voice retorted, sending a shiver down Brenna's spine. "Remember, you can disappear as easily as Prescott."

The line went dead in her ear and Brenna dropped the receiver onto the cradle.

"Who was it?" Mitch demanded.

You can disappear as easily as Prescott. The threat was unmistakable and effective. "Someone wanting to know where the formula is." She forced herself to meet his cold, green gaze. "One of your friends, perhaps?"

"Not a chance." Mitch glanced at the stainless-steel watch on his wrist. "What did he say?"

Brenna studied his impassive expression. "Please don't play games with me, Agent Carlisle," she said finally. "If this is some new tactic the FBI has come up with..."

He shook his head impatiently. "Professor, I give you my word, none of my people placed that phone call."

They stared at each other for several seconds before she trusted the instinct that told her Mitch was telling the truth. "As I said, the caller wants the formula and, like you, he obviously believes I know where it is." She shivered involuntarily and pulled her knees protectively up to her chest.

"And," Mitch prompted, noting her actions, "what else did he say?"

Unaware that her eyes had taken on a pleading expression, Brenna concluded, "He warned me that what happened to Mark could happen to me, as well." She tried to smile but failed miserably in the attempt. "I really wish you could tell me that the FBI is prone to playing practical jokes."

Mitch drew a deep breath and exhaled harshly. "I wish I could, too, Brenna." After a moment's hesitation, he asked, "Did the voice sound familiar?"

Brenna shook her head.

"Was there anything distinctive about his voice—a speech impediment perhaps?"

She shook her head again, trying to shake off the fear as well as reply to his question. "And in answer to your next question, I am quite certain he didn't have a Russian accent."

Mitch settled on the edge of the mattress. "Do I have your permission to put a tape recorder on your phone?"

Her gaze, which had wandered to the foot of the bed where Hobo had been silently assessing the two of them since his sleep had been interrupted, returned to Mitch and his puzzling request. "I thought you had already placed a tap on my phone."

"The Bureau has," Mitch hastily agreed, realizing his error. "This would be for us . . . you, actually. If the guy calls back, I'd like you to be able to listen to the tape—see if you can recognize his voice."

Why couldn't he simply request a copy of the Bureau's tape? she wondered, then mentally shrugged off the question. If he wanted to duplicate effort and equipment, that was hardly her concern. "Go ahead."

"Thank you." He ignored the sharp pang of his conscience. Catching Fedoryshyn was what mattered, not the fact that he was lying to Brenna. Or the fact that the phone call had definitely frightened her, and that fear still clouded her eyes. He had wanted her intimidated; she would be much easier to manage in this frame of mind.

But she looked so vulnerable huddled there, her arms wrapped around her legs. So frightened . . . and alone. He reached for her and tucked one of her ice-cold hands in both of his. The hostility that had existed between them fell away at the simple gesture, and the beseeching look she gave him was awe inspiring.

Gently disengaging one of his hands, he cupped her cheek in a callused palm. Her skin was like silk, and he brushed his thumb against her bottom lip. "Don't be afraid." Whether he meant to reassure her about the threatening phone call or his own actions, he wasn't sure.

"No," Brenna whispered, mesmerized by the way his eyes were darkening to pure emerald. She should call a halt to this, but the enticing rasp of his thumb stopped the protest. His mouth lowered over hers; her breath caught at the first, tentative brush of his lips.

Unexpected desire traced its way up Mitch's spine and demanded more than a mere touch. Insanity, his mind whispered, but his body obeyed its own dictates. He slid closer, tunneling his fingers into Brenna's long auburn hair in order to tilt her face to just the right angle.

Her hands came up—to push him away?—and encountered the warm wall of his bare chest. Her eyes widened in shock; until now she had somehow ignored the fact that he had charged into her bedroom clad only in his briefs, but she realized that some distant, primitive part of her had seen the hard, muscular strength of him and appreciated the sight. This is getting out of hand, she thought wildly. This man, this formidable, dangerous man had no part in her serene world.

"Don't be afraid," he soothed again when her hands clenched into fists against his shoulders. Her lips parted and he ruthlessly took advantage of the moment. His mouth claimed hers with a sudden, burning passion that swept away rational thought.

Searing heat curled through Brenna when his mouth grew demanding. She was vaguely aware of her hands unclenching long enough to slide around his neck, and then her eyes fluttered shut and she was rejoicing in the fierce way his tongue invaded her mouth.

A low groan issued from his throat as he tried to draw Brenna closer and realized that her legs were in the way. One hand manacled her ankles, straightening her legs and gently pushing them aside. Madness, he thought again, fleetingly, and then she was lying across his lap, her arms like silken ropes around his neck, holding him still while she returned his kiss.

Instinctively she molded herself against the hard planes of his body while his hand caressed her spine. A sharp, unfamiliar ache rose within Brenna, and she cried out, twisting a bit desperately in his embrace.

The little sound she made brought Mitch out of his trance. Heart pounding, he tried to catch his breath while he pressed Brenna's head into his shoulder. They were both trembling, and her heartbeat was even more uneven than his.

"Mitch?"

Her voice, sweet and husky, sent another shudder through him. "Hold still, Brenna." God, he ached! He was fully aroused, and the feel of her was a torment. Almost as much of a torment as knowing that the desire flowing between them would go unfulfilled.

Brenna sighed, resting comfortably within the circle of his strong arms. She thought she had understood passion, but she had been wrong. Her relationship with Brian had been comfortable, companionable. Until tonight—until this man—she had never experienced all-consuming desire.

Sanity slowly returned to Mitch, and with it the realization this situation was, literally and figuratively, unacceptable. He swore inwardly as he carefully deposited Brenna back in her original position and rose. "You look a little pale. Why don't I get you a drink or something?"

His withdrawal was unexpected, and Brenna couldn't help feeling hurt. "I don't need a drink."

He nodded, two gliding steps taking him to the doorway, where he stood and addressed the empty hallway in order to avoid her eyes. "Look, Brenna, I'm sorry about this."

Her heartbeat stumbled. "Why?"

"Why," he echoed with a harsh laugh. "I should think the answer to that is obvious. The Bureau frowns upon its people getting involved with suspects."

"Is that what's happening?" she asked hopefully.

It was the hopeful note that made Mitch realize what he had to do. "I mean that you're an attractive woman, and I'm no saint. I would enjoy going to bed with you, but that's all it would be—a physical relationship."

"Would that happen if I weren't a suspect?"

"Probably," he answered bluntly.

"I see." Embarrassed, Brenna slid beneath the covers. "How odd that my virtue should be saved by my supposedly larcenous character."

He winced at the bitterness of her tone. "If the phone rings again, wait until I get here to answer it." He started through the door, then paused again. "Don't worry too much about the caller. I'm not going to let anything happen to you."

She listened to him pad along the hallway back to his room and sighed. Nothing had gone right since Mitch had first appeared in her life, and it seemed as if that wasn't going to change. Even his promise of protection—and it was a promise, Brenna sensed, not a macho affectation or a throwaway line—did nothing to ease the pain of wanting a man who obviously thought so little of her.

Chapter 6

By Monday morning Brenna had decided Mitch was an immovable object who had planted himself firmly in her life and she had best learn to tolerate his presence. In spite of her protests, Mitch had assumed the responsibility of preparing meals for the two of them, and Brenna had silently conceded that he was better at it than she. Meals had to be given one's undivided attention in order to turn out properly, and, except for special occasions, she rarely managed such single-minded determination in the kitchen.

And Mitch's intervention had proven timely, allowing her to catch up on the briefcase full of paperwork she had brought home on Friday. Even the cats—except for Jasper—had come to accept his presence in their home, although the scowl Mitch sent their way whenever one of the them appeared to be considering the suitability of his lap as a resting place did tend to put a damper on their feline enthusiasm. Mitch's arrangement also had the desired effect of separating the two of them for long periods of time, making his presence less intrusive and easier to bear.

As for Jasper, Brenna thought with a sigh now as she watched Mitch maneuver her car toward the campus, he still regarded the FBI man as an intruder, refusing to even consider as edible the cat food Mitch poured out for the others.

"Do you hate cats?" she asked suddenly, breaking the silence in which they had ridden.

"Not particularly," Mitch answered, his eyes shifting between the cars ahead of him and the rearview mirror. "Why?"

"I'm trying to understand why Jasper doesn't like you." He grunted, signifying either amusement or contempt—with Mitch it was hard to be certain. "It's just odd, that's all," she continued in her pet's defense. "Usually he cuddles right up to people."

"Probably can't stand the thought of two males occupying the same territory," he offered, downshifting for the exit.

"No, that's not it—after all, Hobo is a male. I think Jasper is waiting for you to apologize for threatening to turn him into violin strings."

Mitch flicked a glance in her direction but said nothing. Cats were animals; they didn't feel or reason, just followed their instincts. The simple fact was that Jasper's life had been upset by the remodeling and he was reacting appropriately, but he doubted Brenna would accept such logic. She was the type who believed that animals had feelings and, probably, souls. A romantic, idiotic notion, but one that suited her. He swung the car into Brenna's parking space and turned off the engine.

"Are you sure you can explain me tagging along with you all day?"

Brenna frowned slightly. "It seems you should have asked that question earlier." When his eyes turned flinty at her mocking reply, she shook her head by way of apology. "Forget I said that. Yes, I'm sure. We have three weeks left before the end of the quarter. Everyone—students and professors—is going to be so caught up in the rush that I doubt anyone will give you a second look."

That assurance proved untrue within minutes of entering Meredith Hall. Penny, the department secretary, swallowed the cousin story whole, but that could have been because she was busy drooling over Mitch three seconds after their introduction. Brenna scowled at them over the rim of her glasses as she checked her mail, feeling an unreasonable spurt of jealousy. Looking away from the offensive scene, she gave a mute groan of resignation when Bradley Jackson stepped out of his office and fixed her with a disapproving look. The knowledge that she had been expecting a confrontation with Jackson for the past week was no comfort when the history chairman bore down upon her.

"I should like to take a few minutes of your time, Professor Hawthorne."

"Let me check my schedule," Brenna hedged, only to swallow the rest of her excuse when Jackson frowned at her.

"I'll meet you in the lecture hall after your first class. Coach Miller will be with me."

Brenna nodded, then winced when Jackson's office door slammed behind him.

"Anything wrong?"

"Possibly." Frowning, Brenna looked past Mitch to the clock on the wall. "But it's nothing I can't handle. Come on, I've got five minutes to get to my office and make it to class."

This time Mitch selected a seat in the front row of the lecture hall, but instead of concentrating on the content of Brenna's lecture, he listened to the flow of her words, the current of excitement that underlined her lecture.

She loved her job, he realized with a start, relished it, in fact. She enjoyed challenging her students, making them work up to—and, perhaps, past—their potential. No question they asked was pointless or redundant to her, no opinion trivialized if grounded in fact. Granted, in a general-requirement course such as this there was the expected percentage of students who were simply marking time, but even some of them found their interest aroused. Those with a passion for history to begin with were soon as lost in the past as their dynamic professor.

Listening to Brenna explain some of the initial causes of the Roman Empire's downfall, Mitch found himself wondering yet again if this woman could possibly be involved with technological espionage. It was a question he had asked himself repeatedly since Saturday's alarming episode. She had appeared truly frightened by the caller's demand, which meant Brenna was either a superb actress or she was telling the truth about her relationship with Prescott. More and more, the latter theory was gaining credence in his mind, and that was upsetting for two very good reasons.

First and foremost, someone—not *someone,* he told himself forcefully, *Fedoryshyn*—believed Brenna knew the location of the formula. Which meant her life might be in danger; better than anyone, Mitch knew just what lengths the Russian would go to in order to protect himself.

Second, Llewellyn was a small college, a community unto itself, and he was sure gossip spread as quickly here as it did in any community. The police had initially questioned Brenna in her office; Mitch didn't doubt that within an hour that news had spread throughout the campus. And while Brenna hadn't told anyone about her home being searched by the FBI, and he and the Bureau had tried to be discreet, the possibility of a leak existed within any organization. If Fedoryshyn hadn't suspected Brenna to begin with, Mitch himself and the two law enforcement agencies may have unwittingly drawn the Russian's attention to her.

If she was innocent, he might be responsible for leading a killer right to her. Mitch stared at her as she paced the dais, her slender figure fairly crackling with energy, remembering the way she had felt in his arms. The thought of her life being snuffed out was a sickening one.

Brenna was in the midst of dismissing the class when the side door opened and Bradley Jackson and Coach Miller entered. She took her time explaining the next assignment, then calmly stacked her lecture notes and answered last-minute questions from students who approached her before turning to acknowledge the two men. Jake Larken had left his seat to stand beside his coach.

Hoping she was as prepared for this confrontation as she thought she was, Brenna drew a deep breath and tried to control the way her heart hammered when she saw the anger in the coach's eyes.

Coach Miller wasted no time on pleasantries. "You failed Jake Larken on his midterm."

"Yes, I did." Brenna folded her hands on top of her notebook and prayed none of the men had seen them trembling.

"You agreed to pass him," Coach Miller exploded. "You sat in your chairman's office and told me you would give him a passing grade!"

"I agreed that his work would receive a passing grade," she interrupted softly, turning her gaze on the football player. "I can't grade a paper or midterm exam that was not handed in, Jake."

The football player's face turned a dull shade of red while Miller sputtered incoherently. "Professor Hawthorne, I don't think you understand the agreement the three of us reached," Bradley Jackson diplomatically intervened. "Llewellyn needs Mr. Larken on the football team, and in order for that to happen, he has to meet the academic requirements."

"No, I fully understand our agreement, and I'm ashamed of my part in it," she said quietly but firmly.

Unnoticed, Mitch left his seat to stand in the shadows beneath the exit door. He was closer to Brenna now, able to rescue her if the situation turned ugly.

"That agreement was in the school's best interest," Miller shouted. "And in Jake's best interest."

Brenna considered the furious coach for several moments before replying. "I don't agree. Llewellyn has a history of academic excellence—faking Jake's grade certainly does not reflect well upon the school." Her eyes returned to the student. "Nor is it in your best interest, Jake. You need help, Jake, a reading tutor—"

"Professor Hawthorne, we will not have this discussion again," Jackson thundered. "You will give this student a C in this course."

"Is that an order?" Brenna coldly inquired of her superior, her nervousness burning away in the face of her rising anger. "If so, I'll gladly comply. But I will also be forced to file a complaint with the committee on student affairs."

Bradley Jackson bit back a nasty retort. There were still enough old-timers in positions of power at Llewellyn who failed to see that alumni didn't simply donate large sums of money out of the goodness of their hearts. Alumni liked to see their donations provide concrete results—such as a division-winning football team. But the odds were that those entrenched hard-liners would take one look at the Larken situation and come down firmly on Professor Hawthorne's side. And it would be his neck on the chopping block.

Sensing his ally's vacillation, Coach Miller strode forward to take matters into his own hands. "Would you really ruin Jake's life—the possibility of a place on a professional team—just to make a point?"

Brenna raised her hands in a helpless gesture. "It's his life I'm thinking of, Coach. Don't you see that? What will his future be if he isn't picked up by a professional team after college?"

The large man snorted derisively and turned to Jackson. "Why are we wasting our time with her? You're the department head, Jackson—see to it Jake gets a passing quarter grade and I'll handle any damn committee inquiries." He tossed a smirk at Brenna. "And come next spring, you'll be looking for a job, Professor. How does that sound?"

"If that's the way you want it," she answered. "Hopefully I will find a position at a college whose standards are in keeping with my own. I wish I could say the same for you."

Coach Miller frowned. "What do you mean?"

"I mean there are several athletic associations, including the NCAA, that would find your methods of maintaining student eligibility rather questionable." With a poise she was far from feeling, she smoothly pushed her glasses to the top of her head and gathered up her notebooks. "What would the alumni association say about *that,* I wonder?"

She was halfway to the exit before Bradley Jackson's voice stopped her.

"What do you want, Professor?"

Closing her eyes briefly in an expression of relief that only Mitch could see, Brenna slowly turned back to the podium. "I want Jake to have a tutor. In exchange I will agree to give him an incomplete this quarter, with the provision that he retake the course—with me—next fall. Agreed?"

Bradley Jackson conceded at once, Coach Miller several seconds later, and with unconcealed rancor. "Jake?" Brenna questioned when her student insisted upon staring sullenly at the floor.

He looked at her then, the resentment in his eyes as clear as a beacon. "What choice do I have?"

Brenna sighed. "None, I'm afraid. I'll see to it the regis trar's office receives the authorization for the incomplete grade." With that, she hurried toward the exit.

Mitch threw open the door for her, allowing Brenna the grand exit her victory deserved. With a brief, hard smile for the three men on the dais, he followed her through the door.

"Thank you," Brenna murmured when Mitch fell into step with her in the stairwell.

"You play rough, don't you, Professor?"

"When I have to."

He followed her into the cramped cubicle of her office. She kicked her chair out of the way in order to get to the window, where she folded her arms across her chest and glared at the winter landscape. "I get the impression neither you nor that Larken kid are too fond of each other." When she answered with a shrug, he prodded, "So why annoy Jackson?"

"Weren't you listening?" she asked, her voice sharp with an anger she hadn't displayed earlier. "This has nothing to do with Jackson or Miller or even Jake, for that matter. This has to do with believing in a principle enough to take a stand."

"Another higher moral purpose, Brenna," he goaded, lighting a cigarette.

She turned on him then, her face aglow with conviction. "If you like."

"And if this little crusade costs you your job?"

A shadow of regret flitted through her eyes as she considered that possibility. "Then I'll update my résumé and sell my home."

"What's the old saying about cutting off your nose to spite your face? That's what you're doing, Brenna. Five minutes after you're gone, no one will remember—or care—that you sacrificed your job over a student who didn't give a damn about you *or* your career!"

Brenna smiled. "But *I'll* have the satisfaction of knowing that that particular student can now read above a sixth-grade level. That he is capable of making something of himself if he never has a chance at professional sports. Don't you see? That knowledge is worth the loss of this job."

Mitch said nothing, retreating behind a screen of cigarette smoke and an implacable expression that told Brenna he thought her a fool. Well, he could add that fault to his list. Brenna sighed inwardly and took her place at her desk, preparing for her next class.

An idealist, Mitch thought, watching as she reached for resource books that were stacked on the desk, next to the desk and on the bookshelf on the wall. She's obviously never learned the fine art of compromise. He was torn between admiration and pity over her attitude; she would always have the satisfaction of knowing she remained true to herself, but in the end the world would deal her a mortal blow and the inevitable disillusionment would follow. He found it sad to think of Brenna without that spark of battle in her eyes.

Having finished her class preparation, Brenna was frowning over a term paper from one of her master's students when her phone rang. She reached for it absentmindedly, only to be brought up short by Mitch's hand on hers.

"I want to listen in," he told her softly, laying aside the book on Elizabeth I he had been reading. "Just in case."

She swallowed nervously, nodded and lifted the receiver. Holding it far enough away from her ear so that he could hear the caller, she said, "Brenna Hawthorne."

"Hi! Met any dead kings lately?"

Brenna chuckled in relief. "Hello, Marcia. No, not lately."

"Good. Listen, George just wanted me to call to remind you not to walk through the kitchen until tomorrow night."

"How could I forget," Brenna inquired wryly, bringing the phone back to her ear when Mitch picked up his discarded book and resumed his seat.

"I was surprised when George came over for the key this morning," Marcia continued easily "I thought Mitch would let him in."

"Um, Mitch decided to spend a few days on campus with me," Brenna explained. When her "cousin" looked up inquiringly, she added sweetly, "We see each other so seldom that there's a lot to catch up on."

"I'll bet."

"Don't lay it on with a trowel," Mitch advised. "The woman's not an idiot."

Brenna grinned, enjoying the thought that she might be making him uncomfortable.

"By the way, best friend of mine," Marcia continued. "Is your gorgeous cousin busy tonight?"

Brenna was immediately suspicious. "Why?"

"My sister is coming by for dinner, and I thought Mitch might enjoy a break from what you laughingly refer to as your culinary skills."

"I can cook," Brenna protested.

"But not well."

Brenna sighed. "I'll ask." Covering the mouthpiece with her free hand, she eyed her watchdog speculatively. "How do you feel about blind dates?"

"What?"

"Blind dates," she repeated. "Marcia appears to have given up on me for a while in order to concentrate on you. Her sister's coming to dinner tonight, and three at a dinner table is an unlucky number." Brenna waggled her eyebrows over the rim of her glasses.

"Three on a match is unlucky, and that's only on the battlefield," Mitch corrected dryly. "I think I'll pass."

"Marcia is a fabulous cook."

"So am I, as it happens. No, thanks."

"Shall I tell her you're married?"

Mitch placed the book upside down on his lap and fixed her with a cold look. "Tell Marcia whatever you want. You and I both know the reason I won't leave you alone."

The teasing expression Brenna had worn during their exchange faded as she uncovered the mouthpiece. He obviously had no intention of allowing her to forget her place. "Marcia? Sorry, but Mitch has other plans for tonight. Sure, I'll tell him." She hung up and went back to reading the paper in front of her.

Mitch let several minutes pass before asking, "What are you supposed to tell me?"

Brenna circled a sentence with her red pen, scratched a note in the margin and turned the page before answering. "Does it matter? After all, we both know why you're here, and it isn't to meet Marcia's kid sister." It was ridiculous, she realized, but her feelings had been hurt by Mitch's cruel reminder of the reason for his presence here. They were not friends, nor even acquaintances, as he had just made clear, no matter how tolerant she and the cats may feel toward him. Maybe Jasper had the right attitude, after all. She made a check mark beside another line and wrote a comment. Glancing at her watch, she reached for her lecture notes. "Time for my next class. I'd ask if you're coming along, but the answer is obvious."

Mitch closed his book and followed Brenna from her office. "Don't you lock your door?" he asked when she started toward the stairwell.

"No, I always carry my purse with me and, besides, I want my students to be able to get in touch with me whenever necessary."

"Let them slip a note under your door or call you," he advised, not comprehending her sudden, biting tone. Marcia's sister notwithstanding, Brenna knew the score. He wasn't about to leave her alone for a blind date or any other reason until this business with Fedoryshyn was finished. "You've got student records and what must be hundreds if not thousands of dollars' worth of research materials in your office. Anyone could walk in there and clean the office out while you're in class."

"No one would do that," she assured him coolly.

"Trusting to the basic nobility of human nature again," he mocked.

"That, and the fact that there are enough instructors running around by the offices to keep the criminal element under control." She stopped beside the classroom door. "Are you planning to monitor this class, as well? Or will you be content to stay in the hall and eavesdrop?"

The dark glint in those sapphire eyes told him exactly how angry and hurt Brenna was. "If you don't mind, I'd rather stay in the class. I've had my fill of standing out in the hall during the past week."

"Suit yourself," Brenna muttered. "But then, you always do. Don't you?"

They managed to make it to lunch without exchanging more than a dozen words or setting off an argument, but Brenna had her doubts about sharing a table with him for an hour. She had brought a book to read, but she was still smarting over his earlier words.

Odd, she thought, selecting a chef's salad and coffee as they went through the line, but she and Brian had managed to live together nearly ten years without exchanging as many barbs as she had with Mitch since their meeting.

"Both," Mitch told the cashier, indicating Brenna's tray and his own.

Brenna snapped her mouth closed around a protest and started toward a table in the center of the dining room.

"Over here." Mitch jerked his head toward the tables by the wall of windows overlooking the now-dormant fountain. "This is where you usually sit."

In other words, don't do anything out of character, anything that will attract unwelcome attention to us, she interpreted moodily. Normally she sat at one of these tables because she enjoyed the view. Today, however, it left her feeling isolated and slightly depressed because she didn't like the idea of being trapped with Mitch Carlisle. Peeling away the plastic wrap, she investigated the contents of the salad bowl for a moment before tearing open the pouch of dressing and adding it to the lettuce.

Mitch chewed his way through half the spaghetti he had ordered before deciding to break the silence shrouding the table. "Brenna, if I somehow offended you this morning—"

"Oh, heavens, no," she broke in sarcastically. "I just forgot my place in your little scheme of things, but rest assured I won't suffer such a lapse again." She stabbed at a wedge of unripe tomato, the kind that invaded Minnesota produce shelves at this time of year.

Scowling, Mitch returned his attention to his meal. Obviously she was in no mood to accept his apology. Not that it mattered. He could accomplish his job whether Brenna talked to him or not.

"Brenna, what happened to you Friday night?"

One couldn't escape destiny, she thought wearily as Aleksei—as he had asked her to call him at their meeting on Friday—bulldozed his way through the crowd to their table.

"Hello, Aleksei," she managed in a normal voice, offering her hand and wondering as she did so if he would no-

Four Silhouette Special Editions FREE! *Plus*

SILHOUETTE
Special Edition
LINDSAY McKENNA
ne Man's War

SILHOUETTE
Special Edition
PAMELA TOTH
Two Sets of Footprints

SILHOUETTE
Special Edition
ERICA SPINDLER
Baby Mine

SILHOUETTE
Special Edition
MARY CURTIS
Loving Arms of the Law

Special Editions bring you all the heartbreak and ecstasy of involving and often complex relationships as they unfold today. And to introduce to you this powerful, contemporary series we'll send you four Special Edition romances, a cuddly teddy bear **PLUS** a mystery gift absolutely **FREE** when you complete and return this card.

We'll also reserve a subscription for you to our Reader Service, which means that you'll enjoy:

▶ **Six wonderful novels** - sent direct to you every month.
▶ **Free postage and packing** - we pay all the extras.
▶ **Free monthly Newsletter** - packed with competitions, author news and much more.
▶ **Special offers** - selected only for our subscribers.

Claim your **FREE** gifts overleaf

FREE BOOKS CERTIFICATE

Yes Please send me four **FREE** Silhouette Special Editions together with my **FREE** gifts. Please also reserve a special Reader Service subscription for me. If I decide to subscribe, I shall receive six superb new titles every month for just £10.50 postage and packing **FREE**. If I decide not to subscribe I shall write to you within 10 days. The free books and gifts will be mine to keep in any case. I understand that I am under no obligation whatsoever - I may cancel or suspend my subscription at any time simply by writing to you.

NAME _____

ADDRESS _____

_____

_____

POSTCODE _____

SIGNATURE _____

I am over 18 years of age.   9S2SE

A MYSTERY GIFT POST TODAY!

We all love mysteries - so as well as the FREE books and cuddly teddy, we've an intriguing FREE gift for you.

Reader Service
FREEPOST
P.O. Box 236
Croydon
CR9 9EL

No stamp needed

tice how cold it was. "How nice to see you again." When he gallantly kissed the back of her hand, she smiled and shook her head over the action.

Time seemed to slow for Mitch. The musky odor of Fedoryshyn's cologne came at him in waves. The Russian's accent grated on nerves already scraped raw, and he seemed to have lost his hearing. Fedoryshyn's lips moved, but he couldn't hear what the man was saying, and a feeling of panic swept through Mitch as he felt himself rising, felt the pull on his shoulder holster increase as he stood and offered his hand in response to the movement of Fedoryshyn's own hand. So simple, a part of his mind whispered. Pull the gun out of the holster and kill him. One bullet—two if the Russian moved. He could be out of the union before Brenna recovered enough to scream for help.

What's the matter with him? Brenna wondered when Mitch simply stared at Aleksei, ignoring the older man's greeting. "Mitch is the reason I missed your party, Aleksei," she hastily put in. "My cousin was supposed to arrive on Saturday, but instead he showed up Friday night, just before your lecture. I'm sorry I didn't have time to stay and explain."

Aleksandr Fedoryshyn waved away her apology. "I understand. Family is important in my country, as well."

Brenna smiled nervously. "Won't you join us?"

"Ah, thank you." Aleksei settled congenially into the free chair at their table and sipped at the coffee he carried. "I am afraid I have not yet adjusted to your students, Brenna. Some of them ask very... difficult questions."

"Pointed, you mean?" At his shrug, Brenna nodded. "I like to think we train their minds well."

"They take nothing for granted, do they? I make a statement, and they find twelve different ways to challenge it."

"Don't take it personally. You should sit in on one of my doctoral classes and see what the students do to me," she invited, keeping a wary eye on Mitch now that he had resumed his seat.

"So," Aleksei sighed. "This is, perhaps, what we have to look forward to at our universities now that our leader has invited diversity of opinion."

"Probably," she conceded. "But as an educator, surely you find that a challenge?"

He slowly shook his head. "It is a different way and will require much adjustment on everyone's part."

"That's the way of the world, though," Mitch put in at last, having regained enough control to speak. "It's called progress."

"I suppose so," Aleksei said a trifle sadly. "But not all the old ways were bad." He swept a hand to indicate the laughter and discussions taking place in the room in front of them. "Forgive me, but to look at your students, it would seem that they do not take their university education seriously."

"Not all of them do, I suppose," Brenna mused.

"A waste."

"I disagree," she argued, smiling at the Russian. "Those who aren't serious about being here will leave soon enough to find their niche in life. We can't force square pegs into round holes, after all."

"So liberal." Aleksei leaned forward to pat her hand. "I suppose you approve of demonstrations on campus, as well?"

"Naturally." His condescension rankled, and she forced herself to keep smiling.

"Cousin Brenna is the radical in the family," Mitch agreed as he lit a cigarette.

The Russian turned his assessing gaze on the other man. The flannel shirt and jeans had seen better days, as had the unbuttoned, fleece-lined jacket he wore. "And do you teach, as well?" he asked in a tone that made it clear he doubted Mitch could do much more than sign his name.

Mitch shook his head, aware of the headache that was suddenly throbbing deep in his temples. "I came down the side of the family that likes to work with its hands—Brenna's side got all the brains."

"And more than its share of beauty," Aleksei gallantly contributed after several moments of awkward silence.

The blatant compliment stunned Mitch almost as much as it did Brenna, if he could judge from her expression. A corner of his mouth kicked upward in a knowing smile. So Fedoryshyn planned to seduce the location of the formula out of Brenna, did he?

"I hope we might have dinner one evening this week." Aleksei continued to speak to Brenna, ignoring Mitch.

Spy or not, Aleksei was definitely adding serious complications to her life, Brenna thought miserably. She would bet her harpsichord that Aleksei was the type who considered himself irresistible to women. An outright refusal would probably only engender a more ardent pursuit. The cold look in Mitch's eyes drew her attention and, thankfully, suggested an escape from the trap in which she found herself. "That would be very nice, Aleksei. Perhaps Mitch and I could show you the sights? Wouldn't that be fun, Mitch?"

Some of his own tension ebbed at the worried look on her face. He had put her in an untenable situation from which she was trying to free herself. He acknowledged the wisdom of her solution by raising his coffee mug. "Sounds fine to me."

Aleksei stared at the woman next to him, amazed at the swiftness with which she had turned his cozy dinner into an outing for three. Could she possibly be so dense as to not know when a man was making advances? Or had he been too oblique?

Whatever the explanation, it would be wise not to press his point now. He would catch her alone sometime this week and clarify his invitation. "I would enjoy that, certainly, but for now I must beg your indulgence," he excused himself politely. "I have another seminar this afternoon. I don't suppose you would drop by for part of it?"

"I'm sorry, Aleksei, but my afternoon is hectic. Office hours, you know."

"Office hours?"

She gestured elegantly. "Time set aside to talk with my students."

"Of course." He smiled and pressed her hand between both of his. "I hope we see more of one another during my stay here."

Brenna gently withdrew her hand. "That would be—wonderful."

He gave a curt nod to Mitch, not bothering to offer his hand to the other man. "A pleasure meeting you."

"The pleasure was mine," Mitch assured him in a deadly purr that brought a look of surprise to the Russian's face, and then he smiled in understanding and plowed his way through the union. Yes, Aleksei thought as he walked briskly to the history building, in order to make progress with Brenna Hawthorne, he was definitely going to have to remove her from the overprotective influence of her cousin.

Alone with Mitch, Brenna lifted her glasses from the top of her head and carefully polished them with a napkin. "Well, is that the Aleksandr Fedoryshyn you know?" she demanded when Mitch pulled an aspirin bottle from his shirt pocket.

"Yes and no." Mitch swallowed four aspirin with a grimace, glancing with apparent indifference around the room. It was a testament to Greg's craftsmanship—and Mitch's own tutoring—that it took the older man several seconds to isolate his younger colleague following the Russian out of the area. "Until a few minutes ago, I had no idea what a playboy Fedoryshyn thinks he is."

Brenna slipped her glasses into their case. "I wonder what it was I did that brought you into my life?" she asked with a certain amount of venom, his cynical comment bruising her taut nerves. "I've always been kind to small children and animals—hell, I was even a Girl Scout. I helped little old ladies across crowded intersections and earned all kinds of badges for being able to find my way through a forest." She fixed him with a blistering glare. "So how come I end up with the FBI's equivalent to the seven plagues of Egypt?"

Mitch frowned. "Don't tell me you're actually upset because you can't go out with good old Aleksei!"

"Don't be absurd! The point I'm trying to make is that you are interfering with my life," she hissed. "I've told more lies since Friday than I have in my entire adult life—and I have you to thank for it!"

"Careful, Professor, your temper is showing." Mitch felt his mouth twitching into a genuine smile. Despite the tensions of the day, seeing the woman emerge from the shadow of the absentminded professor was almost as enjoyable as kissing her. "I think I'm beginning to believe that old tale about redheads."

"I'm lying to my closest friends," she went on as if he hadn't spoken, "lying to colleagues, and you just sit there with that oh-so-superior look and watch all these horrible things happen around me! It's like Alice through the looking glass, and I'm getting really tired of it. I want you out, Carlisle," she muttered at him. "Do you hear me? I want you out of my house, my office and my life."

Mitch leaned forward. "Did you know that when you're angry, your eyes get these gold sparks in them," he observed lazily. "Interesting, really interesting. The blue shade darkens, and then these little, sparkling flecks show up and kind of dance around."

Brenna stared at him, stunned by the outrageous comment. "That's the stupidest thing I've ever heard," she ground out when she found her voice. "My eyes, gold flecks or not, are none of your business!"

"'Stupid!'" Mitch theatrically placed a hand over his heart. "And here I thought I was being charming."

His declaration summoned up the mental image of his half-naked body holding hers. "I don't want you charming," Brenna managed in a furious whisper. "I just want you gone!" She snatched up her book, coat and purse and fled through the milling students before he could stop her.

"Well, that was brilliant," Mitch chided himself, scrubbing a hand over his face. After two weeks of surveillance and three days of living with her, he still wasn't certain what the correct approach to dealing with Professor Brenna Hawthorne was, but he was damn sure finding the ways *not* to use.

He really should go after her, he supposed; after all, she was his primary lead in this case. But they both needed a break from each other's company, and as fed up with him as Brenna appeared to be, it was reasonable to assume she wasn't about to contact the local FBI office.

"Problems, teach?" Greg Talbott, sporting a pair of horn-rimmed glasses and carrying a backpack, eased into the chair Brenna had occupied. It was the simplest of disguises and the more effective because of it. His appearance was altered just enough to confuse anyone—such as Brenna—who might have come into contact with him when he was working with the Bureau, and to blend in with the student population. It had taken Mitch himself several moments to identify his friend.

Mitch grunted. "You might say that." He sipped at the fresh coffee Greg had brought. "Where's Fedoryshyn?"

"Happily chatting away to a dozen graduate students in a first-floor classroom. Their fifteen-minute break is scheduled in—" he consulted his watch "—ninety minutes. I'm planning to nap until then."

Mitch flinched inwardly at the dark shadows noticeable beneath Greg's eyes. "If there was any other way—"

Greg shrugged, trying the contents of his cup. "But there isn't."

"No, there isn't," Mitch agreed unhappily.

"The man has done absolutely nothing suspicious since I've been following him," Greg said in a conversational tone. "He's been wined and dined by the head of the history department and been to more faculty, alumni and student teas than I care to remember. It seems like every department here wants a piece of him." He paused to take another drink of coffee. "The tap on the phone hasn't turned anything, either. No unidentified callers, no significant ringing sequences, and no prearranged codes that I've been able to pick up on. Nothing."

"So the call Brenna received Saturday night didn't come from him?"

Greg shook his head. This was ground they had already covered in the small hours of Sunday morning. "I double-checked the tapes, in case I dozed off. No outgoing or incoming calls. And with the motion sensor I put into the door frame, there's no way he could have left that apartment without setting off the alarm."

"Unless he found the sensor and deactivated it."

"I checked that, too. My two tamper warnings were right where I put them."

"Well, somebody called her!"

"Not Icon," Greg replied imperturbably. "Lighten up, teach. You're showing signs of stress."

"Stress." Mitch laughed thinly. "I'll give you stress. I'm living with a loony college professor whose house is being demolished room by room, said house also being protected by an attack cat which hates my guts. Saturday I went tromping through at least ten acres of forest in order to chop down two trees, and then we spent the rest of the day decorating the house for the holidays. Yesterday morning she decided to make coffee. A friendly enough gesture, I suppose, except that she forgot to add the water. The house still smells like burning coffee grounds. And to top it off, she's got this insane neighbor—"

Greg chuckled. "So what's the problem?"

"The problem," Mitch groaned, "is that I cannot deal with that woman. She's driving me crazy."

The heartfelt admission concerned the younger man. "Mitch, you've dealt with all sorts of people, many of whom were more exasperating than this professor seems to be, and I don't remember ever seeing you lose your detachment before."

"Right. She's just a part of this case, a necessary part. I keep telling myself that, but there are times when..." He shook his head. "That call really frightened her, Greg—I could see it in her eyes, and it made me madder than hell. Stupid reaction on my part, but sometimes I think I don't want anyone intimidating her but me. I've managed to do that a couple of times, but it doesn't last."

"You know what, teach?" Greg smiled at his friend. "I think you like her."

Mitch's jaw tightened ominously. "Bull. She's a tool, nothing more."

Greg shrugged. "Admit it. There's something about her—a vulnerability—that makes you want to wrap her in cotton and keep her away from the big bad world. I feel that way just from meeting her and reading her file."

"She's a crusader, and as a historian, she should know how the crusaders ended up."

"Defeated, dead, broken. But a few managed to survive." Greg finished his coffee and reached for his backpack. "I'm off. Nice seeing you again."

Mitch grunted a noncommittal farewell, mulling over Greg's opinion about Brenna. His friend was right; Brenna Hawthorne had somehow wormed her way into a corner of his heart and settled in for the duration. And to complicate matters, he was beginning to consider her less of a tool than a woman. Hell, physical attraction aside, there were even times when he liked her, and he couldn't afford that luxury. He hadn't survived as long as he had by losing his objectivity, and if he didn't recapture it soon, he was going to blow this opportunity to get Fedoryshyn. During his walk back to Meredith Hall, he found himself wishing for the peace of his secluded château.

The second phone call came that night at nine, and effectively ruined the small pleasure her new kitchen floor had briefly provided Brenna. The tape recorder Mitch had attached to the telephone in the family room was sound activated; Brenna could see the spools begin turning obediently before the first ring was completed. At his nod, she rose and picked up the receiver. Without being prompted, she held the receiver far enough away from her ear so that Mitch could hear the conversation.

"My patience is running out," came the whisper. "What did you do with the formula?"

"If this is your idea of a joke—"

"No joke, Professor. I want that formula."

"But I don't—"

"And if you're relying on your cousin for protection, don't."

The line went dead and Brenna shakily replaced the receiver. "He knows about you," she said in a tone approaching disbelief. This was the first time she had spoken to him all evening.

Mitch rewound the tape. "He knows the story we've told," he corrected.

Brenna swallowed. "Doesn't that make you nervous?"

"No. In fact, that statement tells me a couple of things. Your mysterious caller is nearby. Otherwise he wouldn't know about the cover story. Also, he is apparently keeping a very close eye on you."

"How comforting." Staring at the phone, she gnawed thoughtfully at her bottom lip. "Should I change my phone number?"

"That might not be a bad idea," he allowed.

The carefully neutral tone of his voice drew Brenna's attention. "I sense a 'but' in your statement."

"Who would you have to notify about the change—immediately, I mean?"

She gave serious consideration to the question. "The college history and personnel departments, friends, the utility companies, George. The rest—credit cards and the like—could wait, I suppose."

"Okay, first thing tomorrow we get your phone number changed. Then we make a list of everyone who knows about the change, and you don't tell *anyone* else."

"You're awfully eager for this change."

"Not eager. Curious." He lit a cigarette before continuing. "I'm curious to see exactly what kind of access to your private life this caller has."

Chapter 7

"I want you to do me a favor."

From across the width of her desk, Brenna eyed Mitch suspiciously. "What is it?"

He frowned at the wiring diagram he was drawing on the sketch pad he held. "I want you to start locking your office door whenever you leave for class or lunch."

A small, relatively harmless request, but it followed on the heels of a morning spent being dragged from the telephone company—where Mitch used his FBI identification to cut through red tape and the sheer threat of his presence to enforce cooperation when the federal badge proved insufficient—to an electronic supply house, where he gathered up the rudiments of what he told her would be a simplistic alarm system for her home. He had stoically ignored her argument that she didn't need an alarm system, simplistic or not.

"Brenna, I don't want to fight about this, too," he said wearily when he caught sight of the mutinous set of her jaw. "I just want to limit the caller's access to you and the places where you spend your time."

She pushed her glasses to the top of her head and considered his pronouncement. "Am I in danger?"

The question made his heart race. He had asked himself the same thing during the sleepless night before and he didn't care for the affirmative conclusion he had reached. "I don't think so," he lied blandly, "but I'm the careful sort."

"I've noticed." Last night he'd had her listen to the tape of the caller time after time in the hope that she would hear something—anything—that would identify the man. Brenna sighed at the memory; the FBI could be so horribly relentless when it suited them.

He was pushing too hard, Mitch realized; he had been since the last phone call, trying to force a lead that wasn't there. Leads came from careful research and analysis, not from badgering a woman who had been thrown into a situation that she was ill-equipped to deal with. If he had needed proof of Greg's observation that he was losing his objectivity, his actions at the telephone company were hard evidence. He had nearly blown his cover this morning by using his fraudulent identification simply because a clerk wasn't moving quickly enough to suit him. The clerk he had threatened had turned several shades of red before calling her supervisor, and Brenna had suffered through the scene with a mortified expression on her face.

Although, he reflected, Brenna never really believed she was without options, as last evening's fight had shown him. When, at one in the morning, he had suggested a final playing of the tape recording, she had wordlessly yanked the reel off the machine and sent it spinning across the floor, the plastic tape playing out behind it. The cats had loved what they thought was a new toy. Brenna had merely smiled at his curses and gone to bed. Now, after this morning's scene, she was treating him with a remote civility that was annoying.

"I'm surprised you don't want me to change the locks on my doors," Brenna said finally.

Mitch tapped his pencil against the pad braced on his lap. "I'm holding that in reserve."

Brenna sighed inwardly. She should probably be grateful to Mitch for caring enough about her safety to take on the phone company—even if he was just doing his job. Since she had thrown the tape reel at him, the tension between them had been thick enough to be cut with a knife, and there didn't seem to be anything she could do to reduce it. Or was there? "I'm sorry about last night," she said thoughtfully, her gaze falling to the book in front of her. "I shouldn't have destroyed your tape."

"I deserved it, I guess, given the way I acted." A grudging smile tugged at the corner of his mouth when her eyes met his. "The cats enjoyed it, though."

Her mouth quirked in an answering smile. "Yes, they did." She carefully marked her place before closing the book. "Have your people been able to trace the phone calls yet?"

Her question was innocently asked, and completely disconcerting. The drawing pad slid to the floor; retrieving it gave Mitch a moment to compose himself before answering.

Misunderstanding his reaction, Brenna continued artlessly, "It's all right, Mitch—I know the way the Bureau thinks. When you told me about the tap, I immediately assumed it would also be used to trace my incoming calls."

"So far the caller hasn't stayed on the line long enough for a trace to work," he replied evasively. It was true; the calls were of short duration, guaranteed to prevent even state-of-the-art equipment from discovering the caller's location.

"Maybe I should try to keep him talking," she suggested.

"No." His refusal was emphatic, too much so. At her curious look, he clarified, "It won't do any good. The guy is a professional. He probably uses a stopwatch to time his calls. And we don't want him to get suspicious."

"I suppose we don't," she murmured, "but I'm so tired of all this. I just want it to end."

So do I, Mitch thought, returning to the diagram he was working on. He was being pulled into her life more deeply than he had expected, and he didn't care for it. He hadn't wanted to meet her neighbors, much less like them. He hadn't planned to help Brenna decorate her home for the holidays and find himself enjoying the process. Worst of all, he hadn't thought that a grudging admiration for the absentminded professor would develop after following her around day after day. But all of those things had happened, and he had the uneasy feeling that his life would be permanently affected by his exposure to Brenna.

"I imagine you wish this was over, too," she hinted when he didn't answer, not realizing how accurately she had gauged his thoughts. When he shrugged in reply, she added, "It must be awful, being away from your family during the holidays."

Mitch looked up from his diagram at the not-so-subtle probe. "Wondering if I'm married, Brenna?"

She blushed furiously at his directness. "Not at all. I just assumed..."

"If you're curious, ask."

It was the cool arrogance of his question that overcame her embarrassment. "Is there a Mrs. Carlisle?"

"No."

She waited a beat and then asked, "Was there ever?"

"No." He smiled. "Except for my mother, of course."

"I suppose your life-style doesn't exactly lend itself to home and hearth," she speculated.

You don't know the half of it, Mitch thought, his mind turning to the shadow-life he had led over the past few years. Had he really chosen such an isolated existence, or had it chosen him? A few weeks ago, the answer would have been clear, but here, from the perspective of Brenna's office, he wasn't sure. "Actually life with the Bureau is fairly settled," he replied at last.

He wasn't retreating behind his usual, icy barrier, so Brenna pressed her advantage, finding herself curious about the man sharing her house. "Where do you live?"

Mitch groaned inwardly at the bright interest in her voice. He had encouraged her to ask questions and now he was paying the price. "Out East." It was the truth, he told his chiding conscience. Europe was definitely east of the United States. "Greg and I were assigned here temporarily to reinforce the Bureau's manpower."

"Do you enjoy being vague, or don't you remember where your home is?" she teased.

When telling a lie, the wisest course of action is to stay as close to some grain of truth as possible. His training had drilled that axiom into his brain. Therefore, he borrowed Greg's apartment in Washington and described it to Brenna as his own.

Such a grim man, Brenna reflected, listening to his impassive description. At times he seemed almost inhuman, incapable of any genuine emotion. But there were other times, like last night, when she managed to evoke a response that was almost intimidating in its intensity. As overwhelming as his sensuality. It was beyond her comprehension how he was able to keep such passion in check.

A knock on her door frame drew Brenna's attention. A handsome, bearded man poked his head into her office and she smiled a welcome. "Hello, Steven. What can I do for you?"

"Hi, Bre—ah, Professor Hawthorne." Steven corrected himself when he caught sight of her visitor. "Excuse me, I didn't know you were busy—"

Brenna waved him inside with a laugh. "Steven, this is my cousin, Mitch Carlisle. He's spending the holidays with me." When Mitch rose to take the hand Steven extended, she continued, "Mitch, this is Steven Morrison, one of the doctoral candidates in history."

Mitch muttered something before resuming his seat. He didn't immediately go back to his sketch, however; watching Brenna's student proved more interesting. Morrison was close to Brenna's age, perhaps a couple of years younger, Mitch judged. They were discussing Elizabethan customs, but there was a gleam in the other man's eyes that was more personal than professional. Mitch lit a cigarette and narrowed his eyes at the younger man.

"Anyway," Steven said with a rather subdued laugh, aware of the intense scrutiny, "I just stopped by to deliver your invitation to the annual Christmas party." He handed Brenna a heavy parchment envelope inscribed with beautiful calligraphy. "And to see if you had planned to go with anyone."

Brenna stared at the invitation with a sinking feeling in her stomach. "Actually I'd forgotten about the party," she replied, shooting Mitch an apprehensive glance. How in the world was she going to explain the importance of this annual event to the stoic FBI man?

"You're going to have problems finding a costume," Steven warned.

She shook her head, thinking of Marcia and her closets full of costumes. "I have access to a ready supply of period dresses."

"That's fortunate." Steven cleared his throat, looking uneasily at Mitch. "If you'd like, I'd be happy to provide you with transportation that night."

"That's very kind of you, Steven, but I'm not sure of my plans yet." She laid aside the invitation and smiled. "But thank you for offering."

Obviously disappointed, Steven departed, leaving Brenna with Mitch.

With one hand, he reached out to gently shut her office door, then picked up the invitation and read it carefully. The invitation had been issued by the history, archaeology and music departments. "A madrigal dinner," he quoted silkily. "Join us in celebrating Christmas with an evening of sixteenth-century food and music. The date is a week from this coming Saturday." Looking up, he fixed Brenna with a penetrating stare. "You're not going."

"Attendance isn't exactly optional," she sighed, seeing an argument headed her way. "The staff is expected to be present."

"No." The single word had an air of finality about it.

She had expected the refusal to her appeal, but it saddened rather than angered her. Brenna had hoped that the past few days with her had somehow proved to him that she was not a suspect in his case. Apparently he had yet to be impressed with her sterling character. She folded her hands on her desk, facing him squarely. "Nearly two weeks remain until the party—your case may be solved by then."

He nodded, conceding the point. "But if it isn't, you're staying home."

"No, Mitch, I'm not," she returned evenly. "I'm afraid this is one time *you* will simply have to adjust *your* life to suit my needs."

He glared at her through a cloud of smoke. "If you think for one minute I'm going to tag along and watch what's-his-name drool all over you for an evening, you're crazy."

"Steven?" She blinked in amazement. "I have no intention of being seen at a social event with Steven as my escort—no matter how innocent the circumstances."

"He's after you," Mitch stated bluntly. "A blind man could see it."

Brenna smiled in gentle amusement. "This is not the first time I've dealt with a student's crush."

"He's not exactly one of those uncertain adolescents in your freshman classes," he pointed out, remembering the look in the other man's eyes.

"No, he isn't, but he is a student. My student." She eyed him curiously. "Do you understand what I'm saying?"

"That having an affair with a student isn't your style," he hazarded sarcastically.

"That it would be...unethical for me to allow Steven or anyone else to think that I consider him to be anything more than a student."

"Ah, yes, your professional reputation," Mitch retorted. "What would your department head say?"

The taunt fired her temper. "An abuse of my position," she hissed at him. "Believe it or not, Agent Carlisle, I do have standards, and I would never take advantage of that position!"

Dead silence followed her outburst. Mitch crushed out his cigarette with an air of grim finality. "Unlike me, you mean," he said finally, holding her gaze, recalling, as he knew she was, the scene in her bedroom.

"I—I didn't mean it that way," she began lamely. "I only wanted to explain—"

"The difference between us." His hard mouth twisted briefly. Rising, he came around the desk and put his hands on the arms of her chair, trapping her. "You made your point, Professor, but you don't know me all that well...yet." His eyes swept boldly over her. "Pay attention, I'm about to show you just how ruthless I can be."

His mouth descended violently upon hers, effectively crushing any resistance she may have put up. Crowded into the vinyl cushions, Brenna held herself motionless, stunned by and a little afraid of the ferocity of his attack. When Mitch finally lifted his head, she could barely meet his eyes.

Her lips were already swelling from his assault, Mitch saw with a pang, and her eyes were clouded. It had been a mistake to pursue Fedoryshyn, a bigger mistake to wander into this woman's life. Where the hell was his celebrated control, the vaunted detachment he had always been able to bring to his work? "I want you and I shouldn't," he rasped, his lips lightly brushing hers. "What are you doing to me, Brenna?"

She pulled in a shattered breath, unable to answer. Her hands found his and settled onto them with the softness of a butterfly's kiss. His hands were lean and hard, just like his body. They were so wrong for each other, so different, that nothing lasting could ever develop between them, and yet the physical attraction between them was potent and undeniable.

The confusion in her eyes echoed his own, and Mitch tentatively brought their mouths together. "I swore this wouldn't happen again," he breathed against her lips. "But I can't seem to help myself. Tell me to stop."

"I can't," she whispered, tilting her head to allow him access to the sensitive flesh of her throat.

He wasn't thinking of intimidation or retaliation this time, just surrendering to some primordial instinct. Insanity ruled. He trailed a sensual caress over the strong tendons of her neck and then plunged into the moist cavern of her mouth. Her tongue met his with a hesitant stroke that tore a moan from deep in his throat.

She was shattering, held together only by the cage of Mitch's arms. He pressed closer and her hands slid upward to curl into his hair. Wrong or not, the sensations washing through her were too powerful to deny. She reveled in the smell of soap that clung to his skin, at the gentle touch of his callused hand on her throat. Brenna stopped breathing when his hand fell to the front of her blouse and opened the top three buttons.

"Beautiful," he murmured, his eyes feasting on the creamy skin visible above her camisole. Tracing a finger around the globe of her breast, he smiled as her nipple sprang to life to push impudently against the satiny material. "Brenna—"

Whatever he would have said was lost when the shrilling of the phone broke them apart. Mitch took one last, regretful look at the dreamy expression Brenna wore before forcing himself to move away.

Mitch's physical withdrawal was tantamount to being hit with a bucket of cold water. Brenna fumbled with her buttons as she reached for the phone, and the enormity of what had almost happened hit her. After her fine speech, all Mitch had had to do was kiss her and she forgot everything except the craving his touch instilled in her. Thank heavens her voice sounded halfway normal, she thought as she managed to concentrate on what the student at the other end of the telephone was saying, because the rest of her was shaking like a leaf.

Mitch picked up his sketch pad and jabbed viciously at the paper with the pencil, breaking the lead. With a curse, he tossed the instrument into the wastebasket and lit a cigarette. He slowed his breathing, concentrating on the sight of the fresh snow drifting past Brenna's window. They couldn't go on this way; *he* couldn't continue giving in to the temptation to touch her, because one of these times he wouldn't stop. His self-control was rapidly eroding, and he couldn't depend upon another timely interruption. This had to end, here and now, before he found himself in Brenna's bed, making wild, violent love to her.

Minutes later, when he heard her return the receiver to the cradle, he spoke carefully without looking at her. "This was by way of a demonstration, Professor, a crash course in ruthlessness. It won't happen again. For the remainder of my stay, it would be best if we keep our relationship as professional as possible. Do you agree?"

Brenna nodded mutely, appalled by his ability to play at passion when every cell of her body was still humming from his touch. With trembling hands she reached for the book she had been reading earlier and pretended to be engrossed by its contents. The tears she felt burning her eyelids would be shed later, in the privacy of her bedroom.

The week proceeded with no change in the level of tension between Mitch and Brenna; civility and politeness were the standards by which they lived, and they avoided one another as much as was possible under the circumstances. Mitch cooked the meals; Brenna complimented him on his efforts and then retreated behind a paper wall of lecture notes and research while he devoted his evening hours to the new alarm system. Sensing a rift, the cats restlessly prowled the house, pausing to meow plaintively at their mistress and avoiding Mitch unless he made a friendly overture.

They did not discuss, nor did either mention, Fedoryshyn, Mark Prescott or the attraction that shimmered between them like a living thing in spite of their efforts to ignore it. The one bright spot in the week was that changing her phone number to an unlisted one had put a stop to the threatening phone calls. Small comfort, Brenna admitted to herself, but one had to take what one could.

Even Marcia, during one of her unannounced evening visits, was not immune to the underlying discord in the house. "So what's wrong?" she asked, throwing herself into one of the leather armchairs in Brenna's office. "Fed up with the relatives so soon?"

Brenna scowled at her friend. "What makes you say that?"

"I'm an actress, remember? One of the things I do well is read body language, and you and your cousin are stiff as boards around each other."

"He irritates me." Using the slippered toes of one foot, she propelled her swivel desk chair back and forth in a short, agitated arc.

Marcia chuckled. "So send him to a hotel. The last thing you need is a houseguest with the state your house is in."

"I can't do that," Brenna mumbled. "Though God knows I'd like to."

Amusement fading, Marcia leaned forward and lowered her voice to a confidential tone. "We've been friends for a long time, Brenna, so level with me. Exactly what is going on around here? You've been giving off some really strange vibes ever since this cousin of yours appeared."

What a relief it would be to confide in Marcia, she thought longingly, even while part of her mind searched for a convincing lie. And knowing Marcia as she did, Brenna could just imagine the good-natured teasing she was going to take when the FBI finished its investigation and she was finally able to tell the truth about Mitch. Before she could come up with a reply or a way to distract her friend, however, the brunette actress began speculating aloud.

"What's really interesting is that Brian doesn't remember a Carlisle branch in your family tree," Marcia informed her airily.

The swivel chair came to an abrupt halt as Brenna sat bolt upright, startled. Damn! "H-he doesn't," she finally stammered inquiringly.

"No." Marcia gave her an impish smile. "Why is that?"

It was an excellent question; Brenna just wished she had an excellent answer. "We—Mitch and I—aren't exactly cousins," she haltingly began.

"Do tell?"

"I mean, we're cousins . . . but we're distant cousins."

Marcia nodded in understanding. "How distant?"

"I'm not really sure." Brenna gulped. "Second or third, once removed—something like that."

"Hardly a relative at all—more like kissing cousins," Marcia decided, looking for all the world like a cat who had just cornered a particularly delicious canary. "Listen, friend, if Mitch is your lover, why not just tell me?" At Brenna's stricken expression, Marcia laughed. "Don't look so horrified—*I've* been waiting for this day for ages!"

"N-no, Marcia, you don't understand—"

"Of course I understand. Or have you forgotten my matchmaking efforts over the past few months?" She giggled, savoring her discovery with obvious relish.

Brenna regarded her friend sourly. Leave it to Marcia to jump headlong to an erroneous conclusion and not even consider the possibility that she might be wrong. She should be grateful for Marcia's impulsiveness, Brenna supposed—after all, explaining the truth could prove to be a great deal more embarrassing—but given the physical attraction between them, the very thought of having an affair with Mitch played havoc with her mental health.

The repressed—but unforgotten—image of a practically nude Mitch standing on the staircase flitted through Brenna's mind, bringing with it a wave of warmth that washed her from head to foot. The idea of allowing Marcia to believe that she and Mitch were lovers grew more disturbing by the minute, but she couldn't work up the nerve to correct her friend.

"Look, Marcia, keep this to yourself. Okay?" she asked finally.

"Brenna, we have long since passed the stage where an unmarried woman was supposed to be ashamed of taking a lover," the actress teased, her laughter ringing through the house when her words brought a flood of color to Brenna's cheeks. "Honestly, Brenna, you can be such a *prude!*"

"Please, Marcia," she implored. "Things aren't exactly at their best between Mitch and me right now. I'd rather not have to do a lot of explaining if our relationship fizzles."

"Mum's the word," Marcia promised. "I won't tell a soul except Ted."

Brenna dropped her head into her hands in a gesture of despair.

"Well, you can't expect me not to tell *someone,*" she exclaimed dramatically. "I'd simply die!"

"Tell anyone but Ted and you'll die, all right," Brenna promised grimly. "By my hand."

Marcia grinned and snuggled back into her chair. "I take it I'm the first to know about your big romance?"

"Yes, you're the first," Brenna assured her on a sigh. Her friend could be such an incredible busybody when she chose!

"I'm flattered." Marcia picked up one of the packs of cigarettes that were now scattered around Brenna's home and shook one out. "Is he going with you to the Christmas party?"

"That has yet to be decided. Mitch has a certain reluctance to wearing tights."

Marcia sniffed longingly at the tobacco. "Why? Are his legs ugly?"

Brenna nearly choked. "N-no, his legs are fine," she stammered. And they were, she remembered. Long, beautifully muscled, with well-developed thighs and calves.

"If it's the fit he's worried about, I can take care of that for him." She replaced the cigarette with a sigh of regret. "There are days when I wish I hadn't quit," she said parenthetically. "Now, what were we talking about? Oh, yeah. Some of the actors face the same problem, you know."

"Problem?" Brenna stared blankly at her friend. "What problem?"

"A sudden attack of shyness." Marcia gave her an exasperated look when Brenna simply looked even more confused. "They like to keep a few things a secret," she hinted, her eyes widening suggestively. Her gaze strayed to the door and she grinned. "Isn't that so, Mitch?"

Brenna could feel the blood race up her throat to suffuse her face and she couldn't bring herself to turn around. How much of their conversation had he heard? Torn between embarrassment and tears, she sat stiffly in her swivel chair, praying that she would simply disappear.

"Actually, Marcia, I hadn't give the problem much thought." Mitch sauntered into the room, throwing Brenna a knowing look as he passed by.

"You don't even have to wear the hose," the brunette cheerfully informed him. "A costume isn't mandatory for anyone but faculty. Didn't Brian wear a suit?" she questioned a mortified Brenna.

"A tux," she replied in a strangled tone. "Brian wore a tuxedo."

"See, no problem. Just go rent a tux." Marcia glanced at her wristwatch. "Oh-oh, bedtime for my monsters. I'd better get home before Ted loses control."

Ted will be in good company, Brenna thought direly as she watched her friend bundle herself into her coat.

"If you change your mind about a costume, just let me know," Marcia was saying. "See you later, *Cousin* Mitch."

Brenna rose and by sheer willpower put one foot in front of the other in order to escort her neighbor to the front door. When Marcia was gone, she leaned weakly against the wood and reluctantly met a pair of emerald eyes that sparkled wickedly at her.

"What was that about my legs, Brenna?"

"With some help from my ex-husband, Marcia has discovered that you and I are not cousins," she informed him broodingly. "And she has reached her own conclusion about our relationship."

Mitch lounged against the doorjamb, his arms crossed over his chest. "Let me guess—she thinks you and I are playing house, right?"

"Got it in one," Brenna mocked. "You're as bright as you think you are."

His eyes narrowed at the jibe. "Use a bigger knife, Professor. I barely felt that one."

"I'd like to use a bazooka," she shot back before she could stop herself. Instantly appalled by her behavior, she raised her hands in a defensive gesture. "Sorry. Don't worry about Marcia—I'll make sure she doesn't try to turn you into a Tudor courtier." Pushing herself away from the front door, she headed for her office.

Mitch blocked her path by simply placing a hand, palm down, on the other side of the doorway. "You're determined to go to this damn party, aren't you?"

Brenna nodded, her eyes fascinated by the way the gold hair on his arm cradled his black-faced watch and its matching leather strap. It was a blatantly masculine picture, and her body reacted accordingly. Her mouth went dry and there was a definite weakness in her legs that she tried to tell herself she wasn't feeling.

Knowing only that she avoided looking at him, Mitch sighed inwardly and bowed to the inevitable. "I draw the line at wearing tights."

The warmth of his breath on her cheek jerked Brenna from her reverie. "W-what?"

"No tights," he reiterated bluntly. "I'll wear a tux, but no frilly shirt or patent leather shoes. Deal?"

Brenna considered arguing, even reminding him that she had withdrawn her invitation for him to act as her escort, but something in his expression warned her not to press her luck. She cleared her throat. "What if you solve the case by then?"

He straightened as if slapped; his arm fell back to his side. "Then your ex-husband can take you." With that, he turned on his heel and disappeared back into the dining room.

Expelling a shaky breath, Brenna retreated to her office. They did not speak for the rest of the night.

Chapter 8

On the Thursday-evening news, the weather forecaster's prediction of record-breaking amounts of snow for the next three days caused Brenna to sigh inwardly. Since her confrontation with Mitch over the Christmas party, the tension level in her household had escalated from high to volatile, and it wouldn't take much to cause an explosion. Absolutely the last thing they needed was a weekend of enforced confinement. But I can get through it, she told herself with grim determination as she watched the snow fall on campus Friday morning. After all, Mitch didn't allow her to leave the house by herself anyway, so the only difference was that the snowfall would simply reinforce the psychological prison he had erected.

Upon arriving home, Brenna discovered two things. One, George and his crew had installed her new cabinets, and the sawdust from their enterprise had sifted throughout the first floor of the house; and, two, the task of clearing the accumulated snowfall from her driveway and sidewalk would take a good three hours. The combined mess of sawdust and snow was enough to make a grown woman cry—unless the said woman happened to be in the company of an ever-so-practical government employee.

Mitch drew a finger over the dining room table and stared wordlessly at the track it made, then turned an assessing gaze on Brenna.

"The snow first," Brenna decided. It would be dark soon, and she didn't relish having to guess where the driveway and sidewalk were. "I'll worry about the house later." She turned on her heel and left the room before he could argue.

Minutes later, dressed for the elements in an outfit that caused her to bear a striking resemblance to the French tire man, Brenna slogged her way behind Mitch to the garage. He was still using the heavy jacket and boots he had borrowed from Ted, but she had come to the conclusion that, regardless of his attire, the cold and snow would not have affected him. The man was simply impervious to anything that might stand in the way of whatever he wanted to accomplish.

He could have dealt with this on his own, Mitch thought as he plowed through the snow, but he hadn't wanted to risk an argument with Brenna over the issue. He had finally managed to erect a mental barrier between the two of them, which had allowed him to regain a portion of his former objectivity. An argument now could damage that wall, make him forget that he was here to catch Fedoryshyn, not make love to an absentminded college professor. It was as he was exploring the garage that Mitch found a perfectly serviceable snowblower sitting beneath a tarp.

"Why don't you use this?" he called to Brenna as she started outside with two shovels.

Brenna glanced at the machine with magnificent distaste. "It doesn't like me."

"I beg your pardon?"

"It doesn't like me—I don't like it. Take your pick."

When that defiant note crept into her voice, Mitch had learned, he had definitely struck a nerve. "Don't tell me you don't know how to run this thing?"

"Of course I know how to run it. I simply choose to use a shovel—at least it won't sputter and die every foot or so."

Mitch grinned. "You won't mind if I give it a try?"

Brenna shrugged. Attired as she was in a bulky, one-piece insulated snowsuit and heavy boots, what should have been a delicate movement looked more like a convulsion, and Mitch choked back a laugh. "Suit yourself."

While Mitch tinkered with the recalcitrant snowblower, she turned her efforts to clearing the sidewalk. Brenna didn't doubt for a minute that the machine would purr like a kitten for Mitch, just as she had no doubt that if she so much as touched it, it would cough, wheeze and die, as it had since the day she had brought it home. She didn't get along well with mechanical things, with the exception of her car. Of course, she reasoned, at least twice a year she paid a man nicknamed Smitty a small fortune to ensure that the car knew it was loved.

There was a loud roar from the direction of the garage, and a moment later Mitch appeared, the snowblower rolling triumphantly in front of him. Giving in to a childish impulse, Brenna stuck out her tongue at the pair before bending to attack another snowbank.

By the time she was ready to tackle the sidewalk leading up to the house, Mitch had cleared the driveway and was advancing on her position, the mechanical monster devouring every snowflake in sight.

"Get out of the way," Mitch yelled, gesturing for her to move. "I'll take care of this and then give Ted a hand."

Brenna glanced across the street. The entire Thompson clan was outside, Ted shoveling furiously while Marcia tried to keep their four sons from throwing the snow their father had already cleared away back onto the driveway.

"Move, Brenna!"

It was his impatient tone that made her bristle. The man insisted upon giving her orders, and she was sick of it. Eyes sparkling dangerously, she edged past Mitch so that he had a clear path to the front steps. Ignoring her, he put the snowblower in gear and followed in its wake.

Before she could think better of the idea, Brenna sliced her shovel into the snow and loaded it so heavily she had trouble lifting it. She followed behind man and machine, then stopped, waiting patiently for Mitch to reverse direction.

Mitch was about to shift from reverse to forward when he became aware of the figure blocking his path. "Will you get out of the way?" he bellowed, the fact that she was carrying a loaded shovel not registering. It was getting late, he was cold and sweaty and at this moment he wanted nothing more than to sit in front of a roaring fire with a glass of Scotch.

"Not until you apologize," she shouted back, her voice carrying clearly over the roar of the engine.

"For what?"

"For yelling at me," she screeched, her temper overriding common sense. "For giving me orders!"

Something snapped inside Mitch. Every time he turned around, the woman was challenging him and he was more than a little tired of it. He had been doing his damnedest to keep their relationship impersonal, to deny the attraction growing between them. The only way either of them was going to survive this situation was to remain cool and detached, but Brenna simply wouldn't do her part to keep up the pretense. Twisting the key to silence the snowblower, he started down the cleared path toward her. "You need a keeper, lady! Why are you so mad? All I'm doing is helping you."

"I don't need your help! Who do you think did this little chore before you showed up? Who do you think is going to do it when you're gone? I'll tell you who—me, that's who."

"Shall we discuss just how inefficient your method is?"

"It works!"

"Not very well. That's why I give you orders—because you don't have the sense God gave a duck." He came to a stop a scant three feet in front of her.

Across the street, Marcia and Ted were staring in amazement at the scene unfolding in front of them. Even the four boys had abandoned their play in favor of watching Aunt Brenna yell—something that, in the course of their short lifetimes, they had never witnessed.

"It must be true love," Marcia sighed blissfully.

Ted graced his wife with a wry smile. "How can you tell?"

"They sound just like us," she returned triumphantly, then focused her attention back on her best friend.

Brenna's mouth worked silently for a moment as she searched for a particularly scathing retort to this latest insult. Her brain, unfortunately, must have been numbed by the cold, because all she could come up with was an unsatisfactory, "You take that back!"

"You're a loon," Mitch continued, his voice rising with every word. "It comes from living in that snooty ivory tower of yours. What's the matter, Professor, afraid to face the truth?"

"Oh-oh," Marcia groaned. Brenna had been given red hair for a reason, and it wasn't to compliment her complexion.

Later, Mitch would remember that when he had been wounded in Vienna, he hadn't heard the shot directed at him. The loaded shovel functioned the same way. One minute he was ready to tell Brenna that if she had cared for Brian as much as she did her cats, she would still have a husband, and the next his face was stinging like hell from the snow she had thrown at him.

He started to yell, choked and spit out a mouthful of snow. "You little witch," he purred in a deadly tone, feeling the snow that had found its way inside his jacket trickle down his chest as it melted.

Brenna scooped up another round of ammunition and smiled, sure of her control over this situation as she watched Mitch give a vigorous shake of his head to rid himself of the snow in his hair. "I am *not* a loon. Say it."

Judging the distance between them, Mitch made a few rapid, mental calculations and parroted, "I am not a loon." Then he moved.

Brenna felt the shovel being torn out of her hands, and then she was flat on her back in the snow, Mitch straddling her hips while he pinned her gloved hands over her head. His movements had been nothing more than a blur; only now did she feel the imprint his hands had left at her waist when he had thrown her to the ground. *Too close—he was too close!* Instinct made her arch against his hold in a futile effort to free herself. "Let me go," she demanded, trying to bluff her way past the primal fear inundating her.

"Not until you apologize."

"For what?"

"For starters, the snow in my face," he told her silkily. God help him, he liked the feel of her beneath him; liked the way her eyes widened in awareness when he allowed more of his weight to fall on her.

Mitch wasn't hurting her, she realized, simply holding her in place in a manner guaranteed to raise the hackles of any modern woman. He was calling her bluff. "You deserved it—you were being high-handed and dictatorial again."

He chained both her wrists in his left hand, then scooped up a handful of snow with his right. "Apologize, Brenna."

"You wouldn't," she said, trying to sound positive about her assessment, but keeping a wary eye on the weapon. Could she have misinterpreted the threat in his emerald eyes?

"I would. Didn't that afternoon in your office teach you anything, Professor," he inquired menacingly.

Brenna gulped and nodded. Bravado was fading fast, yielding to memories of that afternoon and the desire that had surfaced between them. That was surfacing now, in her.

"Apologize, Brenna."

"I'm sorry, please let me go." The intimacy was growing between them, threatening her sanity with its intensity. She had to fight the urge to reach for him, beg him to kiss her again.

He barely heard the breathless, hurried words; his body was too busy reacting to her closeness. Desire was constricting his throat, causing his breath to come in short, painful gasps.

"Mitch—" Brenna whispered in bewilderment, wanting him but afraid of the strength of her own passion, and knowing somehow that he felt the same way. And there was something else that lay between them. "Do you still consider me a suspect?" she forced herself to ask.

The question brought Mitch back to reality. As abruptly as he had grabbed Brenna, he released her, rising swiftly to his feet. "Go in the house," he gritted, not extending a hand to help her up. "Don't come out here again."

Brenna scuttled into the house as fast as her bulky clothing would allow, realizing how narrow her escape had been. She needed time to think, get a grip on her turbulent emotions, she told herself as she paused in the kitchen to yank off her boots. Most of all, she had to get away from Mitch Carlisle before—

She didn't want to carry that thought any further. Leaving her boots on the large braid rug to dry, she stripped off her outerwear and hung it on the coatrack before running for the safety of her bedroom.

Crystal gave a sharp meow of shock when Brenna slammed the bedroom door and leaned against it to catch her breath. "I know, this is ridiculous," she told the white cat. "I don't like him—he doesn't like me. What's going on between us is nothing more than plain, old-fashioned lust. Nothing to be scared of. Right?"

From her position in the middle of the bed, Crystal regarded her explanation with feline contempt. "Right," Brenna sighed. "That's why I'm scared to death." The sound of the snowblower starting again drew her to the window. She watched Mitch finish the sidewalk, then walk the machine across the street to the Thompsons.

She was feeling more than lust, and she knew it. As absurd as she told herself it was, she had never felt more alive than she had since Mitch walked through her door, and she wanted to capture that feeling, enhance it. For once in her careful, secure existence, she wanted to revel—no, wal-

low—in pure sensation. The sensations only Mitch seemed
to generate in her.

Turning from the window, Brenna stared at the four-
poster bed. The bed was new, purchased after her divorce.
It was also as chaste as her life had been since the separation. She had a sudden, vivid image of Mitch in a sensual
sprawl on her rose-spattered linens and gave a low moan of
protest. If she didn't stop fantasizing, she was only going to
make matters worse. After all, she was only his suspect,
something to be watched, like a bug in a jar. If she allowed
herself to forget that fact, she was going to find herself in the
middle of one giant mess.

With another groan, Brenna made a beeline for her bathroom and a hot shower. She left the shower stall only when
the water heater had been drained and then, to her chagrin,
discovered that there were no towels in her bathroom. They
had been dropped down the laundry chute that morning for
the load of wash she planned to do when she returned home.
Shivering, she struggled into her robe and took a quick
glance out the bedroom window. The snowblower and
Mitch were still merrily chugging away in the Thompsons'
driveway, so it was safe for her to venture down the hall to
the linen closet.

She was returning to her bedroom with a set of towels,
pulling off her shower cap with her free hand as she walked,
when Mitch suddenly appeared at the top of the steps. Her
first thought was that the man had a definite aversion to remaining fully clothed; her second was that she had never
seen anything sexier in her life than the way his flannel shirt
gaped open over his furred chest.

Mitch's fingers tightened on the leather holster strap
dangling from his hand at the vision in front of him. Brenna's hair was an untamed mass of waves and her pale skin
was lightly flushed from the shower. Both seemed to beg for
the touch of a man's hand. His gaze dropped briefly to the
towels she held before returning to her face.

"No towels in my bathroom," she explained unnecessar-
ily, her heart thudding madly. When he continued to stare

at her, she nervously wet her lips and searched vainly for something else to say.

Part of his mind told Mitch to stay right where he was until Brenna could retreat to her bedroom. The rest of him—the predator in him—urged him forward in a smooth, gliding motion, his stockinged feet silent on the hardwood floor.

"You have the loveliest skin," he said hoarsely, stroking a finger down her throat. "Like cream."

Brenna shuddered at his touch. "Don't."

His eyes searched her face for a long moment before he took the final step that brought his body into contact with hers. This time the shudder racked both of them.

"You—you said this wouldn't happen again," she shakily reminded him.

"I was wrong," he admitted, still moving, forcing her back against the wall. His mouth skimmed her temple.

Brenna swallowed convulsively and wedged a fist between them to push against his chest. When his eyes finally met hers, she managed to say, "Please, don't. You won't learn anything new about Mark or his project by taking me to bed."

Mitch searched her eyes. "Baby, if I thought seducing you would elicit a confession, I would have tried it days ago," he murmured, his free hand sliding around the back of her neck.

"I don't know anything about any formula," she whispered brokenly, needing desperately for him to believe her.

He nodded, unsmiling. "I know." His lips settled on hers at the same moment his legs moved, making a place for himself between her thighs.

It was like being struck by lightning. Brenna stiffened at the invasion, then felt her legs give out. She was vaguely aware of the towels falling from her arm, followed quickly by the thud of Mitch's holster hitting the floor, and then his tongue was seducing hers, inviting her to indulge in pleasure.

Mitch cupped his hands around her buttocks, lifting her against the hard ridge of his arousal. The little mewling sound that forced its way out of her throat at his action drove him wild, as did the sharp sting of her nails sinking into his chest.

"Not here," he gasped when he managed to tear his mouth from hers. Gathering her in his arms, he strode down the hall to her bedroom.

Wave upon wave of sensation washed through Brenna as Mitch allowed her to slowly slide to the floor. Laying a cheek against the silky mat of hair on his chest, she gave a little sigh of anticipation when his hands worked at the knot of her robe. A moment later, the robe was gone and she was bared to his hungry gaze.

"Beautiful." He turned her slightly so that his hand could travel unimpeded over her breast. "So perfect." He cupped one breast and squeezed gently.

Brenna cried out as pleasure flooded her and she buried her face in the hollow of his shoulder. When his fingers plucked enticingly at her nipple, she nipped at his throat, then instantly bathed the wound with her lips and tongue when he trembled under the attack.

Her hands seemed to float over his back and chest, sensitizing his flesh to her slightest touch as she stripped away his shirt, and Mitch closed his eyes in surrender. He caught his breath when Brenna's mouth lovingly explored his chest, stoking the fire within him by finding and teasing his nipples with the edge of her teeth. When she seemed reluctant to explore further, he took her hand and guided it to his waist.

With a soft sigh Brenna worked at the button and zipper of his jeans, then stripped the denim down his lean hips. Mitch impatiently kicked the jeans aside and, wearing only his briefs, hauled her back against his chest.

As his mouth found hers, the savage glitter in Mitch's eyes frightened Brenna and she knew a moment of panic. What were they doing? They couldn't—

"Don't think, Brenna," Mitch murmured hoarsely, sensing her withdrawal. "Just feel, just..." His voice trailed off as he brought their hips together, rubbing himself against her in an age-old movement of need.

"This is so right," he growled, catching her up in his arms and carrying her to the bed. "Nothing in my life has ever been this right." Holding her with one arm, he stripped back the comforter, blanket and sheet in one swift movement, then gently deposited her in the middle of the floral linen.

Brenna cried out as he crowded her into the mattress, his greater weight fusing bare flesh to bare flesh. The feel of his skin and the smell of his cologne were overloading her senses, spinning her out of control. When his tongue probed the line of her mouth, her lips parted eagerly, greedily, and Mitch groaned his appreciation of her welcome.

He felt Brenna's hands flutter across his back and down to his waist, to the elastic of his briefs. Muttering an oath, he levered himself away from her in order to dispose of this final barrier, but before he could sink back to the silken cushion Brenna offered, her hand stole between them and touched him intimately.

"Oh, Brenna, yes," he whispered brokenly, feeling her touch vibrate throughout his body. "I want you, too, so much..." His own hand dropped to the triangle of auburn curls at the apex of her legs and probed gently. She was moist and warm, as ready for him as he was for her, and the knowledge threatened his sanity.

Her reaction to his caress was purely instinctive; Brenna arched against his hand with a wordless little cry that was his undoing. He entered her swiftly, easily, and had to suppress the shout of triumph that welled in his throat.

"Like lightning," Brenna gasped out, even as she was adjusting to his possession.

"*La petite mort,*" he whispered, feeling her legs wrap themselves around his waist. "I finally understand." And he did; his heart told him that he would never find this quintessential pleasure with any other woman. Bending, he took one rosy nipple into his mouth and suckled gently, his

eyes closing in almost painful ecstasy when her body reacted to his latest ministration by tightening around him.

"Mitch!" His name was little more than a quivering expulsion of air, and Brenna was shocked by the helpless
sound. His blond head came up and she found herself staring into those green eyes that could be so cold and unfeel-
ing. But they weren't cold now; they were ablaze with
masculine intent and promise as he moved inside her, and
her fingers curled around the straining muscles of his upper
arms.

He continued the smooth, provocative strokes that soon
had Brenna writhing beneath him, and smiled down at her.
"Am I hurting you?"

Brenna managed to shake her head.

"Because I don't want to hurt you, baby," Mitch rumbled, lowering his head to nuzzle at her breast. "I want to
make this so good for you that just the memory will drive
you crazy."

She laughed shakily as his mouth continued to torment
her. "You're succeeding..."

Speech deserted her when his arms freed themselves from
her hold and his hands found her hips. "I've wanted this for
days," he murmured impulsively, guiding her frantic
movements when she twisted against him. "Dreamed about
it, fantasized about it—but even my fantasies weren't this
good."

"It's frightening..." Brenna whimpered. Her body was
going up in flames and there was no way to control the in-
ferno.

"No, it's perfect," Mitch told her, remotely aware of the
blatant satisfaction in his tone. "Just feel what we do to
each other."

The fire took her then, searing nerves and flesh and soul
in a wrenching consummation that triggered the same response in the man above her. Trembling, Brenna cried out
again when Mitch growled his satisfaction and collapsed on
top of her.

They lay motionless for several minutes, their perspiration-drenched bodies slick against one another. Eventually Mitch rolled to his side and tucked Brenna securely against his chest. The room was lit only by the streetlights now, and Brenna was grateful for the shadows—they hid the furious blush in her cheeks and the way she was worrying her bottom lip with her teeth.

Aftershocks ran through her limbs, a vivid reminder of what they had just shared. She had never before reacted like this to a man's touch; her physical relationship with her ex-husband had been as placid as their marriage, pleasant but hardly earth-shattering. With Mitch, however, something buried deep within her seemed to come alive, to revel in the ferocity with which he made love. The discovery was shocking and more than a little upsetting, for it meant she was capable of experiencing desire without love.

Her hand stroked thoughtfully through the mat of hair covering Mitch's chest, and she felt the tempo of his heartbeat increase. But then, what was so terrible about pure physical attraction? His arm tightened, and before she realized what she was doing, Brenna had planted a warm kiss in the hollow of his throat.

"You make me ache, Brenna," Mitch breathed into her hair, feeling desire stir again.

The quiet admission embarrassed her more than lying naked in his arms, more than her own doubts, bringing her back to reality with heart-stopping swiftness. What had she done? My God, she had gone to bed with a man she barely knew! A man who until a few minutes ago had suspected her of technological espionage.

Truly panicked, Brenna pushed against him, freeing herself from his lazy embrace, and hurried into the bathroom. Switching on the light, she caught sight of her reflection and stared in disbelief at her image. Her mouth was swollen from Mitch's kisses, and there was a red patch on her neck where his beard had unwittingly abraded her flesh. Auburn hair formed a wild cascade around her face. All in all, she looked well and truly . . . satiated. Oh, damn, damn, damn!

She needed to get away from him, away from his touch, his scent and *think about what to do next!* Swallowing a sob, she turned on the shower and stepped under the spray.

Mitch watched her retreat with a puzzled frown and lay for several minutes listening to the running water. He had looked forward to holding Brenna in his arms, drowsing in the aftermath of spent passion and then making love again, only this time in a slow, leisurely fashion. Instead, she had torn out of the bedroom as if her life depended upon putting as much distance between the two of them as possible.

"Oh, hell," Mitch swore under his breath, suddenly realizing what must be bothering her. Swinging out of bed with a lazy grace, he silently stalked into the bathroom.

Brenna shrieked as the shower curtain was torn open, exposing her to the emerald gaze of the hard man who had turned her entire life upside down.

"I accept full responsibility," he informed her in a tone that brooked no disagreement.

"Wha-what," Brenna stammered, wrapping nervous fingers more tightly around the bar of soap she held.

"Responsibility," Mitch repeated, stepping into the tub with her and pulling the curtain back into place. "From now on I'll take care of the precautions—unless you already have?"

She stared at him in bewilderment, knowing she should understand what he was talking about but unable to gather her roiling thoughts long enough to make sense of his words. "Precautions?"

Mitch sighed and ran an impatient hand through his hair. "Yes, precautions," he ground out. "Normally you aren't this slow." When she simply shook her head in confusion, he clarified dryly, "As in contraceptives? As in are you using anything?" He received his answer when the bar of soap squirted out of her reflexively tightening grip and hit him on the bridge of the nose. Pain rocketed through his head and Mitch closed his eyes against it.

"Oh, I'm sorry!" Her horrified gasp was drowned out by the muttered curses filling the bathroom. "I didn't mean..."

Unable to form a coherent apology, she bent to retrieve the soap from the bottom of the tub before it could injure him further.

Unfortunately Mitch could feel the soap lodged between his foot and the side of the tub, and decided to recover the offensive object without bothering to open his eyes. It was inevitable that the top of Brenna's head would meet his chin with a resounding crack.

Brenna saw stars and reached out to steady herself. When her hand encountered the shower curtain, it tightened gratefully around the plastic just as she lost her footing. She hit the bottom of the tub with a deafening thud, but she could have sworn she heard each individual curtain ring crack as the shower curtain gave beneath her weight.

Mitch opened his eyes just in time to see the shower curtain fall into the tub, and then there was a screech of metal and he looked up. Fortunately he had enough warning to throw his arms over his head before the curtain rod surrendered to the pull of gravity and fell on top of him.

For several moments the only sound was the hiss of the shower, and then there was a frantic rustle as Brenna fought her way out of her plastic shroud. Mitch gallantly picked up the curtain rod and propped it against the wall outside of the tub, where it could do no further damage.

Humiliated beyond belief, Brenna kicked at the curtain, which insisted upon tangling around her ankles, and pushed the wet, streaming hair out of her face before looking into piercing green eyes that harbored a suspicious glint in their depths.

Mitch felt his lips twitch in amusement and tried to control the reaction. "I take it the answer to my question is no?"

His matter-of-fact tone was the last straw; Brenna gave in to her emotional turmoil and burst into tears. Burying her face in her hands, she turned away from the man looming over her and tried to disappear under the stream of water.

Any amusement he was feeling evaporated in the face of her embarrassment. Sighing, he reached around Brenna to turn off the shower and then, when she showed no sign of being willing to face him, he simply picked her up and carried her back to the bedroom.

Snatching Brenna's terry-cloth robe from the floor, he bundled her into the garment and sat her on the bed before going down the hall for the towels she had dropped earlier. Winding the bath towel around his waist, he returned to the bedroom and closed the blinds and turned on the light before sitting down beside Brenna.

"Go away," she sniffed when his arm came around her shoulders. "Just go away and we'll pretend this never happened."

"Don't be an idiot," he snapped, turning her toward him and forcing her hands away from her face. "Damn it, look at me!" When she reluctantly obeyed, when he saw the confusion and anguish in her eyes, he groaned and pulled her into his arms. "Don't cry, baby, please. Everything is fine."

"No, it isn't," she argued tearfully. "Everything is awful."

Brushing a kiss against her temple, he sighed. "Tell me what you're thinking," Mitch cajoled, his hands moving in long, soothing strokes up and down her back.

The request was so simple, so heartfelt, that it eased some of her tension. Maybe it would be easier to talk to Mitch if she didn't have to look at him. Swallowing a sob, Brenna burrowed farther into his shoulder. "I'm—I'm not using anything," she finally whispered. "I haven't…that is, since my separation…." She gave up trying to explain and simply cried, "What if I'm pregnant?"

The frisson of pleasure that ran through Mitch at her fearful question was so strong it took some time for him to find his voice. He had a fleeting image of Brenna growing heavy with his child that was so beautiful it made his heart ache before he brought his imagination under control. "If you're pregnant, we'll deal with it," he told her evenly.

Brenna stilled. "We?"

Reining in his impatience, he tightened his embrace in a gesture of reassurance. "Yes, Brenna, we. I always take responsibility for my actions."

Something about the way he said "responsibility" made her wary. She had the feeling that if Mitch had a child, he would insist upon being part of that child's life. Which was, of course, a mature, adult attitude she should appreciate. So why did she suddenly feel as if a trap had closed around her? Pulling away, she said nervously, "I don't think you have to worry, though. Fortunately this happened during the wrong time of my cycle."

Framing her face in his hands so that she had to meet his eyes, Mitch smiled. "I'm not worried, baby—next time I'll use something."

"Next time," Brenna choked, appalled. "Listen, Mitch, I think we have to talk—"

"Talk about what?" he asked good-naturedly.

"Ab-about what just happened!" She gestured vaguely at the bed. "About this."

He considered her answer while his forefinger rubbed across her lips. "Thinking of me as a one-night stand?"

"N-no, but—"

"Good, because I won't let you," he murmured, feeling renewed passion curl through him. "We're both adults and we want each other."

Brenna gulped. "There should be more." But she couldn't deny the truth of his words, not now, when his touch was arousing those wild feelings again.

"Love?" Mitch slowly parted her robe and skimmed it from her shoulders. "I've never been in love. What does it feel like, Brenna?"

Her mouth worked soundlessly for a moment before his lips postponed her reply. When the long, drugging kiss ended, Brenna had to force her eyes open. "You frighten me," she admitted softly. "I don't know anything about you, except that you work for the FBI."

Mitch stiffened briefly, then drew her down on top of him. "You know that you make me go up in flames, that I want you so badly I can't think of anything else." She was sprawled across his chest now, and he could feel the jack-hammer rhythm of her heartbeat. "Follow your instincts—I've found they're usually right."

Brenna gave a soft moan and brought her lips to his. He was offering passion and desire, nothing more, but she sensed he didn't bestow either lightly. Perhaps for a man like Mitch, a man so obviously alone, passion was the equivalent of love. Not that it mattered; the words he had spun around her like a seductive web had convinced her to take a chance on desire. This was the first kiss she had initiated and he let her control it, set the pace and the intimacy. By the time she was finished, he was breathless with need.

Feeling his hardness against her, Brenna smiled regretfully. "I shouldn't have gotten so carried away," she whispered, running her fingers through his damp hair.

He smiled lazily. "I'm enjoying it."

"But..." She blushed and her color deepened when he gave a low chuckle.

"Such a mass of contradictions, Professor," he teased. Then he chuckled again at the delight he was discovering in being *able* to tease this woman. "We both know the facts of life."

Brenna blessed him with a disgruntled look. "Some of us aren't quite so blatant about it. Besides, you know what I mean. We can't, um, do anything until, well, until you—"

This time he laughed outright. "If you can control yourself long enough to let me run to my room, we can do something about this, ahem, mutual urge we seem to have," he finished with a devastatingly accurate mimicry of her hesitancy.

"You mean you..." Brenna's accusation died when he moved, flipping her onto her back so that she was pinned beneath him.

"This has been building between us for some time, and I believe in being prepared," he murmured outrageously. "But you took me by surprise in the hallway. All I could think of was touching you, holding you. Being inside you," he breathed into her mouth. "Am I forgiven?"

With a sigh of surrender, she arched upward and brought their lips together in reply.

Chapter 9

Brenna woke to the rich smell of coffee and she sniffed appreciatively before deciding she needed sleep more than caffeine and burrowed farther under the covers. Outside, the wind was howling, rattling the windows with its ferocity, and she smiled, thinking how delightfully snug her bed was by comparison.

"There's a real blizzard out there," a low, masculine voice close to her ear informed her. "Nothing is moving. It looks like we're trapped here for the duration." A finger stroked down her cheek in a soft caress and she shivered. "What are we going to do with all this time, Professor?"

Sighing sleepily, Brenna opened her eyes and focused first on the alarm clock—which read seven o'clock—and then on the man crouched beside the bed. "You could come back in here where it's warm," she suggested, noting that Mitch was wearing his jeans but had neglected to button his shirt. "Some of us need a full eight hours."

Deliberately choosing to interpret her words to his own advantage, Mitch teased, "Insatiable woman." Setting aside the coffee cup he was holding, he grinned wickedly and bent forward to nuzzle the curve of her neck. "Now you're getting the idea."

One of her hands crept out from beneath the blankets to comb through his hair. "Who kept waking whom?" she asked blithely, recovering her equilibrium.

"I'd say it was fifty-fifty," he retorted, his lean, muscled body flowing upward over the side of the bed to come to rest beside Brenna, pinning her beneath the covers. Turning his head, he pressed fleeting, burning kisses against her fingers and the palm of her hand. "As I recall, I was sound asleep at three this morning when these inquisitive fingers of yours came wandering over to my side of the bed—"

"You were on my side," Brenna felt obliged to point out. "In fact, I couldn't move because your leg—" The rest of the teasing remark died a quick death as she watched his eyes darken with desire. "This happened so fast," she whispered. "And it's so intense."

Mitch nodded and propped his chin in his hand, studying her. Incredibly, after the night they had just shared, he found himself as hungry for her as he had been the first time. "That doesn't make it wrong." If she was trying for a tactical retreat at this point, she was in for one hell of a fight.

"No, it doesn't." Brenna smiled, feeling the force of his not inconsiderable will emerge from beneath his civilized veneer. She loved tampering with his iron control; it was a constant challenge that attracted her on a very elemental level. "But since I've never had an affair before, this is all quite new to me."

His heart tightened at her choice of words. "Affair," he repeated softly, severely. "You make this sound very transitory."

She regarded him silently for several moments, puzzled by the flash of pain she had seen in his eyes. "We live in two different worlds, Mitch," she said at last, trying to clarify exactly what she was feeling—for both their sakes. "And these worlds just happened to overlap. Given that, our relationship can only be transient in nature."

"The old live-for-today philosophy," he growled. She was right, of course, and for more reasons than she knew, so why was he fighting so hard against the truth?

"If you like," she sighed.

"Well, I don't," he informed her threateningly. "I don't want an affair—I want to be your lover."

Brenna frowned. "I fail to see any difference between the two, except for the semantics involved."

"Oh, there's a difference, all right." Mitch's gaze grew more intense. "I know you very well, Brenna. You think that by categorizing what we have as a fling, you'll be able to view our relationship as an aberration, a moment of insanity to be forgotten as soon as I'm out of sight."

"Won't you?" she challenged, wanting him to deny the accusation. It hurt to think that she might mean nothing more to him than a pleasant interlude in a case.

He shook his head warningly. "Don't interrupt. We're talking about you, not me. You relate people to situations, not the reverse. That's why I want to be your lover, not have an affair with you. I want to be burned into that phenomenal—if highly selective—memory of yours."

Mitch didn't give her time to question the fierce declaration; he couldn't give her the advantage of discovering that she had become as much a part of him as breathing. Nor could he bring himself to put a name to the aching, possessive feelings she aroused. He had come of age in a hard, unforgiving world, where to admit to needing anything was to give the other person a weapon to use against him. All he could admit to was a desperate sense of wanting Brenna to find him unforgettable.

So instead of telling Brenna what he was experiencing, Mitch made fierce love to her, swamping her with height after height of such intense pleasure that in the end she lay limp and gasping in his arms. When she fell asleep, her breath warm and moist against his chest, he combed his fingers through her rich fall of auburn hair and tried not to think about what would happen when she learned the truth about him.

* * *

When Brenna next awoke, the filled coffee cup on the nightstand had been replaced by an empty one and a thermos, and she smiled to herself. Mitch took such very good care of her. Glancing at the alarm, she saw it was midmorning, and if memory served, she had an entire first floor covered with sawdust to clean. Levering herself up on her elbows, she searched the room for the cats, but discovered Mitch sitting in the armchair, frowning over his alarm system diagram while sipping coffee from a cup that matched the one on the nightstand.

Brenna remained motionless, enjoying the picture he presented. What would it be like when he was gone and she and the cats were left to ramble through the house by themselves? When he looked up and found her watching him, she put aside the sad thought and smiled. "Good morning. Again."

"Sleep well?" Mitch asked, a decidedly smug curl to his mouth.

Nodding, she reached for the thermos. "What are you doing?"

"Making sure that I have the IR receivers placed exactly right." He flipped the pad around so that she could see the drawing and indicated the multicolored lines drawn on the paper.

"IR?"

"Infrared," Mitch clarified, uncoiling his length from the chair to cross the room and sit beside her on the bed. "If the magnetic contact on the switch is broken, the receiver is activated and sends an IR beam to the main box." Scowling, he lit a cigarette. "Right now the receivers and main box are battery powered—they should be wired into the electrical system, using batteries only as backup power. You'll have to hire an electrician to do that."

"I doubt that will be necessary," Brenna demurred. "Once this business with Mark is over—"

"This system isn't a temporary measure," he interrupted. "Your house is an open invitation for everyone from vandals to rapists—you have absolutely no protection here, and there are at least a dozen ways for someone to break in.''

''You worry too much.''

Mitch snorted derisively. ''It's an occupational hazard.'' When she didn't reply, he said, ''I mean it, Brenna, have this alarm system permanently installed. You'll need the protection.''

When I'm gone. He didn't say the words aloud; he didn't have to. Brenna knew exactly what he was thinking.

Setting aside her coffee, she started to rise, then thought better of the idea when she realized she was naked beneath the covers. ''I've got cleaning to do.'' She eyed Mitch expectantly, waiting for him to do the gentlemanly thing and leave the room.

Instead, he curled a restraining hand around her wrist, holding her in place. ''I've already installed the switches on the front and back doors and the windows in your office. I want to finish the rest of the first-floor windows today. Once that's done, I'll give you a hand.''

''You don't have to help,'' she began in a strangled tone. ''I'm capable of dusting.''

Mitch sighed. ''I don't do anything I don't want to,'' he explained carefully. ''I thought you realized that.''

''Like planning this system so that when you leave—'' She swallowed the rest of the condemnation, not wanting to mar whatever time together they might have.

Pain sliced through Mitch's heart. ''Do you want me to lie? Promise you forever?''

Brenna hastily shook her head. ''No. It's just that I can't help wondering how quickly you'll forget me.'' The fingers around her wrist tightened painfully, and she gave a tiny gasp as she met his eyes.

Dismayed that she could think so little of herself, he said thickly, ''I couldn't, even if I wanted to.'' He couldn't bear to crush the tiny flicker of hope that appeared in her eyes at his confession. ''Washington isn't that far away.''

''No, it isn't,'' she agreed, smiling shakily.

"And the flight schedule from Minneapolis to Washington is pretty good," Mitch continued, silently damning himself for the fantasy he was spinning. Don't hate me, Brenna, he pleaded silently; please, don't hate me for what I'm doing. But how could he tell her, now, that he had lied to her from the beginning?

Brenna nodded, unable to speak for the heady emotions singing through her at the possibility Mitch was offering. Desire may have drawn them together, but it seemed obvious he wanted more from her than fleeting satisfaction of a physical need. She gave a little sigh of relief, realizing she had been figuratively holding her breath since last night, wondering exactly what he was feeling.

Long-distance romances were becoming more prominent in this day and age, and while she would miss having Mitch close by, Brenna was elated that he was as anxious to pursue their relationship as she. "I guess I'm not as modern as I thought I was," she apologized with a little smile.

"I don't want a modern woman. I want you," he told her fiercely. "Just don't ask me for promises, Brenna—don't ask for something I can't give you."

"I just want you," she answered just as fiercely. "I don't need any hearts and flowers."

But you deserve them, he thought bleakly. Just like you deserve the kind of man who will cherish you to eternity. Forcing himself to relax, Mitch released her wrist. "Get dressed before I take this as an invitation."

"I wouldn't mind."

He smiled thinly. "Neither would I, but the cats are scattering sawdust all over the house. First things first."

Laughing, Brenna threw back the covers and padded into the bathroom. There she discovered that Mitch had fixed the curtain rod and draped the shower curtain over it. As a stopgap measure, it worked beautifully. In fifteen minutes Brenna had showered, applied her usual light makeup and was making her way downstairs.

* * *

By nightfall Brenna and Mitch had accomplished their objectives for the day and the cats were intensely put out at having had their adventure in sawdust put to an end. Jasper, who had hissed at Mitch all day, curled himself into a ball on his mistress's lap and gave an ominous growl when Mitch sat down beside Brenna on the yellow sectional sofa and draped a possessive arm around her shoulders.

Mitch sighed, conceding defeat. "I apologize for the violin string remark, Jasper. Pals?"

Jasper's answer was another rumble, accompanied by a furious spit.

"He sure carries a grudge," Mitch commented, lighting a cigarette with his free hand. "Of course, the fact that I've usurped his place in your bed probably has something to do with his attitude."

Reddening slightly, Brenna chuckled. "Only another male would consider that a rational explanation."

"Only because it's true." He grinned down at her. "Hungry?"

"Starved," she admitted. "I was just thinking about the pizza I have in the freezer."

Mitch shook his head. "You eat too much junk food."

"And you smoke too much." She glanced at the cigarette he held. "That could be contributing to your headaches."

"Does it bother you?" he asked, choosing to ignore her observation.

"Only because you're hurting yourself," she replied seriously.

Crushing out the cigarette and ignoring an incensed Jasper, who agilely jumped to the floor, Mitch hauled Brenna across his lap. "Give me a pleasurable alternative," he demanded.

Brenna complied, looping her arms around his neck in order to pull his head down to hers. This kiss was the antithesis of those they had previously shared. It spoke of compassion and concern and, when her tongue shyly explored his mouth, it expressed the awe they were discovering in one another.

Mitch had never experienced anything so earth-shattering and when he sensed she was about to withdraw, he tightened his arms, prolonging the incredible feeling of sharing. He was storing up memories, he knew, sensations and images that could be pulled out at a later time and turned over and over with the same fascination as watching a crystal prism reflect light. In the end, memories were all he would have of Brenna Hawthorne.

When he finally allowed the kiss to end, Brenna felt a tear roll down her cheek.

"Don't," he whispered, catching the drop with a fingertip.

"I'm not unhappy," she sighed, knowing he misunderstood. "Far from it. I just never knew that a kiss could be so beautiful."

"Neither did I." He pulled the clip out of her hair, smiling as the auburn mass fell across his arms. "It beats the hell out of a cigarette."

His unexpected humor made her laugh, and she hugged him. "Anytime."

In the end the pizza stayed in the freezer, and while Mitch prepared a salad, Brenna was assigned the task of cutting cheese and buttering several slices of French bread.

"Somehow I expected you to be demanding a steak," she told him when they were seated at the dining room table.

"Since you don't have any in the house, there's no point in my demanding one," he said reasonably.

"You don't like it rare, do you?"

Mitch looked up at the unabashedly disgusted tone of her question. "As a matter of fact, I like mine well-done."

Brenna grinned and made a mental note to buy steaks the next time they went to the store.

When the dishes were done, Mitch disappeared into the family room to watch the news and Brenna took the opportunity to unearth the container of microwave popcorn she knew was hiding in one of the boxes holding her kitchen.

When that effort met with success, she melted butter while the popcorn snapped merrily away and then carried the huge bowl in to Mitch.

She held up a hand to forestall the comment regarding junk food she knew he was going to make when he raised an eyebrow at the concoction. "No salt, just butter. Lots of butter," she added with relish. Filling the small bowl she carried with popcorn, she set it on the floor before joining Mitch on the sectional.

When Brenna didn't explain the placement of the small bowl, Mitch surrendered to the perverse curiosity that seemed to go hand in hand with living here. "It's a little early to leave a snack for Santa, isn't it?"

"Don't be absurd," Brenna sniffed. "I leave cookies and milk for Santa. The popcorn is for the cats—otherwise they'll be all over us during the movie."

"Movie?"

"A Humphrey Bogart movie," she informed him, switching to the station she wanted.

"Not *Casablanca,*" he groaned.

"We're No Angels."

"Speak for yourself."

Brenna laughed. "That's the movie, you nut. Bogart, Aldo Ray and Peter Ustinov as inmates on Devil's Island. Don't tell me you've never seen it?"

Mitch shook his head. "Not that I can remember."

"Well, you're in for a treat," she assured him, curling up beside him on the sectional. "This is a classic."

And Mitch, who hadn't had time in his life for movies, classic or otherwise, found himself thoroughly enjoying the next two hours. As predicted, the cats were content to eat from their bowl of popcorn and left the humans in peace, although they eyed Mitch curiously when his laughter occasionally rang through the house. By the end of the movie, the large popcorn bowl had been relegated to the cocktail table, and Mitch's head was resting comfortably in Brenna's lap.

As the halos appeared on-screen, Mitch heard a noise that sounded suspiciously like a sniff, and turned so that he could look up at Brenna. "Don't tell me you're crying."

"Of course not," she retorted, blinking away the moisture in her eyes.

Reaching up, he grasped a fistful of hair and tugged gently, forcing Brenna to lower her head. "Such a sensitive little creature," he murmured against her lips. "Do you really leave milk and cookies for Santa Claus?"

Mitch definitely had some things to learn about bedroom etiquette, Brenna decided when she woke up alone for the second morning in a row. Small, insignificant things, like the fact that on a cold winter morning, some women, such as herself, enjoyed waking up in the arms of the same warm body beside which they had fallen asleep. Or that a good-morning kiss was the perfect way to start a day. As if in answer to her thoughts, Jasper put his cold, wet nose against her cheek and gave a loud purr of contentment.

"Thanks, Jasper," Brenna muttered, scratching him behind his ears. "But it's just not the same."

Sighing, she stretched, then winced when several muscles that felt themselves to have been abused in the past forty-eight hours made their protests quite clear. Not even the twinges could keep the smile from her lips, however, when she rolled over and found the thermos and a cup and saucer waiting for her on the nightstand. "You can be a very sweet man, Mitch Carlisle," she said aloud as she filled her cup.

As Brenna lifted the saucer, she found a neatly folded piece of gray paper that had come from her stationery supply. Her name was done in an arrogant scrawl that she instinctively knew was Mitch's handwriting, and frowning curiously, she opened the note.

"Storm's over," she read to Jasper. "Gone to help Ted dig out the neighborhood. Sleep in." She raised an exasperated eyebrow at the cat, who was regarding the note with distrust. "He also has a lot to learn about love letters."

Jasper meowed an agreement and leaped off the bed with his usual feline grace while Brenna rose and went to the bedroom window. A quick look through the blinds showed that, just as his note had said, Mitch and Ted were intent upon clearing the Thompsons' driveway, using both shovel and snowblower. Her driveway, Brenna noticed, had already been cleared. At least two feet of snow had fallen, and with yesterday's severe wind, there were now drifts of snow that reached mammoth proportions scattered throughout the cul-de-sac. Men, she decided as she headed into the bathroom, could be very handy creatures to have around.

Brenna had thoughts of going outside to help with the snow removal, but by the time she had showered and dressed, another look through the window showed that the men were finished. While she watched, the Thompsons' front door opened, followed swiftly by four small figures bundled in snowsuits, scarves and mittens. Brenna grinned. Marcia was undoubtedly hoping that a few minutes outside would tame the Thompson terrors. A moment later she saw Ted and Mitch follow the children into the yard.

Each adult chose two boys, retired to opposite corners of the front yard and began forming an arsenal of snowballs. Within minutes they were engaged in a battle royal that soon had them all resembling animated snowmen. Even inside the house, Brenna could hear the boys' shrieks of delight in the play. Marcia really should put a stop to this, Brenna thought fleetingly. After all, it was precisely this type of learned aggression that triggered global conflicts. On the other hand, she mused, she did have fond memories of cold days and the fierce satisfaction she derived from perfecting her aim against her older—and oh-so-superior—brother, so perhaps there was no real harm in this type of play. Neither she nor her brother had triggered a war recently.

What happened next brought a sweep of emotion through Brenna. The smallest figure on Mitch's side took what appeared to be a direct hit from an opponent and fell to his knees. Mitch was beside him in a flash, tilting the child's face upward to check for possible damage. Apparently satisfied that all was well, Mitch swung the boy up in his arms for a brief, reassuring hug, and the play resumed. You could tell a great deal about a person by the way animals and children reacted to him. Mitch might have struck out with Jasper, but he was obviously batting a thousand in the little-boy department.

"A regular guardian angel," Brenna whispered tenderly, seeing that Mitch now took special care to protect the boy from further harm. "You're not so tough."

The ringing telephone drew her away from the window, but she kept an eye on the scene across the street as she answered.

"I'm coming for the formula, Professor."

Cold fear replaced the warmer emotions Brenna had been feeling. The knuckles of her fingers turned white as her grip tightened on the receiver. "Who is this?" she choked out.

"Did you hear me, Professor? I'm coming for the formula and you and your cousin will be as dead as Prescott."

"I don't know anything," she cried. "Leave me alone!"

There was no reply, only the click of the line going dead. She was trembling so violently that it took several tries before Brenna was able to replace the receiver, and then she realized the significance of this latest call. The man had discovered her new phone number. Stark terror replaced the fear she had been feeling. One thought sliced cleanly through her emotional turmoil. Mitch—she had to get to Mitch.

It took a few moments for her legs to find the strength to work, and then she was moving, practically stumbling down the staircase in her haste. She didn't bother with a coat or boots; in fact, she didn't even think about such mundane things. Unlocking the inside front door, she wrenched it open and ran across the narrow porch. Usually left open for the paperboy, this second door refused to yield to her panicked efforts before Brenna remembered that Mitch now kept it locked. She fumbled with the dead bolt, and then the door came open and she was through the glass-and-metal storm door.

The scream of the alarm system sliced through the morning air, bringing an abrupt halt to the activity in the Thompsons' front yard. The sound sent adrenaline pumping through Mitch, as did the sight of Brenna fleeing the house as if chased by demons. Or an intruder.

Not wasting time by taking the cleared sidewalk and driveway, Mitch bulldozed a more direct way through the drifts and carefully constructed banks, his gaze alternating between Brenna and the front door of her house. She was in the unplowed street now, awkwardly slogging through the accumulated snow, but there was no sign of pursuit. Unzipping his jacket, Mitch felt for the familiar shape of his pistol, only to realize that he had left it in the drawer of Brenna's nightstand. A hell of a lot of help he was going to be if the caller had decided to come out of hiding.

"God*damn* it!" It took forever to come within reach of her, to grab her shoulders and throw her to the ground, out of the line of fire.

Brenna didn't even feel the discomfort of being trapped between Mitch and the snow. The arms holding her were hard as steel bands, reassuring in their strength, as was the way his breath rasped against her ear. She buried her face in his jacket and clung to him, taking refuge in the safety he represented.

"What happened?" Mitch demanded, looking over his shoulder at the house.

"H-he called again, just now," she managed, shivering at the memory of that cold, deadly voice.

Mitch closed his eyes against the heady rush of relief her answer left in its wake. Just a phone call this time, thank God, but he could easily imagine a different scenario.

The alarm was still shrieking as Mitch rose, pulling Brenna up after him. "She forgot about the burglar alarm," he lied when Ted puffed to a halt beside them. "Scared the hell out of her."

Ted frowned at Brenna, shivering now from the cold. "You okay, Brenna?"

She managed a shaky nod.

"Come into the house. I'll get Marcia to make some cocoa."

"No, Brenna needs to get out of these wet clothes and I have to turn off the alarm," Mitch explained, wrapping an arm around her shoulders and starting back across the street before Ted had an opportunity to argue.

Once inside, he keyed the cancel command into the control box that was attached to the wall next to the front door and hustled Brenna upstairs and into the bathroom. "Your teeth are chattering."

"It's nothing."

"Right." He spun the taps on the bathtub. "I'm going to draw a bath for you, and while you soak you're going to tell me exactly what happened."

Minutes later Brenna, her hair pinned to the top of her head, occupied the tub, listening to Mitch move around in the bedroom. When he came to the bathroom door, the first thing she noticed was that he was once again wearing his shoulder holster.

"What did he say?" Mitch braced an arm against the door frame and fixed her with a dangerous look.

Sighing, Brenna repeated the brief, one-sided conversation. She didn't doubt that Mitch would listen to the tape later, but at the moment she was still feeling shaky enough to want him to stay with her.

When she was finished, he studied her silently for a minute before saying curtly, "I'll put on some coffee. When you're dressed, I'll show you how to turn off the alarms."

When he turned to leave, she said, "Mitch?"

"Yeah?"

"I'm sorry about the alarm," she nervously apologized to his back. "I just forgot—"

"Don't worry about it," he told her gruffly. "It's my fault—I should have shown you how to operate the system yesterday."

He disappeared and Brenna thoughtfully moved her hands through the water, trying to ignore the uneasy feeling that this latest phone call had just caused a significant change in their relationship.

Mitch's attitude throughout the day did nothing to alleviate Brenna's anxiety. Listening to the tape recording of the morning's phone call, his expression grew bleak, his eyes as cold as twin chips of green ice. When he had finished reviewing the tape, he reset the machine and downed several aspirin with a bottle of mineral water.

"What time does the secretary open the department office?" he asked after lighting a cigarette.

"Just before eight," Brenna answered, curled up in a corner of the yellow sectional. "Why?"

Mitch finally looked directly at her, something he had avoided since this morning. "I want to find out how difficult it is to gain access to her desk and the personnel files. Odds are, that's where the caller got your new phone number."

Brenna folded her hands together, watching mutely as he ejected the magazine from the handle of the automatic he carried and checked both weapon and cartridges. "This is the third time you've done that," she observed when he rammed the magazine home with a threatening snick and returned it to the shoulder holster. "You're making me more nervous than the caller."

"I'm here to protect you, not soothe your nerves. If you're that tense, call your ex-husband—I'm sure he'll be more than happy to prescribe something."

"Don't do this," she said quietly, her gaze holding his. "Don't push me away."

Mitch's jaw tightened. "I'm not. I'm just doing my job." He glanced at his watch. "Come on, let's find something for lunch."

He was friendly enough after that, but in the old, remote manner of the previous week. Nothing he said or did could be vaguely construed as intimate; in fact, he once again put as much physical distance between them as possible—but she was never out of his sight.

When Marcia called in the afternoon to invite them to dinner, Mitch was instantly at her side to listen to the conversation. When Brenna cast him an inquiring look, he simply shook his head and returned to the newspaper he had been reading.

"It might be fun," Brenna ventured warily when she had hung up. "And you wouldn't have to cook."

"I'd rather cook than have to search the house for an intruder," he told her brusquely. "I don't intend to argue about this—I said no and I mean no."

Brenna swallowed an angry reply and headed for the door of the family room. Whatever was bothering him, he was obviously in no mood to discuss it.

"Just where do you think you're going?"

"Upstairs," she answered with more equanimity than she was feeling.

What was needed was to indulge in something that would absorb all her emotions without requiring intense concentration. To that end, Brenna went into the music room, selected several pieces of music from the bookshelf and seated herself at the harpsichord. That Mitch appeared a minute later came as no surprise. He had obviously resumed his watchdog role.

"You're going to be very uncomfortable," she warned him with a certain degree of satisfaction. "No chair."

Mitch dropped the newspaper onto the floor and sat down beside it. "No problem."

He buried his nose in the paper with an eagerness Brenna found insulting. Grinding her teeth together, she flipped open the sheet music and worked out her frustration by dealing with a Mozart composition.

After five minutes, Mitch gave up any pretense of reading and, leaning his head against the wall and closing his eyes, listened to Brenna play. She had a light touch, uncertain in spots, but soothing nonetheless. Rather like her lovemaking, he thought, feeling his body stir in reaction. Although he would hardly define what she did to him in bed as soothing. The music came to an end, he heard the rustle of paper and she began another, brighter piece. Concentrating on the music, he could almost forget that he had spent one day and two nights losing himself in the wonders of her softly rounded body and then, this morning, he had left Brenna defenseless. Almost—the ice surrounding his heart was a constant, bitter reminder of his lapse, of what could have happened because he had lost his perspective.

Suddenly aware that she had stopped playing, Mitch opened his eyes to find Brenna regarding him intently. He sighed inwardly, knowing what was coming. My little absentminded professor, you won't let it die quietly, will you, he thought with a fleeting tenderness that he couldn't afford to show.

"Explain to me," Brenna said slowly, distinctly, "exactly what happened between last night and this morning. Tell me how it's possible for you to look at me and not truly *see* me."

Mitch fumbled for a cigarette, then realized he had neglected to bring an ashtray with him. Shoving the pack of cigarettes back in his shirt pocket, he folded his arms across his chest and fixed her with a blank stare. "Let's not play this scene out, okay?"

"Why not?" Brenna persisted, her voice frighteningly controlled. She pointed to the hallway. "Forty-eight hours ago you had me backed up against that wall, kissing the life out of me. Now you're acting as if we've just met. One of us is sending out some very confusing signals, and I don't think it's me."

He looked away then, seeing her pain, feeling it. Brenna didn't deserve this, any of it, least of all becoming involved with someone like himself. "I forgot why I'm here, that's all," he told her finally. "My assignment is to nail Fedoryshyn and keep you safe at the same time. I haven't been doing either lately."

Brenna thoughtfully drew the covers over the double-banked keyboard and studied the grain of the wood. "I've felt very secure the past two nights."

He shook his head. "I left you alone—exposed. Suppose the caller had decided to show up this morning instead of phoning? What do you think would have happened?" He didn't give her a chance to answer. "He could have killed you, and I wouldn't have known you were in danger until I finally came back to the house and found your body."

"I think you're exaggerating—"

"No, I'm not, and you know it. Do you know what I did after Ted and I finished clearing the driveway? I went inside with him and had a cup of coffee. What a *stupid* thing to do!" Even now, he found it hard to believe that he had been so careless.

"Mitch, nothing happened," Brenna soothed, her heart aching at what he was doing to himself.

"That's not the goddamn point!" He had been a fool to think he could actually fit into an average, secure world again. He had seen and done too much to ever have a normal life.

She left the harpsichord and knelt in front of him, not speaking until he met her gaze. "Right, the point is, you made a mistake. We all do, Mitch—we're only human. You make a mistake and learn from it and live with it. You don't wear it like a hair shirt." She touched his cheek. "Don't punish yourself like this. Please, don't."

"You don't understand," he said, feeling her fingers scrape over the stubble on his face. "In my business, mistakes are a luxury I can't afford."

Brenna gave a little chuckle. "I'm sure even J. Edgar erred a time or two," she chided.

Her words cut like a knife and he closed his eyes against the rush of pain and guilt they left in their wake. He should tell her the truth now, end the deception. She would understand why he had lied, perhaps even believe him when he explained that his gut instinct told him that danger was closing in on her.

And then he looked into those incredibly blue eyes, so full of compassion and trust, and knew he had to continue the charade. She was an honorable woman who believed in such things as honesty and commitment. Once he admitted his betrayal, Mitch was certain Brenna could never trust him again.

Odd how that knowledge hurt, he thought, feeling his insides twist into knots. When had her opinion of him started to matter? From the beginning, he admitted to himself. From the night she had found him searching through her desk and bristled with moral outrage. Damn you, Brenna, he cursed, facing the truth at last. You were only supposed to be a means to an end, not someone I will spend the rest of my life wanting. Someone I'll never have.

Mitch took her hand in his, marveled at the odd combination of fragility and strength he found there. "You're in danger, Brenna, more danger than I originally thought. I would never forgive myself if anything happened to you."

"Then stay close to me," she replied softly. "Nothing will happen as long as we're together."

His lips twisted into a cynical smile. "A nice fairy tale, but I know from experience that no one is invincible." When she merely smiled at him, he groaned and pulled her onto his lap. "I was so damn scared this morning," he whispered against her hair.

"So was I," Brenna whispered back, smiling slightly at the way his arms tightened around her. "That's why I ran to you. And then you pushed me away."

"I'm sorry." He feathered a kiss over her temple as he pulled the clip from her hair.

Brenna wondered if this was the first time he had ever apologized. The words sounded rusty, unused. "Just don't do it again," she ordered, snuggling closer.

"I won't." Another lie he would have to answer for, but what did it matter? Their time together was stolen, and he was greedy enough and selfish enough and weak enough to want to lose himself in her, in the illusion she offered. You're a bastard, Carlisle, he berated himself as his mouth came down on hers.

Bit by bit, Brenna felt the tension that had gripped her since morning ebb away as their embrace became more heated. He really wasn't the man she would have chosen for herself, she acknowledged as his hand found its way beneath the yellow sweater she wore. They really were wrong for each other. But then he had undone the front clasp of her bra and Brenna dismissed the thought in order to concentrate on the touch of his hand on her skin.

There had always been an element of leashed aggression in Mitch's lovemaking, but tonight the aggression was transmuted into something more primitive, a savagery that soon had them tearing at each other's clothing in a frantic attempt to get closer. Brenna, her flesh sensitized to his lightest touch, cried out when he stabbed the hard point of her nipple with the tip of his tongue, and sank her fingernails into his shoulders.

"No," she moaned when he levered himself away from her. "Don't you dare."

Mitch's body was vibrating with need. "I just want to get rid of my jeans."

Brenna forced her eyes to open and languidly ran a fingertip down the line of hair bisecting his stomach. The waistband stopped her. "Let me."

"Oh, God." Mitch's hand clenched into fists as she rose above him. Her sweater and bra were gone, somewhere beneath the harpsichord, he guessed, so her breasts rose and fell invitingly with each breath she took. She reached for him, one hand slipping inside the waistband of his jeans while the other danced across his chest, branding him. One swift motion took care of the snap and then her hand fell to his zipper. "Don't stop now," he gritted when her hand remained motionless, pressing against the swelling behind his fly.

Brenna felt an age-old smile curve her lips as the heady awareness of female power spread through her. "Not just yet."

Her mouth replaced her hand on his chest and then his bones dissolved when she drew one of his nipples into her mouth to experiment with it. He collapsed onto the floor, muttering words that dealt with love and lust, and then the breath was sucked out of his lungs when her mouth trailed its way down his stomach.

He tried to stop her, tried to regain the dominant position he had thus far enjoyed, tried to sink his hands into the wealth of hair tumbling around her shoulders, but his reflexes seemed to be off. Instead, Brenna caught his wrists and forced his arms back to the floor as she swung one leg across his lean hips to straddle him.

The sight of Mitch drowning in passion could become addictive, Brenna discovered as she smiled down at him through half-closed eyes. Her smile disappeared, however, at the one discordant note in the picture he made. Frowning, she bent forward to correct the error.

The tugging at his shoulders brought Mitch temporarily to the surface. "What—"

"I don't like this thing," she informed him petulantly, pulling at the shoulder holster. "Take it off."

"But—"

"Take it off," she repeated, her tone gone from petulant to persuasive. But not half as persuasive as the way she dipped her tongue into his mouth. "It's ruining my pretty picture."

"Can't have that," he agreed, not sure what she was talking about, but not really caring, either. He shrugged out of the leather harness and then the shirt, but made sure the holster remained within reach.

Brenna smiled in satisfaction. "Much better."

Mitch's sanity deserted him again when her mouth returned to its teasing exploration of his chest. She paid a great deal of attention to his nipples this time, apparently fascinated by his reaction to said attention. After exploring the cavity of his navel, she paused to catch her breath and lightly rested her cheek against the now-strained zipper.

"If you stop now, I'm dead," Mitch rasped.

"Who's stopping?"

She gave a seductive little wiggle and he pried an eye open in time to see her jeans land in a heap on the floor. The little piece of nothing she still wore hardly qualified as panties.

Mitch's mouth went dry. "Damn," he whispered. Usually she wore staid white cotton briefs.

"Like them?" Without waiting for an answer, she returned to his side and tugged at his zipper. "I've had them for years, but never had the, um, opportunity to wear them until now. I'm glad I saved them."

So was he, but all his attention was focused now on the way she was smoothing first the denim, and then the cotton briefs, down his hips and legs. The release from confinement provided a momentary relief, but her mouth soon followed the path of the material and the agony renewed itself. When she finally straddled him again, he groaned and rubbed himself against that equally vulnerable part of her in a paroxysm of need. His hands found her hips and moved her in an urgent response to his body's need.

Brenna shivered, feeling her own control slip away. "M-Mitch?"

"Okay, it's okay." His reassurance was harsh, guttural. His fingers slipped inside the panties, and with a fleeting regret, he ripped apart the fragile satin-and-lace barrier.

She fell against him, hot and moist, and Mitch shuddered, reaching the end of his control. "Get my jeans."

Brenna fumbled for them, then smiled when she saw him remove a foil packet from one of the pockets. "I wouldn't have minded." She meant it; right now, at this moment, the thought of carrying Mitch's child filled her with an unexpected delight.

He understood instantly, of course. How could he not, when the one thing he wanted was to permanently mark Brenna as his? His gaze locked with hers as he took the necessary precaution, and he shook his head. "You're too precious to waste."

"Oh, Mitch." Brenna's eyes brightened with tears when the full impact of his words and actions hit her. Though he had never said the words, he made her feel extraordinarily loved and cherished.

"Now, I want you to try that again," he growled, his fingers clenching into the resilient flesh of her buttocks. "Let's see just how inventive you can be, Professor."

Her smile was flirtatious, almost challenging, as she reached between their bodies to guide him.

"God," he moaned, arching upward until they were completely joined. Her hair fell in a curtain around them, deepening the intimacy of their act.

She was shattering under the impact of his possession, drowning in sensation. If only she could make him feel a fraction of the desire that was threatening to tear her apart . . . She rocked forward and felt his body tighten beneath hers, rejoiced in the harsh cry he uttered.

"Oh, baby, you feel so good," he growled, meeting her urgent movements with his own. He watched her through eyes grown hot with passion, saw the desperation she was feeling when she bit down on her lower lip. "I'm right here—let yourself go."

Brenna shook her head in despair, unaware of the tear that squeezed its way from between her eyelids. "It's too soon. I want this to go on forever."

"It will," he promised, insinuating a hand between their bodies. He didn't want this to end, either; he didn't want to return to reality. "Let yourself go," he repeated huskily. "Show me what I do to you."

Moments later the house echoed with the sound of their mingled cries.

Chapter 10

The following week was a hectic one. George and his crew were working at a fever pitch in the kitchen and Mitch soon gave up trying to create order out of the chaos they left in their wake. Instead of fighting with the hot plate, he and Brenna stocked up on disposable plates, silverware and glasses and fell into the habit of picking up dinner on their way home from campus.

On Monday evening they drove into downtown Minneapolis. There, Mitch was fitted for a tuxedo and, against his better judgment, allowed Brenna to drag him into the fray of maniacal shoppers while she searched out gifts for those on her list. Once he suggested using the skyway system, the enclosed heated corridors elevated above the streets, and she gave him a look of pure horror.

"The skyway is for wimps," she informed him loftily, buttoning her coat in preparation for stepping outside. "Why live in this country if you don't want to experience winter firsthand?"

A typical Brenna sentiment—romantic and wholly impractical, Mitch thought, following her through the revolv-

ing door. Personally he had had enough of winter to last him
for the next several years.

"When can we go home?" he asked, stepping onto the
sidewalk beside her.

"Soon." She was frowning over her list.

Mitch groaned. "Define soon." He had volunteered to
carry her accumulated packages and was beginning to regret his atypical gesture of chivalry. The lesson of the
weekend had not been forgotten, however; he constantly
swept the faces around them, searching for the one that appeared too often and showed too much interest in Brenna.
What concerned him most was that his hands were full;
presented with danger, he would be able to do nothing more
than knock her to the ground while he fumbled around for
his pistol.

"Just another hour, I promise," Brenna answered
laughingly.

There was something to be said for abandoning the sky-
ways in favor of strolling down the decorated Nicollet Mall,
he conceded as they walked past the beautifully adorned
store windows. Miniature lights were strung through the
bare branches of the trees interspersed along the mall and
swept around the modern streetlights lining the sidewalks.
The result was a dreamy, fairy-tale effect that lessened the
impact of the cold winter night.

Brenna turned from a particularly inventive window display to smile at him, and Mitch felt the breath catch in his
throat. Her cheeks were rosy, and her eyes reflected the
lights around them. She was, he decided, the most beautiful creature he had ever seen. And he was an absolute *fool*
to have allowed her to place herself in this precarious position.

"We're leaving now," he said gruffly, shifting the packages to one hand in order to take her by the arm.

"But, Mitch," she protested. "You agreed—"

"You're too exposed here," he interrupted flatly. The fear
that clouded her eyes caused him to soften. "Please,
Brenna, don't argue. I know you feel like a prisoner in your

own home, but at least I can protect you there. Once your life is back to normal, I swear I'll bring you back here and you can shop to your heart's content."

"I'll hold you to that," Brenna warned, freeing her arm in order to hold his hand.

Mitch's anxiety didn't ease upon returning home. Ordering Brenna to stay by the kitchen door in case there was trouble, he meticulously checked the alarm system and then searched each room for any sign of an intruder.

Brenna waited impatiently, even though she was accustomed by now to his precautions. Daily she grew more concerned over the fact that Mitch had no qualms about risking his own life to protect hers. The thought chilled her to the bone.

Later that night, lying in the cradle of Mitch's arms, Brenna listened to his deep, even breathing and admitted to herself that she had fallen in love with the man now holding her so closely. It wasn't the safe, sane love she had known with Brian; this was a wild emotion that consumed her, body and soul.

But Mitch didn't want love, or promises of forever. He had made that painfully clear on more than one occasion, and she, like a fool, had agreed to his terms. So what was she to do, now that she realized she had fallen in love with this man?

Brenna spent a long, sleepless night mulling over that question without reaching an answer. Nor did the answer come to her during the next two days. Instead, she tried to put some distance between herself and Mitch, as if a new perspective would give her the answer she sought.

The effort was a vain one, doomed from the start. He was so thoroughly entwined in her life by now that trying to ignore Mitch was like trying to cut out her heart with a dull knife. Such an act was beyond her, and Brenna found herself brooding over what would happen to their relationship once Mitch was no longer acting as her guardian angel. And that time was fast approaching, though she had managed to keep the knowledge from him. Last week, Steven had told her when Fedoryshyn was scheduled to leave Minneapolis.

"Professor Hawthorne?"

Brenna blinked owlishly, startled by the sound of her name, and brought herself back to the present. She was facing the blackboard, a piece of chalk in her hand and...she glanced over her shoulder. Eight bewildered faces returned her gaze, and Brenna sighed inwardly, remembering where she was. It was Wednesday evening, and the eight faces belonged to the graduate students enrolled in her night class. Seated in the back of the classroom, Mitch shook his head and grinned at her. Uncharacteristically her mind had drifted to the upheaval in her personal life instead of remaining on the lecture. And now Mitch—the man she loved to distraction—was laughing at her. Wretched man!

Embarrassed, she cleared her throat. "I seem to have forgotten what I was saying."

"You were discussing Robert Devereaux and the truce with Tyrone," Steven supplied from his seat in the front row.

That sounded about right, but Brenna had by now completely lost her train of thought, so she stepped back to the podium to consult her lecture notes. Eyeing Steven over the top of her glasses, she asked, "Then we covered Tyrone and Tyrconnel and the Ulster revolt in 1595?"

"Yes." Steven smiled reassuringly, adoringly. "And the two fleets Philip of Spain sent to Ireland."

Which brought her to 1599 and the truce with Tyrone, Brenna concluded, turning back to the blackboard to write the date there.

Brenna resumed the lecture, hesitantly at first, then with greater assurance, and Mitch chuckled to himself. Until now, her absentmindedness hadn't extended to the classroom, and he had been more than a little alarmed when she had walked to the blackboard and then just stared at it in silence. Where had her thoughts wandered? What was so important that it could distract her so completely? Mitch considered the questions for the next few minutes before giving a mental shrug. Whatever had preoccupied her, it seemed under control now.

Brenna's distracted air continued to grow throughout the week, however. She managed to hold herself together during lectures and discussions, but outside of the classroom her behavior was another story. It grew almost impossible to draw her into a conversation for any length of time; she seemed to tire of a subject and withdraw into that private world of hers where Mitch could not follow. He said nothing to Brenna, telling himself repeatedly that she was simply reacting to the strain she had been under lately. When she stopped talking to the cats, though, he became really concerned. This was definitely not his Brenna.

On Friday afternoon they returned to downtown Minneapolis to pick up his tuxedo. Brenna barely spoke to him during the ride home; her attention was all for the snow-lined streets.

Once inside the house, Brenna headed directly for her office and Mitch followed. "Okay, Professor, let's have it. What's bothering you?"

Brenna frowned at him with the same distracted air she had displayed all week. Waving at the tuxedo he had draped over one shoulder, she said, "You'd better hang that up before it wrinkles."

Mitch tossed the plastic-wrapped garment onto an armchair. "To hell with the monkey suit—I want to know what's wrong."

"Nothing's wrong," she answered, shrugging out of her coat and draping it over the back of the desk chair. "This is just a busy time for me, that's all." She turned on the computer and began rummaging through a box of diskettes. "Look, I have some final exams I want to prepare tonight. Could we talk later?"

He was about to reply that they would talk right now when the doorbell rang. Sending Brenna a sharp look, he inquired, "Are you expecting anyone?"

"No."

Sliding his right hand inside his jacket, Mitch unsnapped the safety strap on the holster and folded his hand around the pistol's handgrip. "Stay here," he ordered tersely.

Before stepping onto the porch, Mitch turned off the front-door alarms and flipped on the outside lights. A rather stocky masculine figure regarded Mitch curiously through the storm door as he crossed the porch. "Yes?" Mitch didn't open the outside door.

The other man appeared taken aback by his presence. "Is Brenna home?" he asked, trying to peer over Mitch's shoulder into the house. There was a certain amount of suspicion in his tone.

"Not if you're selling something." Mitch's grip tightened on the pistol when the other man reached for the door handle.

"Hardly," the stranger said dryly. "I'm Brian Hawthorne."

Mitch stared hard at the man. He had often wondered what kind of a man Brenna had married. "Really?"

"Yes, really," the visitor answered impatiently.

Even if Mitch had been inclined to believe the man—which he wasn't—the statement would only have added to the aggravation he had been experiencing. "What do you want?"

"To come inside and see Brenna before I freeze to death playing twenty questions," the man calling himself Brian Hawthorne snapped. "Any objections?"

"Not if you are who you say you are," Mitch answered tightly. "Show me some ID."

The man's suspicious expression changed to one of outright hostility as he yanked futilely at the locked storm door. "Brenna," he yelled, his voice echoing through the night air. "Brenna, are you all right?"

The menacing gesture was the last straw. In one swift movement, Mitch opened the door, grabbed the other man's jacket collar and hauled him into the porch. By the time the man opened his mouth to protest the rough treatment,

Mitch had already drawn his pistol and now jammed the barrel into his ribs. "Not a word. Inside."

Brenna stared in horror as the man Mitch shoved into the foyer fell to the floor. "Oh, my God!"

Both men spoke simultaneously: "Brenna, do you know this guy?"

It took Brenna several seconds to find her voice again. "Put the gun away, Mitch." Bending, she offered her hand to the man on the floor. "I'm so sorry, Brian."

Brian Hawthorne rolled to his back and glared at the armed man hovering above him. "Who the hell is this guy, Bren?"

"It's kind of a long story," she sighed, following his gaze to the unwavering pistol barrel.

"Is he going to shoot me if I get up?"

"No, he isn't," she said firmly, helping her ex-husband to his feet. "Mitch, please, you're making Brian and me very nervous."

Shrugging, Mitch jammed the pistol back in its holster. He had taken an instant dislike to Brian and honestly didn't care how nervous he made Brenna's ex-husband.

Brian unzipped his jacket and gave his former wife a long-suffering look. "Good God, Brenna! What have you gotten yourself into now?"

"Nothing," Brenna protested.

"Sure. That's why I'm nearly killed knocking on your door." He frowned. "Is this the cousin Marcia told me about?"

Mitch took off his own jacket and hung it on the coat tree. The holster and its contents were a none-too-subtle reminder of what had just transpired. "I'm going to make the coffee for tomorrow," he informed Brenna. "In the meantime, why don't you explain things to your ex?" Pivoting sharply on his heel, Mitch strode through the hallway to the dining room.

Brian stalked into the family room, leaving Brenna to trail reluctantly after him. She had no sooner entered the room than he turned to her with a glare. "What have you done this time?"

"I haven't *done* anything," she raged, her voice rising an octave. "Why do you always assume that I've done something wrong?"

"Remember me, sweetheart? I'm the guy who bailed you out of jail on more than one occasion." Tossing his jacket on the bar, he perched on one of the leather stools there. "What's going on here?"

Brenna tucked herself into a corner of the sectional couch and explained as clearly and quickly as possible why she was sharing her home with an armed man.

"Why didn't you tell Marcia that Carlisle is with the FBI?" Brian asked when she fell silent. He had poured himself a drink while she spoke, and he still held it in his hand, untouched.

"I didn't want her involved any more than was necessary," Brenna conceded. "And Mitch thought the story about his being my cousin would answer all her questions."

"Obviously he never met her at the door looking like Rambo." Brian smiled apologetically. "I think I blew it for you, Bren. I told Marcia I'd never heard of any Carlisle cousins on your side of the family."

"I know."

"So how did you explain my comment?" he asked.

Brenna blushed. "Yes, well, Marcia sort of made some rash assumptions that I didn't bother to contradict."

"This I've got to hear." Brian laughed. "You are such a lousy liar." When she simply stared at the unlit Christmas tree, he prodded, "Come on, Bren, let me in on the latest cover story so I don't make another mistake."

Sighing, Brenna said bluntly. "Marcia thinks Mitch and I are lovers."

Brian's reaction was unexpected; he burst into incredulous laughter. "What would give her a crazy idea like that?"

It had been a long, trying week, and the fact that Brian obviously considered her love life a laughing matter angered Brenna. "I did, as a matter of fact."

"Brenna the puritan involved with someone she just met," Brian chuckled. "Marcia knows you better than that."

"Or maybe you don't know me as well as you think you do," she retorted, her hands curled into small fists on her lap.

He eyed her indulgently. "I lived with you long enough to know that you don't take such things lightly. And besides, we both know you're not exactly a femme fatale."

Coupled with the uncertainty she felt over the future of her relationship with Mitch, Brian's remark, said with such casual certainty, cut deep. Avoiding his gaze, Brenna forced herself to reply calmly, "Yes, you're right. But that's the story Marcia believes and I'd appreciate it if you didn't tell her the truth."

Looking up, Brian found Mitch standing in the doorway of the family room, watching the two of them with what seemed to Brian an unnatural intensity.

Mitch had been eavesdropping and was unashamed of the fact, but he could hardly believe what Brian had just said. A cold anger flooded him as he took in Brenna's defensive posture on the couch. She wasn't aware of his presence yet, but she would be in a few moments.

Brian smiled politely, rose and offered his hand. "Brenna just explained everything, Agent Carlisle."

Mitch felt Brenna's startled gaze fall upon him. Ignoring Brian's civilized gesture, he made his way to the bar. "You're a real bastard, Hawthorne. Did you take cheap shots like that at Brenna while you were married?"

"Cheap shots..." A look of puzzlement crossed Brian's face.

"You didn't even hear what you just said, did you?" Mitch queried, unable to believe that the man could be so blind.

"Hear what?" Brian demanded in exasperation.

Mitch shook his head. "It doesn't matter." He took the glass from Brian's hand and gently set it on the bar. Scooping up the other man's jacket, Mitch thrust it against Brian's chest, then grabbed a handful of his sweater and lifted him off the bar stool.

Brenna was on her feet in an instant, protesting the potentially violent action. "Mitch, put him down!"

"This doesn't involve you," Mitch snapped. "Back off."

His will seemed to roll over her in an invisible wave, threatening, indomitable. "I will not," she argued, fighting the sensation.

"Just what the hell do you think you're doing?" Brian demanded belligerently, waging a losing battle as he was dragged into the foyer.

"I think it's obvious," Mitch replied, opening the front door and hauling his unwanted guest across the porch. Wrenching open the storm door, he launched Brenna's ex-husband down the steps and out onto the sidewalk. "And here's a piece of advice for you—stay away from Brenna."

Brian struggled to his feet and started back up the steps, his jacket and the cold forgotten. "Until now I never agreed with Brenna's views regarding the FBI and CIA, but I'm beginning to see her point." He hesitated before taking the final step that would bring him back to the doorway, level with the other man. "And I don't care for the way you're burying yourself in the role of outraged lover."

"Brian, no." Sensing the barely suppressed violence simmering in Mitch, Brenna tried to push her way past him, but he simply wrapped an iron arm around her waist, pinning her to his side. "Go home—I'll explain everything later."

Mitch fixed the younger man with a stony look, infuriated by the fact that Brenna felt she owed him any sort of explanation. But if that was the way she felt . . . "Explain it to him now, Brenna," he commanded, his voice harsh. "Tell your ex-husband all about my 'role.'"

Brenna paled as Brian's focus shifted to herself.

"What is he talking about, Bren?"

And in a sudden burst of insight, she realized what Mitch was doing—that he was forcing her to admit the truth. What she didn't understand was why Mitch wanted her to choose between himself and Brian.

The truth, Brenna instinctively knew, would end her friendship with Brian. Her tie to him would be irrevocably severed because of a man who may or may not be part of her future. Mitch wanted some kind of a declaration on her part without making any commitment himself. It was an unfair demand. He was asking too much of her. Drawing a shaky breath, she said quietly, "It's not an act, Brian, not anymore." She felt Mitch's fingers dig into her waist, and then he was pushing her behind him.

"You wanted a divorce," Mitch told Brian coldly, "you got it. Now live with it and stop hanging on to Brenna." He closed the door in Brian's astonished face and locked it, then urged Brenna into the house ahead of him.

Brenna stood uncertainly in the foyer, watching Mitch as he locked the inside doors and reset the alarms. She had made the declaration he had apparently wanted. Now it was his turn. "Why?"

Mitch stiffened at the single word. Turning, he met her gaze. "I lost my temper."

"You're a dangerous man, Mitch Carlisle. I knew that the first time I saw you. But you're dangerous because you're always in control." She slowly shook her head. "No, you didn't lose your temper just now, but you did use your anger. There's a big difference."

"Why, Professor, I didn't realize you also had a degree in psychology," he taunted.

"History is in many ways a study of psychology," she answered steadily. "Why did you want me to tell Brian about us?"

Mitch lit a cigarette before replying. "You don't need a jerk like that in your life, not even as a friend."

That was hardly the answer she was looking for. "Don't I?"

"No, damn it, you don't," he flared. "Hell, Brenna, he insulted you."

Brenna gave a sad little smile. "What he said was the truth. I'm no Helen of Troy—my face couldn't launch a rowboat, let alone a thousand ships."

Green eyes narrowed as they swept her from head to toe. "Don't sell yourself short," he ground out. "Men have killed each other over women like you."

She laughed softly, wryly. "Over an absentminded professor? I don't think so."

"The attraction has nothing to do with your vocation, or the way your face is arranged," he told her, his voice vibrating with intensity. "Although I find your face... unforgettable. Your attraction has everything to do with the passion you radiate, the strength and serenity that shows in everything you do. You make a man—" He stopped abruptly, realizing he had been about to say "feel whole." Until just now, he hadn't known how incomplete he had been. How incomplete he would be again, when he had to leave her. "Brian Hawthorne threw you away, and he's just beginning to understand what he lost. You deserve someone better than him the next time around," he finished lamely.

Without giving her a chance to reply, he reclaimed his tuxedo from her office and went upstairs. Brenna stared after him, astonished by his words. Returning to her office, the professional part of her mind went through the routine of preparing the tests while the rest of her considered what Mitch had said.

She was in the middle of the first test when she realized the sound of harpsichord music was floating through the house. The source wasn't her stereo; the music came from the second floor. He had lied about his keyboard abilities, she decided after a few minutes. He played beautifully, with a technical accuracy that would always be beyond her capability. He also instilled the notes with an incredible depth of emotion, causing the music to wrap around Brenna's heart and brand it with passion. It was also strangely calming after the turmoil of the evening. She smiled, letting the music surround her as she worked on the tests.

Two hours later Brenna turned off the computer and printer and slowly followed the music to its source. She watched Mitch silently from the doorway, fascinated by the ease with which his long fingers caressed the keys and the way his bright head was bent in concentration over the music.

"That was beautiful," she said softly when he completed the piece.

"Did I disturb you?" His gaze never wandered to her as he exchanged one piece of sheet music for another.

"No." So intense about everything he does, she thought, making no move to enter the room. She remembered the night he had lain her on the Persian carpet here and made wild love to her. He had been intense then, too, focusing exclusively on her. She shivered involuntarily. Sometimes his intensity could be frightening. "It's late," she observed.

Mitch's hands stilled on the music. There was an implicit invitation in her words and he forced himself to remain on the bench. He wanted her, accepted the fact that he would go on wanting her for the rest of his life, and the knowledge was cutting him to pieces inside. He knew also that there was no possible future for them, that by denying that simple truth he was causing them both pain. "Go to bed, Brenna." It cost him dearly to say those words, to keep his voice even, unemotional.

If he had expected an argument, he didn't get one. Instead, he listened to the sound of her retreating footsteps, heard the sound of the shower being turned on. Only when he was certain that she would not return did Mitch rise and replace the music he had taken from the shelves. Turning off the lights in the music room, he made his way to the bedroom Brenna had first assigned him and stretched out on the bed, wishing he could turn off his thoughts and emotions as easily as he had the lights. He couldn't. He kept replaying the scene in which, earlier this evening, Brenna had chosen him over Brian. Chosen a man who was living a lie over the one she had once married.

Mitch swore bitterly. Everything he did hurt her—or would, once he was gone—and he had never intended that. He had thought . . . what? That whatever was between them could be chalked up to lust and then forgotten? That he could take Brenna in his arms, into his bed, and then be on his merry way without having to pay a price for his manipulations? Yes, he admitted wearily, he had hoped that was exactly what would happen. How could he have known that the price of his time with Brenna would be his soul?

His only salvation now lay in not making the situation any more painful than it already was, in living out the deceit without loving her again. He prayed that Brenna did not feel for him what he felt for her, that she would be spared the agony of having another man betray her love.

Brenna lay on her side, watching the red digital numerals count the passage of time. It was now one o'clock in the morning, and she had long since exhausted her supply of tears. She had known what lay ahead when she emerged from the bathroom and found Jasper curled up in his usual spot on the bed—the side that Mitch had recently occupied. Why? she wanted to scream at Mitch. Why are you pushing me away again when we have so little time left?

Saturday passed quickly, despite the gloomy atmosphere that had fallen on the house. George and his crew worked all day, giving Brenna an excuse to retire to her office and close the door against the noise of their hammering. Mitch spent most of the day in the kitchen, helping where he could and making an endless supply of coffee. His head throbbed painfully, and he downed so many aspirin that by midafternoon his stomach was upset.

Needing to get away from the din for a while, he went into the family room and called Greg. Yes, his friend told Mitch, Fedoryshyn was planning to attend the dinner tonight. And yes, Greg planned to keep him under surveillance. Mitch hung up and sat down on the couch, resting his aching head against the back of the upholstery. He dozed, waking an hour later when he heard the scrape of furniture being moved.

"All done." George grinned at Mitch when he came back to the kitchen to investigate the sound. The crew had already replaced the kitchen table and chairs and was now working on the appliances. "What do you think?"

Mitch surveyed the reconstruction. The kitchen was all warm wood and ceramic tile; he could almost imagine the aroma of freshly baked bread. This room, like the rest of the rooms in the house, reflected Brenna. This was a home, an island of peace meant for loving and living. And he could never belong here.

"I think it's perfect," Mitch finally answered gruffly.

George nodded. "It suits the Doc."

"Yes," Mitch murmured. "It does."

"Well, I guess I better get her opinion."

"I'll get her," Mitch volunteered before George could take a step toward the hall door. He knocked at Brenna's office door, waiting until she called "come in" before entering.

He found her curled into the armchair, a stack of papers in her lap and her glasses firmly in place. She glanced up, then hurriedly returned her gaze to her work. "George is finished," he said when it became obvious she had nothing to say to him. "He wants your approval."

Pushing her glasses to the top of her head, she rose gracefully, placed the papers on her desk and walked past him. All without a word, her silence shredding his heart. He trailed Brenna and stood behind her when she entered the kitchen.

"Well," George inquired gaily, waving a hand at the room at large, "is this what you wanted?"

It was exactly what Brenna had wanted, right down to the old-fashioned drawer pulls, but she found no joy in the sight. She forced a smile. "It's perfect, George. Thank you."

George's enthusiasm flagged at her tone. "I told you we'd be done by New Year's and here it's not even Christmas. How's that for beating a deadline?"

Brenna nodded. "You and your people did a superb job."

"Is something wrong with the room," George inquired with a frown. "If there is, just say so and—"

"No, George, really, it's beautiful," Brenna assured him. "I—it's just been a long week. I'll get my checkbook."

"We'll bring the storage boxes up from the basement," George told her, "but we'll leave the unpacking for you."

"Fine." She went in search of her purse.

"She's had a lot on her mind," Mitch felt compelled to explain when the older man looked at him inquiringly.

Shrugging, George followed his crew down to the basement.

That evening Brenna studied her features in the mirror and sighed heavily. The sleepless night had taken its toll, so she tried to hide the shadows beneath her eyes and conceal her pallor by applying more makeup than she normally used. The last thing she wanted to do right now was suffer through the Christmas party with Mitch as her escort, but she couldn't back out at this point. Last night had proven that she had to be prepared to return to her old life once Mitch was gone.

Satisfied at last with her appearance, she added a final coat of mascara to her eyelashes and pulled her hair into a neat chignon, allowing a few wisps to escape at the temples and nape in order to frame her face. Moving to the bed, she donned the gown Marcia had delivered several nights earlier. She hadn't bothered to try it on; Marcia had promised that she would look fabulous in it, and Brenna had been too distracted to go through the effort of modeling the gown for her friend.

Thankfully the gown was historically accurate, with none of history's fashionable tortures such as the corsetlike farthingale. Instead, the gown, made of black velvet, had an inverted pyramid of a bodice that was boned and lined in order to achieve the narrow-waisted look that had been so in style centuries earlier. Brenna drew the material over her head, then struggled with the hooks—bless the modern convenience that could be concealed by seamstresses—that drew the cloth tightly against her waist.

Stepping to the cheval mirror in the corner of her bedroom, Brenna gasped when she caught sight of her reflection. Marcia had told her that this gown was not what she normally wore to the Christmas party, but she hadn't mentioned that its wide, square neckline cut across the top of her breasts before sharply angling upward so that her neck and most of her shoulders were bare. Appalled by the décolletage, Brenna barely noticed that the long, bell-shaped sleeves and the skirt's pyramid inset were made of a silver brocade that set off the black velvet to perfection.

Gathering up the full floor-length skirt in one hand—again, someone had been clever enough to build the padded bolster directly into the skirt—she scrambled to the phone and dialed Marcia's number.

When her friend answered, Brenna wasted no time on pleasantries. "What have you done to me?" she wailed.

Marcia chuckled unrepentantly. "Doesn't Mitch like it?"

"Never mind Mitch, *I* don't like it," Brenna cried. "Doesn't this little number come with a jacket, or a shawl or something to make it less . . . less . . . ?"

"Revealing," Marcia prompted. "Sorry, buddy, but what you have on was all the rage at the Tudor court. You might try a strand of pearls—Elizabeth I loved them."

"I don't own any pearls large enough to cover what needs covering," she gritted out, eyeing her reflection and trying to adjust the neckline with her free hand. "Marcia, I can't go out in public like this."

"I don't see why not," her friend answered. "This gown is a reproduction of one Elizabeth herself wore."

Brenna closed her eyes and counted to ten. Marcia obviously was not about to offer any of the other gowns in her collection, so she was left with the choice of wearing what she had on or changing into a modern evening gown. The only one she owned—one Brian had bought for her years ago—clashed horribly with her hair. "Didn't they wear ruffs or something?" she asked weakly.

"Not with that dress." When Brenna didn't reply, Marcia added, "Listen, I have some costume jewelry that will go perfectly with the gown. I'll run it over to you."

"I'm tempted to run *you* over," Brenna threatened, but Marcia had already hung up.

Turning to her closet, Brenna dug out a pair of satin-covered high heels that matched a street-length black cocktail dress she owned. Slipping her feet into them, she returned to the mirror and fiddled nervously with the neckline again.

The gown was really quite modest when compared with some of today's fashions, but she still felt—exposed. When the neckline crept back to its original position, Brenna sighed. It was a sure bet that she was going to stand the history department on its ear tonight. And yet...she hesitated, staring more closely at her reflection. She looked like a figure from the past, not herself at all. The gown was a perfect foil for her coloring and she looked...almost beautiful, nearly seductive.

Brenna smiled at herself, suddenly pleased with the image in the mirror. She was conservative by nature; her house, her wardrobe, everything about her was proper. And dull? she wondered suddenly. No, not dull, but quiet, understated. Perhaps Brian had never considered her beautiful or alluring because she had never considered herself to be any of those things. But tonight she didn't have to be herself; this was a costume party and she could pretend—

A sudden, imperious rap at her bedroom door cut into her thoughts. Marcia and her fake jewels had apparently arrived. While she had had time to adjust to the décolletage, she had her misgivings about drawing attention to it. "Come in," she said, not bothering to leave the mirror.

Mitch cautiously entered the room, thinking Brenna was in the bath. The familiar scent of her perfume permeated the air and all his senses kicked into overdrive. Last night had been pure hell; he had had to use every bit of willpower he possessed not to walk into Brenna's bedroom and beg her to take him back into her bed.

"I don't mean to intrude, but Marcia came to the door and practically threw this case at me. I don't..." His voice trailed off when he caught a flash of movement out of the corner of his eye.

At first he saw only her slender, velvet-covered back, then his eyes moved upward and came to rest on her reflection. She met his gaze in the mirror and Mitch lost his breath. "That's what you're wearing?" he managed hoarsely.

Nodding, Brenna did a slow pirouette in front of the mirror. He was wearing his tuxedo, but the top three buttons of the pleated shirt were undone and the bow tie straggled out from under his collar. He looked disheveled and rough and masculine and altogether desirable. Their eyes locked and a current of electricity sizzled between them.

Despite the hurt of last night, at this moment she wanted nothing more than to bring him to his knees with the same passion that was racing through her blood. A most un-Brenna-like thought, but it was in keeping with the evening, so she held on to it anyway. "Like it?" Almost idly she ran her fingertips around the neckline.

Seeing her like this tested the limits of his self-control. He wanted to run all the way back to France, to the château, where he could convince himself that he had not fallen in love. He wanted to kiss her until those challenging blue eyes closed and then carry her to the bed and make sweet love to her until neither of them could move. Dredging up the last bit of control he possessed, he extended the jeweler's box he held.

His eyes were so intense he might as well have been touching her, Brenna thought as she glided across the room. When she stood in front of him, she saw the heat in his glittering emerald gaze and smiled inwardly. "Thank you," she murmured, tugging the box out of his hand.

Nodding in response, Mitch started to back out of the room. Brenna's soft voice stopped him.

"Wait, please. I might need help with the clasp." Opening the box, she removed a wide choker, heavily encrusted with what appeared to be diamonds, and placed it around her throat. "Would you mind?" she asked, presenting her back to Mitch.

Reluctantly retracing his steps, Mitch grasped the ends of the choker and wrestled with the intricate clasp. His manual dexterity seemed to have deserted him somewhere along the way, or perhaps his clumsiness was due to the fact that whenever his fingertips brushed against the nape of Brenna's neck, he felt her shiver. When the clasp finally locked, he breathed a sigh of relief and stepped quickly away. "Done."

Turning, Brenna arranged the choker so that the tear-shaped stone that dropped from the center of it hung directly over the shadowed cleft of her breasts. "What do you think?"

A muscle worked in Mitch's jaw as he struggled with a series of rampant emotions. Shock came first; he'd seen Brenna in everything from demure suits to nothing at all, but wearing this gown and necklace, she positively radiated sensuality. Perhaps, he thought wildly, there was some truth to the theory of reincarnation; she seemed just as comfortable in her present attire as she did in jeans.

Desire came next; pure, unadulterated lust brought about a predictable physical reaction so strong that he nearly groaned aloud. Hard on the heels of desire sprang jealousy; he didn't doubt for a moment that when other men saw Brenna like this, they would react in exactly the same fashion he had.

The thin thread of control Mitch still held snapped. Stepping forward, he framed Brenna's face in his hands and brushed a teasing kiss over her lips. "You take my breath away," he whispered, staring into her darkened eyes.

Brenna's heart pounded wildly against her ribs. "Do I?"

His head dipped again for a more leisurely sampling of her mouth. "You know you do," he answered hoarsely. "Damn you, Brenna, you're not supposed to behave like this!"

Smiling, Brenna looped her arms about his neck, drawing him back to her. "Surprise," she murmured just before standing on tiptoe and pressing her lips to his.

Heat exploded through Mitch and he pulled her hard against his chest, his mouth opening hungrily over hers. Brenna's response was dazzling; her lips parted eagerly for the invasion of his tongue, and then she was answering his sensual quest with her own. A low growl rumbled from Mitch's chest, and she drove her hands into his hair when she felt him start to pull away.

Their kiss turned challenging, almost brutal in its carnality, and Mitch felt himself drowning in passion. Brenna's hands were at his back now, kneading his spine, and then they drifted downward, forcing their lower bodies together. Some part of him screamed for restraint, but his body refused to listen.

So when Brenna tugged at his jacket and let it drop to the floor, then opened the black studs on his pleated shirt, he didn't protest. Sighing happily, she came down off her toes and allowed her lips to trail down his throat for a thorough exploration of his chest.

Throwing back his head, Mitch gritted his teeth against her teasing movements, aware of the primitive sounds issuing from his throat. He slid trembling hands down to her breasts and swore under his breath when he discovered the gown's neckline would not accommodate his marauding touch.

Brenna laughed, the sound somewhat akin to a purr of satisfaction, and stepped back, out of reach. A wanton smile curving her lips, she reached behind her, and seconds later the velvet gown rustled to the floor.

If she had left Mitch breathless before, he was speechless now. Beneath the gown she wore modern, provocative garments guaranteed to bring a man to his knees. His eyes fixed on her black, lacy camisole, reveling in the way the material rose and fell with her breathing, before moving down to discover the black garter belt with matching hose and panties.

"Brenna." Her name emerged as a low moan and he jerked her back against him to reclaim her mouth. Sweeping Brenna up in his arms, he carried her to the bed and followed her down.

When their mouths separated long enough for them to draw a breath, Brenna whispered, "Why did you leave me alone last night?"

He didn't want to talk, didn't want to ruin the web she had spun about them both, so he smoothed away the satin panties she wore and caressed her. The sight of Brenna lying half-clothed with the choker sparkling in the lamplight, her hair a tumbled mass of waves, was the most erotic thing he had ever seen. He fumbled with his trousers, freeing himself from the material.

A sense of feminine satisfaction curled through Brenna as she met his glittering, emerald gaze. Whatever had kept Mitch away last night, she had apparently broken its hold on him, for he was touching her with liquid fire. And she loved him. Later, when all the complications were gone, she would tell him so. But now . . . now she would concentrate on desire, on the way his fingers had slipped inside her. Moaning, she arched against his hand and sank her nails into his chest.

"Love me, Mitch," she whispered, tugging at him.

She was warm and moist, welcoming. Unable to wait a moment longer, he drove into her and they both cried out at the sensations created by their joining.

"Slow down," Mitch rasped when she quickened the pace he tried to set. She ignored him, fought him for the embrace. "Baby, please, it's going to be over too fast if you don't—" And then he felt the contractions grip her and buried himself deeper, surrendering to his own release.

They surfaced long minutes later, their bodies still joined, their heartbeats and breathing returning to normal. He kissed her tenderly, stroking her hair, wanting to say so many things and unable to say anything at all.

Brenna slowly opened her eyes and smiled up at Mitch. "We're going to be late." Her voice was husky with sated desire.

He returned her smile, then frowned. "You do realize that we forgot one important element just now?"

She nodded, no longer smiling but very calm. "I don't mind—it felt so good."

"Yes, it did," he agreed, feeling himself stir once again at her words. Shaking his head when her eyes widened questioningly, he withdrew from her and stood. "We still have a party to attend."

"More's the pity." Brenna stretched languidly and allowed Mitch to pull her from the bed. She slipped into the discarded panties while Mitch put himself in order, then smiled teasingly when he handed her the black velvet gown. "Help me with the hooks?"

"Not a chance," he said wryly. "My helping you get ready is what led to this." He scooped up his jacket and pressed a quick, hard kiss on her mouth. "But later I'll be happy to help you out of the dress."

Brenna laughed delightedly as the bedroom door closed behind him.

The Christmas party was held at the student union, in one of the four ballrooms it offered, and a blast of conversation, laughter and music met them when Mitch followed Brenna to one of the open double doors leading into the area. He caught sight of Greg relaxing in a lounge area—along with several students—directly across the wide hall from the ballroom. Eye contact was all the acknowledgment the two men made before Mitch and Brenna entered the ballroom. Nearly all the women were dressed in period gowns, but only half of the men present were in costume. The other half, Mitch noted gratefully, wore tuxedos.

He stayed at Brenna's side as she greeted the different department chairmen and her colleagues, and then led her to the refreshment table. Wassail punch was poured into earthenware goblets and Mitch sipped at his while he surveyed the room, searching for his old enemy.

"What do you think?" Brenna asked, unaware of his preoccupation while she watched the dancers in the middle of the ballroom perform a stately pavane.

It took a moment for Mitch to realize she had asked the question of him. "I think you ivory-tower types tend to lose yourself in your work." He glanced at her and smiled, eliminating any sting his words may have inadvertently carried. "Actually it's like stepping into history."

Authenticity only carried so far, however. When they were seated at the long tables lining the walls, Mitch was relieved to see that the meal was designed for the modern palate and eating utensils were provided. Throughout the dinner the group of madrigal singers circulated throughout the ballroom, serenading the guests.

It was as the singers were performing in front of the table where Brenna and Mitch sat that he found Fedoryshyn. The Russian, dressed in a black suit rather than a tuxedo, was sitting at the small table reserved for the department heads and their wives.

Glancing up, Brenna saw where his gaze had wandered, and the joy went out of the evening. Mitch hadn't inquired about the length of Aleksei's stay, but everyone in the department knew when the Russian's sojourn would end. It was time to tell Mitch the truth—he would learn it soon enough.

Working up her courage, Brenna leaned toward Mitch. "Aleksei has finished his lecture series." When he turned to her with a puzzled frown, she swallowed nervously before adding, "I understand his flight leaves sometime tomorrow morning."

At first his mind refused to accept what she was saying, but once it did, Mitch felt anger and frustration race through his blood. And pain—he could not deal with the pain of having been deceived by Brenna. "How long have you known?" he asked in a calm, controlled tone that intimidated Brenna more than his shouting ever had.

"About the length of his series?" She shrugged helplessly. "Since the idea was approved."

"I see." His hand tightened around the earthenware goblet until his knuckles whitened. "And how long have you known that he would be leaving tomorrow?"

Try as she might, Brenna couldn't bring herself to hold his accusing stare. "Steven mentioned it to me last week."

Mitch gave a curt nod of acknowledgment. "But you didn't feel this was information I might want to know."

Brenna wet her lips. "I'm sorry. I should have told you, but I was afraid that it would change things between us, and I wanted . . . needed . . . time." Time to have you fall in love with me, she finished silently.

The guests were deserting the tables now, taking their places on the parquet floor to learn the steps to the galliard the dancers were teaching. Grabbing Brenna's wrist, Mitch hauled her to her feet and all but dragged her to an empty corner of the ballroom.

"Do you know what you've done?" he asked, coldly furious now. "Had I known Fedoryshyn's deadline, we might have been able to force his hand. The Bureau would have stepped up surveillance and caught him making the exchange. The fact that he's leaving tomorrow means that he's already accomplished what he came here to do, and thanks to you we missed it!"

"You don't know that." Brenna felt her hand going numb from the pressure he was exerting on her wrist, but she knew it was futile to try to pull away. "That Aleksei has something to do with Mark's disappearance has always been nothing more than an assumption on your part."

"You lied to me." The accusation was accompanied by a rough shake.

Brenna blinked away the threatening tears. "Not really—you never asked me how long the lecture series would run. I just didn't volunteer any information."

Mitch's face was implacable; the only visible expression of his rage was in the savage glitter in his eyes. It crossed his mind that he had not been totally honest with Brenna, either, that her sin of omission was no greater than his of commission, but he quickly pushed the thought aside.

"Mitch, please, I'm sorry—"

He released her wrist with a suddenness that spoke of disgust. "I trusted you, damn it!" That was what cut deepest; that he had finally allowed himself to trust someone and had been burned in the process.

Guilt twisted in Brenna's heart. He felt betrayed and she couldn't blame him. She linked her hands together to still their trembling. "If you'll just let me explain—"

"Save it," Mitch growled, lashing out at the cause of his pain. "I can't believe anything you say."

The tears spilled down her cheeks. "Don't say that."

"Why not, Professor? Does the truth hurt?" He bent toward her. "Is Fedoryshyn's departure the reason for the big seduction scene tonight? Since you knew I'd be leaving soon, did you want a farewell—" The word he used was obscenely explicit.

Brenna stifled a sob, unbearably saddened that he could even think such a thing. "I love you," she told him in a broken whisper.

Mitch laughed, an ugly sound that made Brenna cringe. "Right, Professor, and I love you." A hideous parody of a smile twisted his lips as he straightened, his shoulders squaring. "I have a phone call to make. Stay put."

He strode out of the ballroom before she could say another word in her defense. Mitch had said the words she ached to hear, but he had made them a travesty. Pressing herself more deeply into the shadowed corner, Brenna wiped at her cheeks and forced the tears away. Because of her own insecurity, she had unintentionally ruined their relationship. Knowing that Mitch would now walk out of her life was a mortal wound inflicted upon her soul. She wasn't sure she would ever recover from the loss.

"Brenna, you do not dance?" Aleksei had found her and now stood beaming down at her.

"Not tonight," she said with a feeble smile, wishing the man would simply disappear. If Mitch returned and found them together, there would be hell to pay.

Aleksei chuckled. "Nor I." He gestured at the dancers. "I think it is more fun to observe than to learn."

She nodded wordlessly, watching the couples glide across the floor, but her thoughts were on the man beside her. Mitch was wrong about Aleksei, she told herself. The man might be fatally boring as a teacher, but that didn't automatically qualify him as an agent for the KGB. In fact, there were two or three professors on the faculty who shared his fault, and they weren't associated with the CIA.

"You look most beautiful tonight," he complimented her when they had stood in silence for several minutes.

"Thank you." She had thought so, too, until Mitch had accused her of manipulating their lovemaking. Now she wanted to go home, lock herself in her bedroom and never see a period costume again.

"So sad," Aleksei said with a note of concern, watching a shadow pass over her face. "Come, let me get you something to drink."

The last thing Brenna wanted was more punch or Aleksei's company, but she could find no graceful way to decline. Allowing his hand to rest on the small of her back, she walked beside him to the refreshment table.

"It grows warm in here, no?" Aleksei questioned Brenna when he handed her a goblet.

Brenna nodded and sipped at the wassail punch. Not only the warmth, but the music and dancing, which she normally enjoyed and took part in, were giving her a headache.

Aleksei nodded to the set of doors just behind the table. "Some fresh air, perhaps?"

After a moment's hesitation, Brenna assented. If she could only get away from the noise and the crowd, perhaps she might be able to get through the remainder of the evening without bursting into tears again. Aleksei held one of the doors open for her and she slipped gratefully into a side hallway.

The sound of the party all but disappeared as the door closed behind them, and Brenna gave a small sigh of relief. Leaning against the wall, she closed her eyes. "This is much better, Aleksei," she said at last.

"Very."

She felt the goblet being tugged from her hand and slowly opened her eyes, frowning at him. If the man had brought her out here to make a pass—

"Now, please do not be difficult about this, Professor Hawthorne," he continued smoothly, setting the goblet on the floor and then reaching inside his suit jacket.

Brenna paled when he drew out a snub-nosed pistol and pointed it at her. "Aleksei!"

"We are going to leave now, through this side exit. Do not yell or try to attract attention, or I shall be forced to do something very unpleasant."

"Wha-what do you want," Brenna stammered, dazed by the nightmare quality of the scene.

The Russian smiled coldly. "I want the formula, Professor, and you are going to help me get it."

Chapter 11

It was the oddest sensation, Brenna thought with a clinical detachment, but her own house seemed suddenly unfamiliar to her. As did the man who sat on one of the kitchen counters, observing her with a mixture of frustration and amusement. At this point she had grown numb to the fact that Aleksei stood beside her, still holding a gun on her. She knew she was in danger, but she couldn't seem to keep that thought uppermost in her mind. The feeling of being in danger was superseded by the growing unreality of the situation.

"Aren't you going to welcome me back to the land of the living, Brenna?" Mark Prescott smiled idly and slid to the floor.

"I don't think so," she answered crisply, aware of the white-hot rage that had risen within her when she had recognized the man waiting for them in the dimly lit kitchen. Standing in front of her was the reason her life had been torn apart the past few weeks! Her anger finally had a definite target. "You haven't been resurrected, Mark—you've just reappeared."

Mark's smile didn't waver as he approached. "Mere semantics."

Brenna's rein on her temper snapped. Before she realized what she intended to do, her right arm had swung up and back and hit Mark's smiling face with enough violence to stop him in his tracks. "You son of a bitch," she hissed, bearing down on him to press the attack. An arm snaked around her waist and yanked, stilling her progress. "The FBI was right. You did sell the formula for your superconductor. To Aleksei here."

His smile was gone now. Mark had taken a step backward and was trying to rub away the imprint of her hand upon his cheek. He glanced at Aleksei and then looked back at his attacker. "They guessed that, did they?"

She nodded, holding herself stiffly away from the man behind her. "That's right."

Mark chuckled. "That explains the arrival of your 'cousin' and the new alarm system in your house."

That was what she had been unconsciously waiting for, Brenna realized with a sinking feeling. She had expected the alarms to go off when Aleksei pushed her through the back door into the kitchen. "How—" She couldn't force the rest of the question past her lips.

"Your remodeler's crew stops at the same bar every night after work. All I had to do was sit fairly close and listen." Mark dug into his jacket pocket and slapped four batteries onto the counter. "Once I knew what to look for, the rest was easy."

"Get on with it," Aleksei urged, releasing Brenna and stepping aside. "Sooner or later the agent assigned to watch her is going to look for her here."

Mark sighed. "I'm afraid he's right, Brenna. We don't have the time for a nice long chat. Not yet." Gesturing to the clutter of packing boxes in the room, he continued, "When I left the formula here, sure this was the safest place I could find, I had no idea you were planning to dismantle your kitchen. You can imagine my surprise when I broke in and found this room a shambles. I started to search the rest of the house, but you unfortunately woke up."

"Thanksgiving evening," Brenna clarified, fitting the pieces of the puzzle together. "Were you also my mysterious caller?"

"Guilty as charged—although I did run my voice through some very high-tech equipment so that it wouldn't be recognized."

"Enough!" Aleksei's voice cracked impatiently through the room. "We are wasting time. Get the formula."

A sulky look flitted across Mark's face before he nodded in agreement. "Which box are the wind chimes in, Brenna?"

She frowned at him, nonplussed. "What do my wind chimes have to do with anything?"

"Not your wind chimes," Mark corrected her pleasantly enough. "My wind chimes. I didn't think you'd notice another set, and I see I was right."

"I don't know where the chimes are," Brenna said when Aleksei kicked one of the boxes. "The remodeler packed them."

"Then start looking," the Russian ordered coldly, leveling the gun at her once again.

There was no escape; she had known that the minute Aleksei had shoved the pistol against her ribs. Her only hope was to stall and hope that Mitch would think she had left the party because of their argument and gone home. As she emptied the first box, she prayed that Mitch would come for her.

Brenna alone with the Icon. Alone and undoubtedly frightened, bewildered by the violence she would surely sense in the Russian. A flicker of memory darted through Mitch's brain. A park in Vienna. Death, swift and sudden, dealt out in order to preserve one agent's integrity, to eliminate all proof of his activities. Activities to which Brenna was now a witness. Mitch closed the thought away; to save

Brenna, he couldn't afford the distraction of thinking about her.

"Let me call the FBI or the cops," Greg pleaded from the passenger side of the front seat. "At least they can keep the situation contained." They were headed toward the Hawthorne woman's house now, after having searched for the Icon at his off-campus apartment.

Contained. An innocent word, Mitch acknowledged, but not in the jargon he and Greg used. Another, more appropriate term was *damage control*. The FBI and police could cordon off Brenna's home, make certain that the Icon didn't kill an innocent neighbor, but they couldn't ensure Brenna's safety.

"No. We'll handle it on our own."

"Teach—"

"I said no, damn it! This has to be done my way."

Muttering under his breath, Greg subsided back to his side of the seat.

Hang on, baby, Mitch thought as traffic ground to a halt because of an accident somewhere ahead. Just hang on, I'll get to you.

Brenna wished she had worn a watch. Half a dozen boxes had now been emptied, but how much time had passed? An hour? Surely by now Mitch had grown concerned by her absence. Despite their argument, he still felt responsible for her and was no doubt searching for her. But would it occur to him to look for her here? Never had she been so aware of the passage of time.

Brenna lifted a layer of tablecloths out of the box she was working on to reveal a jumble of wind chimes occupying the bottom. They were a mess, she noted sadly, having simply been tossed into the container without thought, so that wires and rods were hopelessly intertwined. It would take hours of careful work to untangle them without inflicting further damage.

"I've found them." Her voice sounded very small in the room.

Mark roughly elbowed her aside, sending her sprawling, and began pawing through the collection. A set of stained-glass chimes were heedlessly thrown onto the floor and shattered into a hundred shards. Brenna cried out in protest, but fell silent when Aleksei drove his fingers into her hair and gave her a furious shake that ruined the neat chignon.

"Remain quiet," he ordered, looming threateningly over her. "I do not wish to harm you."

Brenna edged away from him before getting shakily to her feet. She automatically smoothed the tumbled mess of hair back from her shoulders. "You mean you're going to let me go?"

"Of course."

The reassurance was smooth, too smooth for Brenna's peace of mind. "You're lying."

Aleksei shrugged. "I have diplomatic immunity. The worst your government can do is force me to leave the country." He jerked his head back toward Mark, who was still busy mauling the chimes. "You can testify against him, of course, but that does not concern me. My task is simply to exchange money for merchandise. Mr. Prescott must make his own arrangements."

"Here!"

The triumphant shout focused both Brenna's and Aleksei's attention on Mark. And the large, pewter-colored wind chime he held clenched in his fist.

Such an ugly thing, Brenna decided, to have caused all the trouble of the past few weeks. And she couldn't imagine why she hadn't noticed it hanging in her kitchen. She would never have chosen such a cold, geometric monstrosity for her home.

"The formula?" Aleksei sounded eager.

Mark took a retractable pointer from his shirt pocket and probed the hollow center rod. A moment later he pulled a rolled sheet of clear mylar from the cylinder. When he unrolled the thin plastic, the symbols written there became all too legible.

"This is the formula," he told Aleksei as he secreted the mylar once again. "The week before I dropped out of sight, I forwarded my lab notes to your people through a series of dead-drops." He lifted one of the angular figures for the Russian's inspection. "These are samples of the ceramic. As you can see, it remains stable at room temperature."

"Excellent," Aleksei breathed, a broad smile lighting his face. Moving away from Brenna, he reached for the chimes.

Mark pulled away before the Russian could touch the ceramic. "There remains the small matter of your final installment payment."

"Of course," Aleksei agreed genially.

The gunshot didn't sound at all like it did at the movies. Instead of a loud report, there came a muffled expulsion of air, and Mark was thrown against the wall. His mouth worked soundlessly for endless seconds before his body sagged to the floor. It took several moments for Brenna to realize that Aleksei had added a silencer to the weapon's barrel—and that Mark was dead.

"Mark!"

Instinctively Brenna started toward the fallen man. She had taken no more than two steps when the back door was blasted off its hinges. Stunned by the onslaught of light and sound, unable to react or think clearly, Brenna felt herself grabbed around the waist by Aleksei and dragged to the far side of the kitchen. Into shadows, she noticed, because the kitchen lights had gone out at the same time the door had been destroyed.

"Professor Hawthorne?" The disembodied inquiry followed a cloud of smoke into the room.

Brenna's heart sank at the unfamiliar voice. She had so desperately hoped—

"Professor Hawthorne?"

Aleksei jabbed the gun against her ribs. "Answer."

It took a moment to find her voice, but she finally replied, "Yes, I'm here."

"Fedoryshyn, I want to talk. Agreed?"

The Russian hesitated briefly. "I have a gun on the woman. If you threaten me in any way, I will not hesitate to kill her."

"Understood. I'm coming in."

The man who came into the shattered doorway was vaguely familiar. When he stepped into the kitchen, into the pool of light created by the moon, Brenna recognized him as Mitch's partner. Her knees threatened to buckle as relief swept through her.

"You know this man," Aleksei demanded sharply with a second nudge at her rib cage.

Brenna nodded. "He's with the FBI."

Greg took another step into the room, his gaze finding the dead man on the floor before sweeping back to the Russian and his hostage.

"You are not alone." Aleksei's voice was flat.

"No," Greg admitted, wishing he really had the backup the Icon thought he had. "I've been sent to deliver our terms. Unless you want to cause a diplomatic incident, we demand you free Professor Hawthorne and return the formula."

The Russian's eyes cut to the body, then back to the man framed by the doorway. "And that?"

"He was guilty of espionage."

"And myself?"

"We'll put you on a plane, quietly, with no fuss or reporters. You'll be back in Moscow before the story breaks. After that, we leave the mess to the diplomats. Your embassy will probably negotiate with our State Department and an accommodation will be reached. You won't be allowed back into our country, of course."

Aleksei gave a soft, unamused laugh. "I find your terms unacceptable."

Brenna felt the recoil of the handgun a scant heartbeat before she heard the puff of air. Mitch's partner fell backward across the threshold.

"Now, Professor." Aleksei laughed in her ear. "Let us see what other surprises the FBI has in store for us." Pausing at

Mark's body, he indicated that Brenna free the wind chime from the dead man's grip.

Brenna did so reluctantly, then clutched the ceramic material in both hands as Aleksei used her as a shield when they stepped from the house into the night. No spotlight greeted them, no voice challenged their progress toward Aleksei's car. Brenna bit her lip in an effort to keep from crying out for Mitch.

Mitch's absence apparently worried the Russian also. "Where do you suppose your bodyguard is?" he whispered, shifting the barrel of the pistol from her ribs to her temple. "And the rest of the FBI?"

She was too frightened to answer.

They had reached the car without incident. "Like we did at the college," Aleksei instructed her. "Open the passenger door and slide behind the wheel."

Brenna fumbled awkwardly with the door handle, dropping the wind chime in her clumsiness. Aleksei swore at her, told her to retrieve it, then went abruptly still.

"Hello, Aleksandr." A form resolved itself out of the shadows by the house.

"Mitch," Brenna whispered, then gave a sharp gasp when the gun barrel dug more sharply against her temple.

"I will kill her." Aleksei made the statement so calmly that he might have been commenting on the weather.

"I know." Mitch stood motionless, the automatic pistol he held pointed at the ground. "I've seen you do it before. In Vienna."

Brenna felt the sudden tension run through Aleksei and wondered at it.

"It was you I shot at?" Aleksei studied the man confronting him. "I thought I killed you."

"Almost," Mitch replied softly. "It took me a while to recover."

There was no emotion in the other man's voice or face, and that worried Aleksei. "So you are here for revenge."

"No—" His eyes flickered to Brenna. He was running out of time. Brenna's neighbors, being the good citizens they were, had undoubtedly called the police at the sound of the plastique blasting through the back door. "I only want the woman."

"I told your friend that your terms were unacceptable."

Mitch didn't look to where Greg was lying. His arm came up, steady as a rock, until his pistol was leveled at the small part of the Russian not blocked by his hostage. "I won't let you leave with the woman. If I do, she's as good as dead."

Brenna shuddered at his words.

"And the formula?"

"You can have it," Mitch replied evenly. "Luckily Prescott's assistants kept a set of lab notes he didn't know about. They can duplicate the ceramic in a month." The lie rolled smoothly out of his mouth. He would do anything—say anything—to keep Brenna alive. Nothing else mattered.

"That is not what your partner said."

"Greg played by the rules—I don't."

Aleksei chuckled. "And I am to believe that I can pick up the formula and drive off unharmed—as long as I leave the woman behind?"

Mitch inclined his head ever so slightly. "Exactly."

"The FBI is suddenly very generous."

"There's no one else here," Mitch said, answering the Russian's unasked question. "No roadblocks down the street, and no one waiting for you at the airport. This agreement is between you and me."

"In that case, I can hardly refuse."

Brenna had heard that complacent tone only twice before, but she recognized its significance immediately. Fedoryshyn used it to lull his victim into a false sense of security just before he struck. And Mitch presented a perfect target.

This time Brenna felt the lessening pressure of the gun barrel against her temple as her captor prepared to turn the weapon on Mitch—the man she loved. "No, Mitch!" She moved at the same time she screamed, throwing her weight against Fedoryshyn and reaching frantically for his arm.

She heard the puff of air that meant Fedoryshyn had fired, and then a deafening explosion from farther away. Mitch had fired also. The Russian released her and threw himself into the front seat of the car.

"Damn it, Brenna, get away from the car!" Mitch had dropped to one knee, the pistol now supported in both hands.

Brenna tried to comply, but the footing was treacherous. She heard the sound of glass shattering, and then her feet hit a patch of ice and she was thrown headfirst onto the driveway. The fall stunned her, and as she lay there fighting for breath, the car behind her roared to life and tore out of her driveway, its tires screeching for traction.

"Brenna!"

Her name was an anguished cry, and then she felt Mitch's hands on her shoulders, gentle, but nothing less than demanding as he turned her over. She winced, feeling the effect of the fall on bones and muscles, and gave a hushed cry of pain as he pulled her into his arms.

Something within Mitch crumbled at the tiny sound. He had seen Fedoryshyn fire wildly through the car windshield and hoped that the bullet had missed Brenna. "Sweetheart, where are you hit?"

She focused on his question, on the urgency behind it, and shook her head. "I just had the wind knocked out of me."

"Thank God." Mitch gathered her close, hearing the distant wail of approaching sirens. Lights had come on throughout the cul-de-sac, neighbors were now hurrying toward them, and he wished that time would stand still. The end had come too quickly, leaving so much unsaid between them—too much to be explained in the few moments of privacy left to them. "I love you, Brenna."

He wasn't sure if he thought the words or whispered them into her hair, but by then it didn't matter. Police cars slid to a halt on the street just as Ted found them huddled on the driveway.

What happened next passed in a shock-induced haze for Brenna. The police drew a chalk outline on the floor around

Mark before allowing the coroner to take the body away. Brenna, sitting on a chair in the kitchen, averted her eyes when the green, zippered bag was brought out. She couldn't bear to witness the gruesome scene.

She was aware of Mitch holding her hand between both of his, of tears coursing down her cheeks, their flow unstoppable. They had started when the paramedic team arrived and discovered that Mitch's partner, Greg, was alive. Aleksei hadn't missed—Greg had two broken ribs to prove that—but the Russian hadn't known that Greg was wearing a bulletproof vest. When Greg had returned to consciousness and grinned weakly at Brenna, she had begun to sob uncontrollably and cling to Mitch.

Nothing was as it appeared, she discovered. Greg was alive and Mitch had lied about the formula to Fedoryshyn. The ruthless, dedicated FBI agent had, in the end, been willing to sacrifice his case for her life. She wanted to tell him how grateful she was, but she couldn't seem to find the words.

Marcia burst onto the scene, her take-charge attitude a blessing. She locked the cats upstairs so they wouldn't get in the way, made pot after pot of coffee for the investigators and directed traffic in and out of the house. The press had arrived, and Marcia made certain that they kept to the street.

It wasn't until the FBI arrived, with Special Agent Keith Johnson in the lead, that Mitch released Brenna.

"Greg is being taken to the hospital," Mitch informed the other man. "I'm going with him."

The FBI agent didn't bother to conceal his hostility. "You do that. When we're finished with Professor Hawthorne, we'll meet you there."

"Mitch?" Brenna swiped ineffectually at her eyes, feeling panicked by the withdrawal of his support. The emotion must have shown on her face, because he gave her a small smile of reassurance.

"I'll be back soon," he promised, ignoring the sharp look Johnson sent him. "Don't worry—you're safe now."

Just that quickly, Mitch was gone and Brenna was left alone with Special Agent Johnson. Accepting a plastic evidence bag containing Mark's wind chime from one of his men, the FBI man crouched in front of Brenna. "Now, Professor Hawthorne, what can you tell me about the wind chime?"

The police and FBI finally left three hours later, satisfied with their preliminary questioning. Both agencies would be back later, to make sure their reports were complete, but for now she and the cats had the house to themselves.

Her neighbors had taken it upon themselves to nail what remained of the kitchen door back into its frame, brace it with an odd assortment of lumber gleaned from their garages and cover the whole thing, inside and out, with plastic. The result wasn't pretty, but it would do until she could contact George to replace it.

Finally, blessedly, alone, Brenna went upstairs to free the cats and indulge in a long, hot shower. When she emerged from the bathroom, she discovered that she was simply too physically exhausted to go downstairs and wait for Mitch to return. She wouldn't be able to sleep, Brenna knew, but the bed offered warmth and comfort. Leaving the bedside lamp burning, she crawled under the covers and stroked Jasper, who was curled into a contented ball at her side.

As she had feared, images of everything that had happened with Mark and Fedoryshyn flashed through her mind, more frightening now, in the aftermath, than they had been when they had taken place. A trick of the mind, she told herself. The shock was wearing off and she could feel herself shaking from head to toe.

She had to think of something else. Something pleasant. Such as the fact that she now remembered Mitch saying he loved her. Despite her anxiety, Brenna smiled. In a way, tonight's terrible events had acted as a catalyst. Left to his own devices, Mitch might have waited months to reach that conclusion.

"Hurry home, Mitch," she whispered aloud. "Have I got a surprise for you."

* * *

His shoulder hurt like hell. Oddly enough, until the paramedic pointed out the dark splotch on his tuxedo jacket during the ride to the hospital, Mitch hadn't been aware that he had once again been the target of Fedoryshyn's bullet. His concern had all been for Brenna.

Fortunately the bullet had missed everything vital and simply caused a clean, in-and-out wound. The doctor in the emergency room had wanted to hospitalize him, but Mitch had vetoed the idea. He and the doctor had engaged in a running argument until Keith Johnson finally arrived. The FBI man filled out the necessary paperwork, and Mitch and Greg had walked out of the emergency room an hour later.

"The Bureau wants you out of the state before the press starts nosing around," Keith informed the two men when they were safely in his car.

"Nothing like ingratitude," Mitch growled from the back seat, trying to brace his aching shoulder in a corner to minimize the jarring.

"The two of you posed as FBI," Johnson said condemningly. "You broke God knows how many laws, and you sure as hell violated the Hawthorne woman's civil rights. My job now is to make a damage assessment and find a way to keep Professor Hawthorne from telling her story to every reporter in the country." He glanced at Greg out of the corner of his eyes. "And Langley is eagerly awaiting your arrival. I think you can both kiss your retirements goodbye."

Greg told the FBI man what the government could do with its pension.

"Where are we going?" Mitch asked when they had been on the interstate for several minutes.

"To the airport," Keith answered. "You're both booked on the five-o'clock flight to Washington. I get the honor of baby-sitting the two of you until you board the plane."

So there would be no opportunity to see Brenna again, to explain everything that had happened. Mitch sighed, lit a cigarette and told himself that it was better this way. Brenna didn't need a man like him in her life and he certainly didn't need her! What good would a history professor be to a counterterrorist?

It was a nice, logical conclusion. The only problem was that his heart didn't buy his reasoning.

Chapter 12

"At least you know who Mitch *doesn't* work for," Marcia offered encouragingly.

It was a February afternoon and the two women were sitting at Brenna's kitchen table, drinking coffee and poring over the books on government agencies Brenna had checked out from the library.

Looking at her friend over the top of her glasses, Brenna uttered a disgusted, "Big deal. I've eliminated one agency out of God knows how many. What I wanted from Agent Johnson was a clue as to which agency Mitch works for." Showing up at the local FBI office this morning to confront Special Agent Johnson had failed to yield any information on either Mitch or Greg Talbott.

Both men had disappeared the night of Mark's murder as if they had never existed. The only proof Brenna had that Mitch had been in her life was the clothing and shaving articles he had left behind. And the memory of him whispering "I love you."

"Maybe you're going about this wrong. Why don't you try reaching him at home?"

"I already tried that. Directory assistance doesn't have a listing for either Mitch or Greg in the D.C. area. If Mitch was telling me the truth, he keeps a very low profile." Brenna sighed, studying the list of names and phone numbers she was working on. "The problem is that Mark's case could fall under the jurisdiction of several different departments. And anyone I speak with could lie to me and I wouldn't know the difference."

"Maybe you should drop the whole thing," Marcia suggested quietly. "I mean, your average guy doesn't just vanish into thin air, Brenna. Maybe there's a reason he hasn't been in touch."

"I'm sure there is," Brenna replied mulishly. "But I've spent a month wondering and worrying and crying over the man and now I want some answers."

The phone interrupted their conversation and Brenna answered it with a frown. There was no immediate response to her greeting, so for several seconds Brenna listened to background noise. Judging by the sounds of voices and footsteps, whoever was calling was doing so from a public phone.

Just when Brenna was ready to hang up, a man spoke. "Take down this number and extension. It will put you in touch with the younger man."

Brenna's pen scratched furiously over her notepad while the man spoke, and then she was listening to a dial tone. She disconnected the portable receiver and stared at what she had written.

"Who was that?"

"He didn't give his name." Brenna slid the pad across the table. "Recognize the area code?"

Marcia shook her head. "What are you going to do?"

Brenna reached for the receiver again. "This is the only clue I've got."

"You think the FBI—"

"I don't think anything of the sort," Brenna interrupted with a smile, wondering what had caused Agent Johnson to change his mind. "The FBI gave me their answer this morning, remember?'' She held her breath as the call went through.

Thinking she was braced for anything, Brenna found herself totally unprepared for what happened when the ringing stopped and a man answered, "CIA, Langley."

She forced the extension number through lips gone suddenly wooden. The call was routed and picked up on the third ring.

"Greg Talbott."

The sunlight was magnifying his hangover into titanic proportions. Mitch slid on his sunglasses as he watched the two cars playing bumper tag along the winding road hewn out of the woods surrounding the château. This was the final day of the evasive-driving course being taught to four corporate chauffeurs. Tomorrow the men would learn to detect and disarm car bombs.

Turning to Maureen, the supervisor of today's activity, he said, "Run them through once more, then call it a day. I want them nice and rested for tomorrow."

Maureen nodded in response and walked off to where other members of her team were standing. Mitch watched for a few more minutes before returning alone to the château.

The château was a busy place now. Mitch's staff stood guard both within and without the building and they all noted his movements. Inside, Mitch nodded curtly to the man standing at the foot of the stairs and retreated to the darkened library. He was spending more and more time here.

Resisting the urge to go directly to the bar and pour himself a large Scotch, Mitch collapsed onto a leather wing back chair and closed his eyes. He must have dozed, for the next thing he knew, Maureen was shaking him awake.

"Lunch is ready."

He shook his head. "You go ahead. I'm not hungry."

Maureen sighed. "The garage called. The Mercedes will be repaired in a week."

"A week." Mitch winced inwardly, remembering exactly why his car was sitting in a body shop. Alcohol wasn't the only cause of his aching head.

"You're lucky the thing is armor plated," she informed him tartly. "Most of the damage was to the tree you hit. Which, by the way, I have two men working on."

Mitch grunted and closed his eyes again. "I always said you were efficient."

"I used to be able to say the same about you," she retorted. "Until you returned from that little jaunt of yours to the States."

"Drop it, Maureen."

She ignored the warning in his voice. "You are fast becoming a hazard around here, Mitch. You snap at everyone and you drink when we're working. You never used to touch anything stronger than mineral water until an assignment was over."

"I've turned over a new leaf."

"Well, turn it back," she snapped, determined to find what had caused such a change in her boss. "Quite frankly, none of us want to work with you tomorrow. The fact that you're carrying a loaded weapon is making us all nervous enough— God knows what will happen if you're handling plastique or dynamite."

"Maureen, I don't need a lecture right now," Mitch groaned.

"I agree. What you need is a hard kick in the butt!" She leaned down so that their faces were within inches of one another. "I'm warning you. You had better get rid of whatever extra baggage you're carrying around up here." She tapped his head—hard—for emphasis. "Until you do, you're no good to anyone here. Least of all yourself."

She was right, Mitch admitted when he was alone once again. His mind hadn't been on his work since he'd returned, and in his business that could literally mean the difference between life and death.

He had thought that all he needed was time—time to forget an auburn-haired history professor, time to convince himself that what he felt for her had been nothing more than lust. He'd had six weeks, and while his shoulder wound was healing, the hole in his heart seemed to be growing. He felt hollow inside, almost numb, except for the night, when he dreamed about Brenna only to wake up to an empty bed. That was when the pain set in, a sorrow so relentless that he was sure he would die from it.

And he was so lonely. Not even the presence of his employees eased that feeling. They seemed to exist in their own world, so that nothing they said or did actually touched him. He had always been alone, and enjoyed the solitude, but this feeling was different.

He felt so isolated, and so flat-out miserable, that he had begun drinking. The accident with the Mercedes had only served to make his problem obvious to the others. Until last night, he had been content to get quietly drunk and fall into bed. Last night frustration and anger had overwhelmed him. Determined to exorcize his demons, he had recklessly taken his prized vehicle to the evasive-driving track and tried to negotiate the hairpin turns.

Now he had a knot on his head from hitting the steering wheel—he hadn't bothered to fasten the shoulder harness—and his Mercedes had a bashed-in front end. Both his head and the car could be fixed, but he couldn't seem to find a cure for his heart.

The library door opened quietly, and looking up, he saw Maureen entering the room with a lunch tray.

"Since you're determined to be a hazard to your employees, you may as well eat something," she said forcefully, practically daring him to argue the point.

"No more lectures, Maureen," Mitch requested.

"Oh, I don't intend to lecture you," she assured him. "After all, you're the boss. You're the one who insists that if anyone exhibits any sign of stress or fatigue, he or she is on a mandatory thirty-day vacation. I want to own my own company—that way I won't have to follow the rules, either."

"You've made your point," Mitch growled. He had to do something, had to snap himself out of the emotional paralysis that was controlling him before he presented more of a danger to his staff and customers than the terrorists did. Scrubbing his hands over his face, he asked, "Can you handle the last phase of the training?"

Maureen widened her eyes in mock horror. "Alone? Without the resident time-bomb walking around? Heavens, whatever shall I do?"

"Can the smart talk," he replied, rising. "Just don't foul up the contract."

Maureen firmly clamped her mouth shut around the words threatening to emerge. She did smile, however, when Mitch used the phone to reserve a seat on the next available flight to the United States.

The music room—the one room in the house that had been her exclusive domain during her marriage—had lost some of its tranquility, Brenna thought as she sat at the harpsichord. Mitch was here, too, just as he was in every other room of the house. She could sell the house, but that wouldn't stop her from remembering. Nor did she want to.

No, what she wanted was to talk to Mitch, find out why he had run away. That was the message she had pleaded with Greg Talbott to get to Mitch. She had to depend on Greg because Mitch wasn't at Langley; he was out in the field and Greg wouldn't say where.

"Professor Hawthorne, I'll do my best," Greg had promised. "But please, don't count on Mitch getting in touch with you. There's too much you don't know about him, about his life."

"So I have no pride," Brenna now muttered to herself as she played. "Everyone's entitled to make a fool out of themselves once in this life."

It was late, and Brenna was making a last check of the house to make sure all the doors were locked when the front doorbell rang. Frowning, she hurried down the hall from the kitchen and opened the door.

And stared at the blond, green-eyed man glowering down at her.

"Damn it, Brenna! Didn't I teach you not to open a door unless you know who's standing on the other side of it?"

To her horror, she felt tears well in her eyes at his harsh attitude. "So stay out there and freeze," she retorted when she found her voice. "Who cares?" She slammed the door in his face, threw the dead bolt and leaned against the wood.

After several seconds of stunned silence, Mitch rapped softly against the panel. "I'm sorry. Please, Brenna, I need to see you." He went weak with relief when he heard the door being unlocked. Brenna stood to one side, allowing him entrance, then closed the door behind him.

The house had changed since his visit. The garland he had strung on the banister was gone, of course, as were the other Christmas decorations. He wondered jealously if Brian Hawthorne had been around to help carry the storage boxes back into the basement.

They looked at each other for a long moment before she gestured to his jacket. "Will you be staying long enough for me to hang that up?"

Mitch shoved his hands into his jacket pockets. "I guess that's up to you."

Brenna relented. "Take it off and go make yourself comfortable in the family room." Her eyes hungrily followed his every action. He looked tired and drawn and he was sporting at least a two-day growth of whiskers, and she was so happy to see him that her heart ached. When he had disappeared into the family room, she drew several deep, calming breaths before following. "Would you like a drink?" she asked, walking through the room to the wet bar.

"No, thank you." Mitch stood uncomfortably in front of the sectional, his hands pushed into the pockets of his jeans in order to keep himself from grabbing Brenna and holding on to her for dear life. "You're looking well." *Except for the shadows under your eyes.*

"Thank you." She perched on one of the stools in front of the bar. "Sit down, Mitch."

He was so caught up in trying to decide what to say first that he didn't hear the invitation. Hell, he might as well jump right in with both feet. "I don't work for the FBI."

Brenna narrowed her eyes at him. "I figured that out when the telephone number Agent Johnson gave me belonged to Langley."

"When—what?" He stared at her in bewilderment.

"I'm just surprised that Greg got my message to you so quickly," she continued as if he hadn't spoken.

"That Greg... What message?" He practically roared the question.

"The one saying I wanted to talk to you," Brenna said pointedly. "I was expecting a phone call, though, not a personal appearance."

Mitch held on to his patience with an effort. "Brenna, I haven't spoken with Greg since we flew out of Minneapolis the night Mark was killed. When did you talk to him?"

"Yesterday afternoon." She frowned up at him. "He said you were out in the field, so I assumed you were out of the country."

"I was. I've spent the last thirty-six hours either waiting for or sitting on an airplane." His gaze locked with hers.

"Then how did you know...?" Her question faded off as she realized what had happened.

Mitch's next words confirmed her suspicions. "I never got your message, Brenna. I just knew that I had to see you again."

Her heart was threatening to beat its way out of her chest. "Why?"

He couldn't say the words, not yet. "There are a lot of lies between us—"

"Finding out you work for the CIA did come as a shock," Brenna interrupted helpfully. "I can't say I approve of the organization—"

This time it was his turn to interrupt. "Brenna, will you please shut up so that I can explain things to you?"

He sounded exasperated and decidedly impatient. Well, he was here and since she already knew the truth, she could afford to be magnanimous. Brenna obediently closed her mouth. The first sentence Mitch uttered, however, punched such a large hole in her composure that she had the feeling she was gaping at him like a beached fish.

"I don't work for the CIA—not anymore. I operate a counterterrorist organization in France." There he paused, giving her a chance to comment. When she did not, he forged ahead with his confession, explaining exactly how he had been living for several years and how he had become involved with the Prescott case.

When he was through, Brenna murmured, "I see," and fell silent, watching him as if she had never seen him before. "So you lied to me."

The flat statement was like a slap in the face, and his heart sank. Mitch nodded.

Brenna bit back another threat of tears. "Did you sleep with me in order to catch Aleksei?"

"No!" His answer was swift in coming, and fierce. "I wanted to tell you the truth after our first time together, but I was afraid to. Afraid that you'd do something foolish, like call the real FBI, and then I wouldn't be able to protect you." He looked down at the floor. "And I was afraid you'd never let me touch you again."

Brenna sighed inwardly. He could be such a difficult, obtuse man. His past didn't matter; what concerned her was the future, their future, together. Didn't he know by now that she would forgive him anything? "Why did you come back, Mitch?"

His head snapped up. She hated him; he could see it in the way she held herself firmly erect on the stool. "I wanted you to know the truth—"

She waved an impatient hand. "Fine, now I know the truth about you and your sordid past. Don't you have anything else to say to me?"

He deserved her scorn. After all she had been through, after the way he had shamelessly used her, Brenna was entitled to her pound of flesh. Even if it was killing him piece by piece. "Just that I'm sorry, Brenna," he replied in a haunted tone.

When she did nothing more than stare at him, he shrugged helplessly and started toward the foyer. Her voice stopped him in the middle of the room.

"I love you, Mitch Carlisle," she said. "And I honestly don't think I can survive your walking out of my life a second time."

His heart started beating again as he slowly turned to face her. "I love you, too, Brenna, but there's no future in it."

"How do you know?" she asked, a challenging smile on her lips. "All you've talked about is the past. Maybe I'd like to live in France."

The very thought of having her in close proximity to the danger inherent in his work sent a chill through Mitch. "No."

"No, you don't want a future with me?"

"Yes!"

"Yes, you do or yes, you don't?" She was pushing him, she knew, but if she didn't, he would kill them both trying to do the noble thing.

"Yes, damn it, I want a future with you," he bellowed, feeling harassed.

Brenna suppressed the urge to giggle. "Then ask me nicely."

Mitch threw up his hands in a gesture of despair. "Okay, what the hell? You want to live with a broken-down ex-spook?"

"No," Brenna replied primly, sliding off her perch. "Really, Mitch, you have to learn to ask the right questions."

His mind hadn't heard anything beyond her refusal. "What do you mean, no?"

"Rephrase your question," she suggested, looping her arms around his neck. "You might get the answer you want."

And Mitch, who prided himself on being able to cut to the heart of the matter, felt his knees grow weak at the look in her eyes. "You don't want to live with me?"

"Yes, I do, very much," she answered, smiling. "But I want it all."

"As in marriage?" He lowered his head and kissed her deeply, delighting in her immediate response.

"As in marriage," she affirmed when she could finally speak. "Are you ever going to ask me?"

"You bet," he promised, lifting her into his arms and carrying her upstairs to the bedroom. "Later."

And he did.

Epilogue

The tall, blond man who screeched the Mercedes to a halt in front of the emergency entrance of the hospital was wearing a tuxedo. He was a successful businessman who owned and managed a security firm in Minneapolis. He and his employees provided everything from home and corporate security to, on occasion, acting as bodyguards. Normally his every action was planned in advance, his reasoning clear and relentlessly shrewd. His employees, in fact, called him the Iceman.

None of that was in evidence tonight, however, as he tore through the electronic doors and announced to everyone present, "I'm having a baby—get a wheelchair."

Before the stunned admitting personnel could react, an auburn-haired woman waddled—there was no other word for it, they all agreed later—through the doors unassisted. Clad in a floor-length evening gown—they had been attending their neighbor's opening night as Lady MacBeth— she was an arresting sight, even in her condition. "Actually," she informed the staff as she moved around her husband, "I'm the one having the baby, but I think you'd better get him a wheelchair anyway." Turning to Mitch, Brenna patted his arm reassuringly. "Why don't you park the car and get my suitcase?"

"Right." He was out the doors in seconds, grateful to have been told what to do next. When he returned to admitting, a chuckling gray-haired woman told him what floor to go to, and he once again happily followed orders.

She had never noticed Mitch's tendency to hover before, Brenna decided later when she was in the grip of another contraction. Nor had she ever seen the lunatic side of him. He was constantly demanding that someone give her a shot. Fortunately the nurses and her doctor were proving adept at ignoring him.

"We're never doing this again," Mitch vowed when her hand crushed his as another contraction began.

"Sure we are," she panted. "We agreed to have three." She thought he groaned, but she couldn't be sure.

The doctor finished his examination. "You're coming along nicely, Mrs. Carlisle. I think it's time we moved you to delivery."

"You'll give her something there, right?" Mitch insisted, gripping Brenna's hand like a lifeline as he walked beside the gurney.

"It's too late for that, Mr. Carlisle," the doctor informed him steadily. "Besides, it's almost over."

"Maybe just a light sedative," Brenna suggested between pains.

"Mrs. Carlisle, I just told your husband—".

"The sedative is for my husband," she dryly informed the doctor. "Frankly he's starting to make me nervous."

When the doctor was scrubbing up, he told his assistant, "I've seen a lot of nervous fathers in my time, but this guy takes the cake. Have one of the nurses keep an eye on him, will you?" The assistant agreed and the doctor shook his head. "I hope this guy doesn't have to deal in crisis situations. He'd have a heart attack."

"If you'll just step aside, sir, we're going to start an IV on your wife now." The nurse had repeated this request several times before she gave up and simply elbowed the expectant father aside.

Seeing the needle slide into Brenna's vein caused Mitch to feel distinctly light-headed, but he willed the weakness to disappear. Thankfully things progressed rapidly after that. He held Brenna upright while she pushed, murmuring reassurances and encouragement as he had learned in their childbirth classes. He even whooped aloud when his daughter was born, exclaiming over her as she was laid on her mother's stomach so that daddy could have the honor of cutting the umbilical cord.

Brenna was cradling her daughter, admiring her thick head of blond hair when a dreadful crash echoed through the delivery room. Turning her head, she saw two nurses rushing to kneel beside her husband, who had passed out cold on the tiled floor. Brenna's laughter mixed with her infant's indignant cries.

SET SAIL FOR THE SOUTH SEAS
with
BESTSELLING AUTHOR
EMILIE RICHARDS

In September Silhouette Sensation begins a very special mini-series by a very special author. *Tales of the Pacific*, by Emilie Richards, will take you to Hawaii, New Zealand and Australia and introduce you to a group of men and women you will never forget.

The *Tales of the Pacific* are four stories of love as lush as the tropics, as deep as the sea and as enduring as the sky above. They are coming your way—only in Silhouette Sensation!

FROM GLOWING EMBERS
September 1992

SMOKE SCREEN
October 1992

RAINBOW FIRE
November 1992

OUT OF THE ASHES
December 1992

Silhouette Sensation

COMING NEXT MONTH

SMOKE SCREEN
Emilie Richards

Take a trip to New Zealand in this the second of
Emilie Richards' *Tales of the Pacific*.

Paige Duvall was soul-shudderingly lonely. She'd
lost the man she'd been planning to marry and her
best friend at one stroke. But Adam Tomoana and
his young son soon made Paige realise that what
she had lost was nothing to what she could
have—with them.

SPECIAL GIFTS
Anne Stuart

Colonel Sam Oliver needed Elizabeth Hardy's help.
A woman was missing, a woman who could be
holding the world's future in her hands, and it
seemed that only Elizabeth would be able to locate
her. But the search could be dangerous . . .

Elizabeth was afraid—afraid of her ability and
afraid to risk her heart again. Sam Oliver was
tough and ruthless but, if she began to care for him,
she would have no idea of any potential threats to
his safety. How could she stay uninvolved?

Silhouette Sensation

COMING NEXT MONTH

ANGEL ON MY SHOULDER
Ann Williams

She *said* she was an angel . . . And she definitely looked the part. But Will Alexander didn't believe in Heaven or angels or anything else. He had business to handle, dangerous business, and she was getting in the way. That was odd, everywhere he went, there she was . . .

Cassandra had to save Will from making a terrible mistake. But she wasn't very experienced and she didn't know how she was supposed to save a man who didn't want to be saved. And why did he make her feel so . . . well . . . *earthly*?

SOMETIMES A LADY
Linda Randall Wisdom

Elise Carpenter wasn't sure she wanted protection, particularly when the protection looked like Dean Cornell, but with her daughters at risk she just didn't have a choice. So Detective Cornell was moving in.

Dean expected a Vet to keep animals, but there were so many and they didn't seem to realise that he was one of the good guys. When the daughters of the house handcuffed him to the bed, he was ready to surrender. But it was Elise who was the real danger—to him!